The Blacksmith's Apprentice

Bey Deckard

Bey
Deckard
Books

*I dedicate this book to **you**.*
Whether you're a fan who's stuck by me through this loooooong dry spell, a reader wanting to give my work another chance, or a newcomer (hello, there!), I couldn't do this without you.

And to Starr, my editor and longtime friend, because she's fucking awesome.

Contents

Themes and Content Warnings

Fantasy-ish setting, non-human, slow burn, erotic elements, grumpy/sunshine, may/december, caste system, slavery, rape/abuse

Soundtrack

https://geni.us/TBAsoundtrack

Kat'hoondeman Breeds and Their Rungs
(as found in Father Sprey's journal)

Samra – Ruler's Rung, pale gold, no markings

Garza & Losano – Teacher's Rung, both spotted brown, but the Garza are bright gold while the Losano are bronze.

Levek & Duval – Trader's Rung, Duvals are pure black; Leveks are brindled black and brown and tend to be on the large side.

Grendall & Ulven – Artist's Rung, Grendalls are light brown with distinctive dark-brown stripes. Ulven are honey/tawny with ivory stripes and are the smallest breed.

Dankel – Farmer's Rung, reddish fur ranging from bright copper to almost mahogany

Kirmen – Slaves, dull, ugly grey, no markings; awful, pathetic creatures, if you ask me.

Father Sprey

Chapter One

Live by the Ladder, cling to the Rungs;
As decreed by the Three Living Suns.
The noble and brave Samra to lead;
Garza and Losano, nurture ev'ry breed.
Levek and Duval create and provide for all;
To charm and regale, Grendall and Ulven's call.
Welcome be the Dankel's harvest feasts;
As Kirmen shoulder the burden of beasts.

E yck smiled and shook hands with Father Tormil. "Take good care of her, Pash. She'll serve you well if you keep her clean and her edges sharp," he said as he handed over the newly finished short sword.

"She's a beauty," Pash replied, sliding the blade from the scabbard to inspect the scrollwork etched into the metal. "You've outdone yourself, Eyck."

"I couldn't let my best friend run around with a second-rate weapon, now could I?" Eyck said with a laugh. "Now, you send your priest friends my way, and I'll make you a matching dagger if they decide to—"

A loud crash followed by furious shouting came from outside. "You *idiot*! You complete *imbecile*! Pick that up. Pick that up now! I swear to the Three Suns if there's a single broken . . ."

Startled, the blacksmith and the priest blinked at each other. They leaned out the open door to see what the commotion was about.

In front of the candleshop on the corner, a Samra man in the lavender sash of a minor lord was striking his Kirmen slave with a crop, over and over again while the lad scrambled to pick candles up off the ground.

The shop's outside display case had fallen over and judging by the torrent of abuse coming from the lord, the blame lay squarely on the slave's shoulders. From the looks of it, most of the candles had survived, but the lord continued hitting his slave even after everything was put back. The lad flinched and cowered with every strike, though he didn't utter a sound. Mrs. Begmard, the candlemaker, stood to the side looking horrified.

"What the fuck?" Eyck said, then grimaced. "Sorry, Pash."

"What the *fuck* indeed," murmured the priest. He shook his head. "I'll never understand a man's need to own another. It's cruel and unnatural—I don't care what the Sun Scrolls say."

"That's blasphemy, coming from you," Eyck joked, but he couldn't bring himself to smile.

He watched the beating taking place down the street with his fists balled and growled low when the lord delivered a hard blow to the slave's face. It made him sick to his stomach that the Samra owned more than three-quarters of the Kirmen still enslaved. Eyck didn't give a damn that the Samra sat at the top of the nine Kat'hoondeman caste breeds and the Kirmen at the bottom—it was an archaic, barbaric system, and he wanted no part of it.

"I have to do something," Eyck said between clenched teeth, watching the lad take another blow to the head.

"Please do," Pash replied, his grey eyes narrowed at the scene.

Eyck grabbed the three-weights hammer by the door and, hefting it to his shoulder, walked out into the cobbled street. "Hello, there," he called out as he neared. "Excuse me?"

The lord started and turned in place still holding the crop aloft. The golden fur on his face was mussed and sweat-streaked, and he stood there panting, his tail thrashing from side to side as he watched the burly blacksmith approach.

"Get along now," the lord said, eyeing the huge hammer resting easily on Eyck's broad shoulder. "This is none of your concern." He was at least a head shorter than Eyck and had to crane his neck to look up at him.

Smiling, Eyck shrugged. "Couldn't help but notice the way you're handling your slave," he replied, looking over at the object of the Samra's ire. He faltered for a second, seeing the slave up close, and laughed to cover his disquiet over the young man's piercing gaze. "Don't you think you're being a tad excessive?" he asked, turning back to the man in the lavender sash.

"*Excessive?*" the lord asked, his eyes wide and voice hitting that high note of incredulous affront so common to his ilk. "Do you know who you're talking to? I am *Lord* Mangley of Stettefyr! Know your place, Levek."

Ignoring the man, Eyck kept his tone light and turned to the candlemaker. "Mrs. Begmard, is there much damage?"

The woman shook her head. "Only a few broken odds and ends, Mr. Stromsmith . . . nothin' even worth mentioning. Wasn't the boy's fault, even."

"It wasn't?"

The stout candlemaker side-eyed the lord then shook her head. "I've been meaning to see you about crafting a new leg for the case. This one's bent, and it was only a matter of time 'fore someone nudged it and the whole of it come down."

Mangley scoffed at her assessment. Grabbing the young Kirmen slave roughly by the shoulder, he gave him a good shake. "This imbecile is a useless fucking wretch if there was ever one. Two left feet, always knocking things over. I should have sold him long ago." The lord's temper tantrum seemed to have run its course, replaced by sneering peevishness.

"I see." Eyck turned to the slave again and furrowed his brow.

The young man held his gaze steady as a big welt swelled up on his cheek beneath the short dull-grey fur that covered his whole body. Eyck tilted his head, appraising him silently.

Naked, except for a dirty loincloth, the Kirmen slave was painfully gaunt. However, he was taller than most of his breed—nearly as tall as Eyck was—with wide shoulders and big capable-looking hands.

An idea took root in Eyck's mind, and he sighed to himself, cursing his soft heart.

"How much do you want for him?" he asked.

"What?" Mangley said, sounding flabbergasted. "You want to *buy* him? But he's a complete imbecile. And dumb as well."

"What do you mean?"

"He doesn't speak a word. He may be near-deaf as well, for all I know—he can barely understand anything said to him. You have to repeat yourself four or five times before he'll obey," the lord replied, screwing up his face with disgust. "The man I bought him from told me his mother was a Kirmen prostitute and his father was a Grendall pirate. No doubt their combined wretchedness worked to create this waste of flesh . . ."

"So, he's of mixed stock," Eyck said, nodding—it certainly explained the young man's height, but there was no way he was an imbecile as the lord claimed. Intelligence burned in the young man's dark-brown eyes.

"*Mixed stock*? That's dainty," said Mangley with another sneer. "He's a *schatten* greyback mutt."

Eyck frowned at the slur. "Turn around for me," he said to the slave.

For a moment, the young man continued to stare.

Mangley gestured toward the lad. "See? I told you that you have to repeat yo—"

The young man turned away from them.

Down the slave's back were the horizontal stripes of his Grendall parentage, but in slate-grey instead of brown. He also had a crest of silvery fur down the length of his spine that disappeared beneath the waist strap of his loincloth. The long tail poking through the hole in the garment was also striped grey like his back, and the tuft at the end of it was the same brown as the hair on his head. Despite how skinny the slave was, Eyck could see potential in him—the young man had obviously only just reached sexual maturity, but judging by his frame, he'd have a powerful build when he finished growing.

Eyck sighed again. "Will you take half a gold?"

"What? You're serious? You still want him?"

"I do."

"Two gold," the Samra replied, lifting his chin in a haughty challenge.

Eyck clenched his jaw—Mangley had obviously grasped that good money could be wrung from Eyck's bleeding heart.

Bloody Suns.

"That's ridiculous. You just said you should have sold him long ago . . ."

"Two gold," repeated the lord.

"*One* gold," Eyck countered in a tight voice.

It was a lot of money, but the slave's shoulders had bowed pathetically at the lord's outrageous price, sealing the deal for Eyck—clearly the lad would rather chance it with a stranger than remain in the hands of his current master.

"One gold and eight silver," replied Mangley, tapping his crop against palm. "Without my slave, I'll need to hire someone to pull my chariot."

"One gold and *three* silver, and I'll find someone to pull your *schatten* chariot." Eyck stared hard at the man.

Mangley's eyebrows shot up at Eyck's language, but he remained silent. Then he gave a brusque nod and held out his hand. "One gold and three silver and someone to get me home."

The slave turned around, his expression completely blank as he stared ahead.

A momentary tingle of doubt coursed through Eyck . . . had he only imagined the lively intelligence he'd seen in his eyes? Did it matter?

"I accept your offer."

They shook hands. Eyck reached into the big pocket of his apron and pulled out the money Pash had just given him. He handed the coins over to Mangley, then turned to look at his new purchase.

"What's his name?"

"Doesn't have one," Mangley replied, waving his free hand as he pocketed the coins. "I just call him idiot or slave. Now, go fetch this man of yours to get me home . . . I've things to do."

"I'll be back in a few minutes," Eyck replied, fully intending on taking his time. He motioned to the slave. "Come . . . uh, young man. Please."

Without being asked twice, the gaunt slave followed Eyck back to the smithy where Pash was still standing in the doorway with a smirk on his face. "Wow, you *really* raked him over the coals . . ."

Eyck rolled his eyes and dropped the hammer by the door. He pointed to the table and chairs by the window. "Sit over there," he told the young man. He turned back to his friend. "Well, what was I supposed to do? Make more trouble for the lad?"

"I don't know. I thought you were going over there to give that little blueblood a stern talking to, maybe wave your hammer around a bit . . . not hand over all your money to the fat little cretin," Pash said with a sneer worthy of a Samra lord on his handsome Losano face. Then he frowned and jerked his head towards the grey-furred young man watching them. "And what in the world were you thinking? You bought a *slave*?"

"He's not a slave anymore," Eyck replied. He looked over at the seated young man. "You hear me, lad? You're not a slave anymore . . . understand?"

The young man gave no response.

Eyck wondered again if there was something wrong with him. "I . . . er, need an apprentice," he said, glancing at Pash.

"Since when? And doesn't he speak?"

"No," replied Eyck. "At least I don't think so."

"I think you made a bad deal," Pash said, but his smile was fondly teasing.

"Maybe." Eyck looked down at his hands. "Can you stay here for an hour? Watch the shop and keep an eye on him?"

"Of course. Why?"

"I have to pull a chariot to Stettefyr." He lifted his eyes to Pash as the priest let out a laugh. "I know. I know . . . bad deal."

WELL OVER AN HOUR LATER, Eyck trudged down Main Street to his smithy, flexing his left hand as he pushed the door open. He'd assumed that half a lifetime of swinging a hammer would have hardened his hands to the point where blisters were a thing of the past, but he'd been dead wrong.

Grimacing, he looked up then stopped in his tracks.

Pash was sitting near the door, his arms crossed over his chest with a dark scowl on his face, but the ex-slave was exactly where Eyck had left him.

"I need to speak with you a moment," Pash said quietly as he rose. He grabbed Eyck's sleeve and pulled him towards the back of the shop, out of hearing but still within sight of the ex-slave seated at the table.

"What is it?" Eyck asked, worried.

"I think you've got a problem on your hands."

Eyck looked over at the silent young man, and they locked eyes for a moment.

"Why do you say that?"

"Olemtil came by earlier to drop off some sort of white powder for the forge. When I went to get what was owed him from the safe . . . well, your 'apprentice' stopped me."

Glancing back at Pash in alarm, Eyck frowned. "You mean, he attacked you?"

The priest shook his head. "No, I wouldn't go so far to say *attacked*. He simply stood in my way . . . menacingly."

Eyck rubbed his hand over his jaw, grimacing as the short coarse fur pricked his tender palm, and stared at the young man again. "I think it's my fault . . . I didn't tell him who you were. I'll take care of it." He walked towards the ex-slave and pointed to the priest. "This is my best friend, Father Tormil. He's allowed to take *whatever* money"— Eyck made a sweeping gesture towards the safe—"out of there because I *trust* him," he said, speaking slowly and enunciating clearly in case the young man really did have trouble with words. "Do you understand?"

Eyck waited a second or two for any sort of reply, but when he didn't get one, he motioned for Pash to step closer. He pointed to him again. "*Father* Tormil. Even if he wasn't my friend, he's a *priest* . . . it's not like he's going to steal from me. Do you understand me at all?"

Again, his question was met with an unblinking stare—was that hostility in the young man's dark eyes? Or was that fear? Eyck clenched his jaw and exhaled in frustration. What in bloody Suns was he going to do with an apprentice he couldn't communicate with?

Pash patted his shoulder. "I'll leave you to it, then. I have to be back for Evenmass. Good luck, Eyck," he said, turning to leave. "Oh, and Olemtil will pass by tomorrow or next for his money."

"All right. Thanks, Pash. Goodnight."

The door closed with a jingle, and Eyck let out a long sigh. He turned his sign around, deciding to close up shop for the night, and grabbed the basket from the shelf beneath the window. He set the basket on the table in front of the ex-slave. Pulling aside the cloth, he uncovered the bean pies Macy Tabor had given him that morning.

"You hungry?" he asked, sitting down. He pulled out two of the small flaky pies and held one out. Slowly, the young man reached across the table and accepted the offering. He brought the pie to his mouth but didn't take a bite.

"Go on . . . they're pretty good. Macy makes them once a week for me since my wife—" Eyck shook his head with a grimace, still unable to say the word after all this time, and crumbled the edge of the crust between his fingers. "I-I usually eat them cold. But I can heat one up for you. I can set it next to the forge for a few minutes—it's still hot."

The ex-slave sat motionless, his eyes on Eyck.

"What is it? You don't like bean pies?"

The young man's hand trembled, and he licked his lips but still made no move to eat. Something occurred to Eyck a second later when the ex-slave's stomach gave a loud gurgle. "Oh, you're waiting for me to eat?" Eyck lifted his pie to his mouth and took a big bite out of it.

The young man started devouring his own pie while Eyck watched in astonishment—it was like he hadn't eaten in days. After the young man had finished the first pie, Eyck reached out, but the ex-slave recoiled and bared his fangs. He was obviously terrified.

"Whoa . . . whoa. I was just going to push the basket closer to you. You can have more . . . go on. Take another. And you don't have to wait for me . . . you're not a slave anymore, remember? Just eat. Go on."

Hesitantly, the young man took a second pie out of the basket, and when he had finished that one, he looked up at Eyck with a hopeful expression.

Eyck laughed and nodded. "Go right ahead."

The young man attacked a third pie, a little slower this time.

"Are you just pretending you don't understand anyone?" Eyck asked.

The young man lifted his eyes and stared at Eyck for an uncomfortably long time while he chewed his food. Finally, he dipped his chin in a very shallow nod.

"Ah ha. And can you talk?"

Again, the stare went on and on. It was difficult not to look away from the young man's penetrating gaze. At long last, the ex-slave shook his head, then went back to stuffing his face with bean pie.

"Were you injured? Is that why you can't talk?"

This time, a shrug immediately followed the questions, as if the young man had decided it was ok to communicate with Eyck. It was a start.

"Do you have a name?"

The reply he got was a lip curled in disgust. Eyck couldn't tell if the lad didn't want to tell him or didn't know—the latter was appalling in its implications.

"Well, I'm not going to call you slave or idiot because you're neither," he said, pulling the wooden crate out from under the table. "We'll just have to come up with something better." He lifted a jar of moonshine out of the crate and set it in front of him with a sigh.

I will not drink the whole jar tonight. I will not *drink the whole jar tonight . . .*

He twisted the cork lid to break the seal, then gasped in pain as the blister on his palm tore. "Schatten," he muttered, grimacing down at his hand.

A popping sound startled him—he looked up as the young man slid the open jar back across the table.

"Oh. Thank you."

Eyck was about to offer some of the moonshine to the ex-slave when he realized the young man was pointing a finger at him.

Frowning, Eyck asked, "Me? What about me?" He lifted the jar to his lips and took a small grimacing sip—the first taste of the harsh liquor was always nauseating.

The young man was still pointing at him, and it dawned on Eyck what he probably wanted to know.

"Oh! You want to know my name?"

He got a nod in return.

"I'm sorry, lad. I should have told you before I left you with Pash. I'm an arse . . . I haven't been myself lately," Eyck said, then held out his hand. "I'm Eyckmigh Stromsmith."

The young man stared at the proffered hand for a couple of seconds, but instead of shaking it when he finally reached out, he held it between his hands and frowned at the oozing blisters.

"I don't know how you pulled that chariot . . . those grips are terrible," Eyck muttered into the jar before he took another sip. The ex-slave's touch was making him feel awkward. "I should really put something on this."

He drank some more moonshine and, looking around for the salve, slowly slid his hand out of the young man's grasp. Spotting the small tin in the rafters above the quenching pail, he retrieved it, then smeared the contents on his blisters. Right away, the salve numbed the pain. It was good for cuts, rashes, and burns—Eyck went through a tin of it every few weeks, treating the latter—and it was even good for bruises.

Remembering the young man's beating, Eyck motioned for him to stand. The poor kid had to be hurting.

"Come here," he said gently. "We should take care of this now."

For a few seconds, all the ex-slave did was stare at him, his mouth set in a grim line and his shoulders hunched. Then he sighed and stood, startling Eyck by dropping to his knees in front of him and reaching for the front of Eyck's pants.

Eyck was so flabbergasted that the young man had two buttons undone before Eyck pushed his hands away, stepping back.

"What are you *doing*?" Eyck rasped, his mouth dry and pulse racing. He quickly rebuttoned his pants, shaking his head as he fumbled for the jar of moonshine on the table. After taking a few deep swallows, he wiped his mouth with the back of his wrist where the fur was sparse and crisscrossed with burn scars. The young man was still on his knees, his expression deeply confused.

"I didn't mean . . . I don't want you to do *that*—that's, well, that's *not* what I wanted you to do. Ever. That's quite all right," Eyck said, his words running together. He took a deep breath, drank more of Pash's homemade rotgut, and shook his head again. "Get up. I'm sorry. You . . . probably had other . . . er . . . duties like that with Mangley, but I don't want that. It's ok. Get up. Come on now." Eyck showed the tin to the young man. "It's for your bruises. At least let me put some on your face . . . where that bastard hit you."

The lump on the young man's cheek was like a marble under his fur. Slowly, he rose, his eyes narrowed in suspicion.

"It's just a salve made of . . . uh, well, to be honest, I'm not exactly sure what it's made of. Mrs. Begmard uses something her bees make plus a few different herbs. See?" Eyck showed the young man his palm and put a little more salve on his blisters. "It's perfectly safe. It's for treating all sorts of things." He scooped some onto the tip of his finger and slowly extended it towards the young man. When the lad didn't back away, Eyck lightly smeared the salve on his cheek.

From this close, Eyck saw the ex-slave had a small stripe of silvery fur between his eyes that fanned up to mid-forehead where it blended in again with the rest of his fur. Like the silver crest on his back, it was interesting, and Eyck had to admit to himself that he found it attractive, which was probably why his heart was still going a mile a minute over what had just happened—and what had *nearly* happened. He felt like a schatten pervert.

Eyck was painfully aware of the young man's persistent stare. He swallowed, looking away. "There we go. All done. It should start feeling better soon." He grabbed his moonshine with a shaking hand and sat back down again to drink. The jar was already half-empty.

After a moment, he cleared his throat, looking down into the golden liquid. "And I just want to make it very clear: you don't have to do those types of things to me. *Ever.* I don't . . . need that. Not anymore."

Quiet footfalls approached, and the chair creaked as the young man reclaimed his seat at the table. Eyck glanced up and then back down again, tapping his knuckles on the scored wood of the tabletop.

"You see . . ." Eyck cleared his throat, frowned, and shook his head. He drank more moonshine, and it no longer burned going down. Lifting his head, he met the ex-slave's eyes—he realized they were the exact same brown as his hair. Yes . . . he was a very good-looking young man. "You see," Eyck started again. "I'm in mourning." He sighed, frowning back down at the jar. "My wife. She . . . uh . . . she passed. She was the love of my life. My soulmate."

Eyck drank from the jar and closed his eyes. He hadn't talked about Manya to anyone except Pash, and even then, he'd said little about her in months despite Pash's worry over his excessive drinking.

But, for some reason, he found himself wanting to open up to the silent young man across the table. Maybe it was because he couldn't speak—his silence projected a quiet sympathy. But was it real? Or was it imagined? For all Eyck knew, the young man was plotting ways to murder and rob him.

What's going on behind those dark eyes?

Eyck rubbed his face, trying to quiet his muddled thoughts.

He started telling the lad about the first time he'd seen Manya working at her father's cooperage across the river in Heldsfirth.

The ex-slave nodded for Eyck to continue every time he was overwhelmed and had to stop, but his expression remained neutral as Eyck told him everything about the woman he thought he'd grow old with—the woman who had died in his arms after a stupid, *stupid* accident.

The sun had long since gone down and Eyck hadn't bothered lighting any candles, so they sat in the near dark, lit only by the street torch outside the shop window.

When the first jar of moonshine was empty, he groped around for another.

"She . . . was . . . oh, she, uh, she was beautiful," he slurred, shaking his head. "Such a *shtupid* accident. I was gonna inshtall a, um, banister on the shtairs. She fell through . . . *Fuck!*" Eyck couldn't find the box of moonshine, but maybe it was because his chair was pushed so far back. He needed another drink to wipe the memory of Manya's broken body from his mind.

Shaking his head to try to clear his double vision, he blinked up in surprise at the figure suddenly looming over him. The young man stared down at him, his nostrils flaring as he breathed slowly.

"What'sh it?" Eyck asked, confused.

The ex-slave seemed pensive.

Eyck squinted—was that sympathy in his eyes? "D'you want somethin'?"

The young man licked his lips, frowning, then turned around.

"What are you . . ." Bleary-eyed, Eyck couldn't finish his thought.

The ex-slave began twitching his tail to the side suggestively, his hips rocking as he stepped backwards, coming to a stop between Eyck's thighs. The young man was close enough that the heat of him radiated through the thick material of Eyck's trousers.

Eyck let out a shaky breath—the lad's blatant mating display was making his head swim. "I don't . . . um. That's not . . . uh . . ."

What are you waiting for? Push him away.

The ex-slave grasped his furry buttocks, pulling them apart, while rhythmically flicking his tail out of the way. Eyck couldn't see anything but the brown loincloth running between the young man's legs, its tail opening snug, but he couldn't tear his eyes away. He felt himself getting hard, something that hadn't happened since . . . since . . .

Shaking his head to rid himself of the thought, Eyck reached out to shove the ex-slave away but instead found himself wrapping his hand around the thick base of the young man's tail.

Suns, what are you doing? He breathed out, feeling shaky and excited.

He drummed his fingers lightly up against the underside of the ex-slave's tail where it poked out of the loincloth, stimulating the nerves there, then squeezed and gave the tail a gentle tug. He panted a few breaths, lifting the tail to stare at the covered space beneath it. Maybe it could be that easy.

What are you doing?

Maybe it could be simple. Eyck shifted in place, his eyes heavy-lidded as he watched himself press a thumb into the thin cloth beneath the young man's tail.

What are you doing!?

He squeezed the ex-slave's tail again, then rubbed his fingers along the underside, feeling the vertebrae in its thick base.

It could be so *easy* to use the young man to forget everything.

Eyck tugged again, a little harder, but when the ex-slave let out a noise, a quiet moan, it startled Eyck out of his fog of lust. He dropped the young man's tail and pushed him away.

"No. No. Go 'way I can't," he mumbled.

Everything was hazy and blurry and dark. So confusing.

"Go th' *fuck* 'way."

Eyck shoved him again, hard enough that the young man fell back.

Eyck covered his erection with his hand, ashamed of himself. Ashamed for forgetting Manya. So much shame.

He squinted up in a daze. The ex-slave was huddled under the table, arms around his knees, his eyes visible above his forearm. Was he furious at the rejection or disappointed? He looked miserable. As miserable as Eyck felt.

So be it. I fuck everything up. I am schatten. I am fucking shit. His fingers closed around the lid of another jar of moonshine.

EYCK SLOWLY LIFTED his sticky eyelids, the sun on his face like shards of hot glass, and he coughed, licking his dry lips before gingerly sitting up. A jar of moonshine was on its side on the table, some of the golden liquid still within, and he wondered how much of it had actually made it into his mouth. Judging by the way his brain was being squeezed by his skull . . . most of it.

"Fuck," he rasped, rubbing his face.

Hard lumps were stuck to his cheek, probably a combination of spilled moonshine and pie crumbs. He picked them out of his fur as he looked around. The ex-slave was nowhere to be seen.

"Fuck," Eyck repeated, then closed his eyes and put his head back down on the table.

Chapter Two

Five Sun-Cycles Later

W ex looked up at the church, trying to figure out if it was the right one. There was a big mosaic on the street-facing side of it, showing the church atop the hill and the town below, the red Mother star centred directly above the tall steeple.

He frowned. *Am in the right place?*

The hill was right, and the church seemed right, but he didn't remember seeing a mosaic before. Then he spotted a small golden statue of a saint holding a sun-topped sceptre in one hand and a miniature stylized ladder in the other. Smiling, he nodded to himself. He remembered that.

Good, I'm getting close.

He passed a crikket field where a few youngsters were playing—another familiar landmark—then followed the cobbled road to the intersection.

He stopped to shade his eyes, looking around. A woman and her child were approaching from the other side of the street, so he put on his friendliest smile and walked towards her, holding out his sheet of paper.

However, when he got close enough to point to the first word on the page, the woman snatched up her little girl and scowled at him, picking up her pace as she muttered, "No money."

"Who is that strange man, Mama?" said the little girl as they passed him. She was a pretty Garza pup with golden fur spotted in dark brown, her eyes green like the sky.

"That's a Kirmen, Della. They're poor and dirty, and he probably has fleas," the woman said, pitched so Wex would hear.

Wex sighed to himself but kept smiling, waving at the little girl. She stuck her tongue out at him and looked away.

Great. Another town full of fucking bigots.

At least, this time, no one threw anything at him.

Shifting his pack on his shoulder, Wex looked up at the sky. It was close to noon. He'd been hoping to find the place before then, but his map of the town was clearly out-of-date. He frowned, trying to remember if he had to go uphill or down when he heard something that brought the smile back to his face: the ringing of metal on metal.

Following the sound, Wex doubled back for half a block, then passed a few storefronts that didn't look familiar. However, when he got to the corner and saw the shop with its display rack full of candles, his stomach gave a nervous flutter. For a second, he couldn't move.

He took a few slow steps, his eyes on the dark brick building farther down the street.

As he reached the door, it swung open with a jingle. Wex dodged out of the way to let pass a skinny little Duval man in a yellow vest who smelled strongly of fresh *chamara*.

Ducking into the shade of the eaves, Wex watched the man walk away, wondering why he felt so anxious. What was the worst that could happen?

The door jingled again, and the blacksmith himself stepped out into the midday sun. Hands on his hips, he stared at the departing customer, and though the man was facing away, Wex recognized the broad back and the crest of stick-straight black hair that led from the top of his head to the back of his thick brindled neck. He even smelled familiar—heated metal and oilcloth.

Up the street, the candlemaker stepped out to water the flowerbox in her shop window, and the blacksmith raised a hand in greeting. Smiling, she waved back at him.

Mrs. . . . Bagderm? Bogram? Birdgam? Wex couldn't remember her name.

After a moment, the blacksmith turned to go back inside but stopped when he spotted Wex in the shadows.

"Can I help you?" he asked, his tone friendly.

Eyckmigh Stromsmith hadn't changed much since the day Wex left —maybe a little more careworn . . . the brown-and-black brindle of his face was now peppered with a few white hairs and a fresh burn mark was visible above the cuff of his work glove—but otherwise, he was the same brawny, lantern-jawed blacksmith.

Eyck's green eyes held no recognition, only curiosity, and Wex tried not to take it to heart. He stepped into the bright sunshine, pulling back his hood, and held out the scrap of paper he'd been carrying for weeks.

On it were the two words Red Falcorr had written out for him before he'd left: *blacksmith apprentice.*

Eyck frowned, tilting his head, and appraised Wex a moment longer before looking down at the paper. His brows shot up, and he lifted his head, surprise making his mouth hang open for a few seconds. "Bloody Suns, it's *you.*"

EYCK COULDN'T BELIEVE his eyes. Five sun-cycles had put over a handswidth of height on the ex-slave so that he stood taller than Eyck, and he had piled on enough muscle to rival Eyck's bulk. The young man's fur was no longer dull, it shone silver with good health, and the haunted, wary look in his dark-brown eyes had been replaced with calm self-assurance.

"Suns. *Is* it you?" Eyck said. "You've . . . changed."

The young man surprised Eyck even further by offering him a wide sharp-toothed smile.

Eyck rubbed the side of his jaw, shaking his head in disbelief. He was so gobsmacked he barely knew what to say. "Uh . . . well . . . uh, come on in. I was just about to sit down to lunch," he said, opening the door to wave the young man in. "You're welcome to join me." Eyck remembered how the ex-slave had devoured the bean pies like a starving man. "There's plenty to eat . . . But, boy, you're no skinny thing like you were, that's for sure. Someone's been feeding you well . . . *really* well . . . maybe even better than I've been eating . . ."

Eyck felt like he was rambling but couldn't stop. The initial shock of finding the runaway on his doorstep was wearing off. Now, all he could think about were the hazy memories of what had happened between them before the boy left—Eyck couldn't recall much, but what he *could* remember was making him tense. If something untoward *had* happened between them, then why would he come back? Revenge? It didn't *seem* like it . . .

Eyck reached into the food basket beneath the window and took out two wrapped sandwiches, placing them on the table. "Why don't you sit and make yourself comfortable," he said. "I don't stand on ceremony here, especially not at lunch." He opened a cupboard, intent on taking out some plates, but obviously, it had been a while since he'd used any—they were covered in mouse droppings. Grimacing, he closed the cupboard. "Yeah . . . no ceremony here. Um, I hope you don't mind eating sandwiches right in the wrapping?"

The young man shook his head, giving Eyck another smile, and took the same chair as he had the last time.

Eyck slid over one of the sandwiches. "They're just cress, tempeh, and mushroom. I made the pepper chutney myself though . . . folks seem to love it, but I hope you like things spicy."

His guest nodded, carefully unwrapping the waxed cloth from around his sandwich.

"Still can't talk, then?" Eyck asked, sitting down.

The young man twisted his mouth to the side and shook his head.

"Well . . . do you have a name this time?"

This was met with a nod. The young man tugged up on the braided cord he wore around his neck, revealing the small bronze medallion at its end. He flipped it over and held it out.

Eyck leaned forward and squinted at it, his eyesight not what it used to be, and frowned. It was just a cheap tourist souvenir from the big cathedral in Wexshire. His mother had bought one just like it when they'd visited the cathedral long ago. On one side was the cathedral, on the other, the one he was being shown, was a likeness of St. Wexelmander, the saint for whom the town was named.

He looked up at the young man, confused. "Your name is St. Wexelmander?"

His guest lifted his other hand, holding thumb and finger far apart . . . then he whistled softly and narrowed the space. The meaning was instantly clear to Eyck.

"Shorter? Your name is . . . *Saint*?"

This was met with a headshake and a smirk as the young man repeated the gesture.

"Uh . . ." Eyck scratched the fur at the back of his neck. "Wex?"

This time, he got a firm nod.

Proud of himself, Eyck stretched out his hand, noticing he was still wearing his blackened chamara work gloves. He pulled them off, grimaced in apology, then held his hand out again.

"Pleased to meet you, Wex."

Brow wrinkled, Wex shook with Eyck, and Eyck found himself experiencing something novel—Wex's hand dwarfed his own. He laughed, realizing this was probably how his customer's felt when they shook with him.

"Bloody Suns, lad," he said, turning their clasped hands to the side so he could see the back of Wex's hand. "You must have Titan blood in you."

Wex's eyes hardened for only a moment, and Eyck remembered the ex-slave's uncertain and unfavourable parentage.

Disconcerted by the young man's brief glare, Eyck released him to gesture to the food. "Well, then . . . Go on, no need to wait."

Wex picked up his sandwich and took a big bite. Sighing contently, he sat back in his chair, chewing as he looked around.

Eyck bit into his own sandwich, scanning Wex's face apprehensively. He seemed to be in good humour, but Eyck couldn't help wondering if it was partially an act. The quick anger in Wex's eyes earlier had unsettled Eyck—it felt like something troubling lay just beneath the surface of his cheerful smile.

After a moment, he put down his food and cleared his throat.

"So, Wex . . . what can I do for you?"

Still chewing with gusto, Wex pushed the crumpled page across the table and turned it to face Eyck. He jabbed at the two words written in block letters with his finger then pointed to Eyck.

"You . . . want to be my apprentice?" Eyck replied, lifting his eyes to Wex's.

Wex nodded and took another huge bite.

"Do you have any experience at all?"

Shaking his head, Wex shrugged.

Eyck leaned back in his chair, crossing his arms. There *was* plenty of work to do—with the fighting at the border, more young men and women were joining the army, and the demand for well-crafted swords was high. Pash was always going on about how Eyck was pushing himself too hard . . . he was probably sick of hearing him complain about his sore shoulders and hands.

Frowning, he looked down. The scars were so numerous he had barely any fur left on the back of his hand, and when he made a fist, his knuckles twinged in protest.

"All right," he said, nodding as he warmed to the idea. "Fine." He smiled at Wex. "We'll start training you up tomorrow. I won't pay you yet, not until you can take on work without my help, but I'll feed you and give you a bed. You'll live here, keep the same hours as me, and you'll do exactly as I say during those hours. Understood?"

Wex nodded once.

"Thing is, I don't know how we're going to communicate . . . can you write?"

Wex shook his head—Eyck had the feeling it was a source of embarrassment for the young man.

"Ok. We'll figure something out. After lunch, I'll show you upstairs where you're going to sleep, and then we'll go to Fagin's to measure you for some gloves. I've got an extra apron but the gloves I have won't fit those giant mitts of yours."

Nodding again, Wex leaned over a bit in his seat and thrust a hand into his side pocket. He pulled out some coins and piled them on the table in front of Eyck.

"What's this, then?" asked Eyck.

Wex lifted a hand and wiggled his fingers, then mimed putting on a glove.

"All right . . . but this is too much for a pair of gloves," he said, lining up the coins. One gold and three silver—exactly how much he had paid Lord Mangley for the slave. "Keep the gold."

He pushed the coin back towards Wex, but Wex stopped him.

The young man pointed to himself, shaking his head.

"*Oh*. Yes, ok. All right," Eyck said, relenting. "You want to pay me back. I understand." He smiled as he pocketed the coins. "Well, I sure appreciate it."

Wex grinned, then licked his finger to pick up the crumbs from his sandwich wrapping.

Chuckling to himself, Eyck pushed the other half of his sandwich towards his new apprentice. "Go on."

Touching his temple in thanks, Wex lifted the sandwich to his mouth and bit down, chewing with relish.

The gold would come in handy—it would cost an arm to keep the young man fed. Sobering, he watched Wex eat, thinking again about that night five cycles back.

"Lad . . . I, ah . . ." he started, scratching the back of his neck. "I want to apologize for whatever it is that happened between us . . . if I did anything wrong . . ."

Wex's eyes widened in surprise, then went flinty, his expression tense—it was a look that made Eyck nervous. After a moment, Wex shook his head emphatically, his expression neutral once more.

"I just want to say I'm sor—" Eyck tried again.

Slapping his hand down on the table, Wex shook his head, the hint of warning back in his gaze. Obviously, he didn't want to talk about it.

"All right. I'll drop it. Sorry," Eyck said, his pulse racing.

Bloody Suns, what in schatten's hell did I do to him?

For the first time in many months, Eyck wanted a drink. Sighing, he pushed the thought out of his mind and leaned his elbows on the table. "Um. I wish you could tell me what you've been up to all these sun-cycles . . . but I guess that isn't really possible, is it?"

WEX SUCKED on the ball of his thumb for a second, licking away the last of the deliciously smoky and spicy chutney. He was going to have to teach the blacksmith some of the signing gestures he relied on to communicate, but he didn't think it would be too hard. He'd already used a few easy ones, and the man had picked up on their meaning almost instantly. Eyck was very observant and eager to understand him. He also seemed quite a bit smarter than he looked.

Lifting one finger, Wex sat up in his chair and tilted his head at the blacksmith.

"Yes?" Eyck said, frowning in curiosity. Though his face was an all-over black-and-brown brindle, salted with a little white, the fur above his eyes was uniformly black and when his brow wrinkled down, the jade of his eyes looked brighter. "Does that mean . . . *first*?"

Wex nodded and made his fingers walk across his palm, then held up three fingers. With the other hand, he made a fist and held it over his head.

"You walked for . . . three—wait, is that supposed to be the sun or the moon?"

Yes, you are definitely smart, blacksmith.

Smiling, Wex made his hand into a crescent shape, the sign for the silver moon that defined the year's months, just to show Eyck the difference, then made the sun symbol again.

"Oh . . . ok. You walked for three *days* . . ." Eyck said, nodding as he caught on.

LITTLE BY LITTLE, Wex explained as best as he could that he walked through the mountains to the north until he reached the sea where he stayed for a few days at a chamara farming village. He couldn't really explain how hard the journey had been, nor could he tell him about the curious sights he had seen along the way, nor about eating grass and twigs to keep from starving when he was alone for nearly a week on the winding path. One day, perhaps, he'd draw pictures for Eyck to explain in more detail—though he couldn't write, his quick drawings were easily read—but for now, simple hand signs would have to do.

He also didn't tell Eyck about selling himself along the way to fellow travellers in exchange for food, water, or clothing. It was none of the blacksmith's business.

Finally, he held up two fingers, then made the sun gesture again, but this time brought it around in a circle in front of his chest.

"Second? Um . . . does that mean second . . . sun-cycle?"

Wex nodded and then swallowed, feeling nervous. He slowly rolled up one sleeve.

Eyck's eyes widened, and he stared at the prison brand for a few seconds before speaking.

"Schatten . . . that's from . . . Hange Prison, right? Uh . . . you *did* wind up far north, didn't you?"

Oh good, thought Wex, relieved.

It seemed his gamble had paid off, coming all the way to South Galetsy to see the Levek blacksmith. Eyck's reaction to the prison brand was rather polite—normally, it was far more . . . unfavourable.

The big sap might actually give me a job. Wex cocked an eyebrow at Eyck, waiting for the inevitable question.

Eyck let out a forced little laugh at Wex's expression and rubbed his big jaw. "All right . . . yes, I *want* to know, but you don't have to tell me. The only thing I need to know is whether you'll do . . . *whatever* it is again."

Wex shook his head, then he rubbed his belly with a sad expression before caging a look to either side as he mimed snatching something and hiding it under his shirt.

"Ah. You stole food?"

Wex nodded.

"Well, that's not so bad. We all have to eat . . ." Eyck replied, sounding relieved. "Is Hange as rough as everyone says it is?"

Wex just shrugged, skipping over the parts where the soldiers had nearly beaten him unconscious; and how he had been spat on and cursed by the townspeople even though they were mostly Dankels who were often just as mistreated as Kirmen; and about the farce of a trial that landed him such an exaggerated sentence. He also kept to himself how he, being younger, smaller, and weaker than some of the men he shared a cell with, had been forced to provide sexual services in return for his safety . . . at least until his growth spurt had put him a head above the lot of them.

Instead, he held up one finger, then a second and mimed opening a door and shading his eyes.

"They held you for *two cycles*?" Eyck said, sounding aghast. "For stealing *food*?"

Smirking, Wex nodded and deliberately stroked the fur on his arm.

"Because you're Kirmen. Well, *half*-Kirmen."

That he was only half-Kirmen hadn't softened the beatings any. The guards and fellow inmates only saw a "greyback," and that was the only thing that mattered.

"That isn't fair. I want you to know I've *never* believed in the caste system, Wex. It's rubbish."

You're Levek, Wex thought. *Believe in it or not, what do* you *have to lose?* However, he smiled and nodded politely.

"What did you do after you got out?"

Wex smiled, then cast around for something he could use to demonstrate. Spying the candles on the windowsill, he pointed to them and looked a question to Eyck.

"You made candles?" Eyck wrinkled his brow at Wex's headshake. "Ok, then . . . not candles. You want to use them to show me something? Go ahead."

Gathering up three of the thick off-white candles, Wex began whistling a lively little tune and then started juggling.

Eyck let out a surprised laugh and slapped his knee, watching Wex deftly juggle the candles under his leg, then higher over his head so he could reach out and snatch a fourth candle to add to the mix. When he was done, he gave a little bow, and Eyck clapped.

"That's very good," Eyck replied. "So, you juggled . . . but why?"

Wex held out a hand for patience. He flexed his bicep and mimed struggling to pick up something extremely heavy.

Chuckling, Eyck said, "Ah-ha! A strongman indeed. You certainly look the part. So, you were with a travelling circus then?"

Wex nodded and sat back down in his chair, carefully putting the candles back on the sill.

"Why did you leave?" Eyck asked.

This time, Wex was caught out by the question. He hadn't prepared a reply, mostly because he hadn't thought he'd be able to talk so easily with the big blacksmith. He frowned, scratching his cheek. The anger was still so fresh.

Chedim Bew had told him he'd always have a place in the troupe . . . but he'd failed to mention that it came at a price too high for Wex to pay. Wex still felt stupid for not realizing the circus doubled as something else: a freak's brothel. Maybe he'd been too busy keeping his head down to notice, trying desperately to learn to form his letters under Red Falcorr's tutelage. The deaf fire-breather had taught him how to use his hands to make words, but he hadn't had any luck teaching him to write, much to their shared frustration.

That the circus's *other* income should have been obvious to him was particularly galling—men lining up at a particular, isolated caravan after the nightly show; the way Saffin and Shaffa, the conjoined Dankel twins had looked at him when he'd said they had the easiest act of them all because all they had to do was sit there; the haunted look in the eyes of Maris, the little Ulven contortionist.

It wasn't even that Wex cared much about prostituting himself—it was the way Bew had brought it up with him, the little snivelling turd:

You've been with us long enough, Wex . . . It's time you start pulling your rather substantial weight. I have a very fancy gentleman who'd like to play slave and master—you're to be his for the whole evening, and for the love of the Living Suns, do as he says? Hm? Why are you shaking your head? If you think you have a choice, boy, you are sorely mistaken. You've been bought and paid for, and you better get used to it. I figure it'll be a long damn time before your backside makes enough to pay back my ample generosity these past months—no one wants to dish out more than a few coppers to stick it into a filthy Kirmen cur, so be glad I was able to find someone who likes his boys brawny and larger than life . . .

Wex had left the next morning with Bew's coin pouch on his belt and Red Falcorr's note in his pocket. He'd forced the troupe master to strip naked, then hung him from a tree by his ankles. Wex had taken the rag he'd used to clean up the mess left on him the night before by the "fancy" gentleman and stuffed it into Bew's mouth to keep him quiet.

Bew had watched him go, eyes wide, his secret on full display for the others to find when they woke up. They'd see that Bew was not fully Grendall, but part "filthy Kirmen cur" just like Wex, and had hidden the truth by dyeing his fur . . . but only from the waist up.

"Wex?" Eyck said softly, his green eyes narrowed with what looked like sympathy. "What is it?"

Sighing, Wex shook his head though his stomach was churning with fresh ire. *I am nobody's slave.*

He reached into his pocket and took out one of the ill-gotten coins, holding it up with a smile.

"You left . . . for the money?"

Wex nodded and repocketed the coin.

"You know it'll be a while before you make any money as a blacksmith."

Wex just shrugged.

THE TAP on the window shook Eyck from his thoughts, and he looked up, startled. Pash's furry bronze face peered at him through the glass. Eyck motioned for him to come in.

"I saw your candle and thought I'd pop in to say hi," the priest said, unbuckling his sword belt to hang it on the hook by the door. He took a seat at the table and looked pointedly at Eyck's mug. "You're drinking alone?"

"Don't worry. It's just tea," replied Eyck with a wry grin. "It's late . . . where are you coming back from?"

"The wounded from the border are being tended to out by the old mill—you know there's a whole tent city there now? I figured I'd lend a hand," Pash replied. He looked down at his hands, the fur stained dark in places. "I'm glad I have a strong stomach."

Eyck nodded, looking over at the staircase, his brow furrowed, listening.

"What's got *you* up this late?" asked Pash, loosening his priest's collar. "You don't look so good."

Rubbing his face tiredly, Eyck pointed to the still-warm teapot and poured his friend a cup when he nodded. "He's back."

"Who's back?"

"That lad . . . you, know . . . the slave boy."

Pash's brow wrinkled up, his grey eyes wide. "Oh yeah?"

"Yup. Showed up on my doorstep around noon."

"Huh. Did he tell you where he's been?"

"He was travelling." Eyck thought about the prison brand on Wex's arm. "Mostly."

"Ah." Pash blew across the top of his cup before taking a sip of the *kamamile* tea. "Well? What did he want?"

"To become my apprentice."

"And you're fool enough to think he'll stay this time?" Pash asked with a little chuckle, then he frowned at Eyck's expression. "What? It's a valid concern, no? But . . . regardless, I think it's a good idea for you to have someone here. You're no kid anymore—who knows how long you'll be able to keep throwing that hammer around."

This time, Eyck cracked a smile. Pash and he were the same age.

"I'm not that old, you arse."

"That's *Father* Arse, to you." Pash's handsome face creased into a grin and, in his teasing expression, lived the ghost of the wisecracking delinquent who'd befriended Eyck when they were children—the brat who'd pulled Eyck out of his shell while getting him into trouble more times than he could count. His best friend, and sometimes more . . . until the Suns had decided they needed Pash's fire for themselves, leaving behind someone who sometimes felt like a virtual stranger even after all this time.

"What is it? What's wrong?" Pash asked again, leaning forward to place a hand on Eyck's forearm. The thick gold ring of his priestly calling glinted in the candlelight. "Tell me?"

Eyck clenched his jaw and shook his head slowly, staring at the ring. "It's not something I can talk about with you . . . *Father*."

"For the love of—" Pash said, exasperated, pulling his hand away. "*This* is your problem?" He pulled off the ring, then drew the stiff gold filigree band out of his collar and set both aside. "Can you tell me as a *friend*, Eyck? What's going on? What did he do?"

Scowling, Eyck looked up into Pash's wide-set eyes. "*He* didn't do anything, Pash. I think, I don't know, maybe it's *me* that did something."

"What in Suns' Light are you talking about?"

Eyck glanced back at the stairs, listening again.

"Oh . . . he's *here*?" Pash said, following Eyck's gaze. "Now?"

Nodding, Eyck leaned forward and lowered his voice. "Yes, but I can't help but wonder if he *should* be . . ." He cleared his throat. "I thought he was being sincere about working for me, but the more I think about it, the more I wonder if he's here for revenge."

"Revenge? Are you certain that's just tea you're drinking?"

Eyck let out a low growl of frustration. "Ok . . . listen. Do you remember how hungover I was that morning?"

"The morning the kid ran away?"

Eyck nodded.

Pash gave a short laugh. "You were sick for two days."

"Well, I don't remember much of the night, only little things, but I think . . . I think I may have taken advantage of him. In a way that he might not have wanted."

Pash's brow wrinkled, but he didn't say anything.

"In a *sexual* . . . way."

"Good Suns, Eyck, I knew what you meant," Pash replied, sitting back. He shook his head and rubbed his forehead. "No, I don't believe it."

"Why not?"

"It's just not something you would do," he said, lifting one shoulder in a shrug. "I can't see you getting drunk enough that you'd go against your very nature."

"I drank a *lot* of moonshine."

"Not enough for you to *rape* someone," Pash replied. "Because that's what you're implying, isn't it?"

The ugly word hung in the air between them, and Eyck stared at his friend in horror, nausea like a lead ball in his stomach.

"How do you know I didn't?" he finally whispered.

"Trust me, if you could see the look on your face right now, I think you'd understand my profound skepticism." Pash took another sip of his tea, made a face because it had probably gone cold, and then tilted his head at Eyck. "What *do* you remember?"

Heart pounding, Eyck licked his lips and thought back to that hazy night. "I . . . I told him about Manya." He closed his eyes. "I just talked and talked . . . don't know for how long. It feels like all night. Then"— he opened his eyes and looked down at his hand, shaking his head— "my hand was around his tail, Pash."

"All right. What else?"

"That's it."

"You could have imagined it," Pash said. "You know how you are when you're drunk . . . Don't you remember that time you were sure you burned down the neighbour's shed?"

"No, I *swear*. I can see it, plain as day . . . I was tugging on it. The same way you used to li—" Eyck stopped himself. "Uh, tugging on it like I *wanted* him."

"Still. Even if that *did* happen," Pash replied, crossing his arms, "it doesn't necessarily mean anything *else* happened. Or that he didn't *want* it to happen."

"*Suns*, Pash . . . I can't believe you'd say that. He was only a kid. And a *slave*." Eyck remembered the way Wex had gone down on his knees, assuming he wanted his needs attended to. He took a gulp of the cold tea, as if it could wash away the sour taste in his mouth.

"You make it sound like he wasn't of age yet, and he was. I saw him too, remember? And, if you're so worried about what happened that night, why don't you just *ask* him?" Pash said, exasperated.

"He doesn't want to talk about it."

Pash's eyes widened, then his expression became a little guarded as if his belief in Eyck's innocence wasn't as concrete as before. "Ah." He cleared his throat. "Well, I'm glad you told me." Finger idly turning the priest's ring on the table, he asked, "Do you want me to talk to him?"

"No. Besides, he still can't talk. Not really. We've been using gestures."

"Oh. Well . . . if you change your mind, I'd be happy to try talking to him, in whatever fashion," Pash said. He knuckled his eye sleepily, then picked up his ring and collar band. "I should go. I'm supposed to lead Mornmass tomorrow . . . I don't want to yawn through the whole thing."

He stood, and Eyck got to his feet, not any less troubled than before.

"All right, Pash," Eyck said wearily, handing the priest his sword. "Thanks for coming by."

Pash clasped Eyck's arm after he'd tied the belt around his hips, his gaze warm. "You can always talk about *anything* with me, Eyck. I'm your *friend*."

"And a priest of the Three Suns," Eyck replied, trying to keep the bitterness out of his voice.

"Yes, but a priest who happens to believe that men have the right to choose whomever they wish to lie with," Pash said, squeezing Eyck's arm again. "When I sacrificed myself and took my vows, it was about serving the greater good, Eyck . . . it was never *ever* over any shame about what happened when we were boys. I've said it before, and I'll say it again: there was no sin in it. When will you believe me?"

Eyck just nodded. *No sin? Greater good? Your Suns think what we did is an abomination . . . and you chose them over me.*

There was nothing he could say. They'd fought over Pash's decision only once, the day Pash had confessed he was going to Walk in the Suns' Light, and it had nearly destroyed their friendship. Eyck could hold his tongue and make his own sacrifice if it meant clinging to what little was left between them.

"Well, good night," Pash said, smiling tiredly. "Sleep well . . . and stop worrying. You're a good man, Eyckmigh. Believe in that."

"Thanks. Good night." Eyck watched the priest walk up the street and sighed, scratching the back of his neck. Maybe it *was* all in his head.

After a quick trip out to the alley to piss against the side of the building, he snuffed the candle and dumped the rest of the cold tea and leaves into the covered pail of table scraps by the door, then he froze, turning to the stairs.

Holding his breath, he stood listening. Had he imagined the quiet tread on the steps? A minute or two went by, and the only sound was the quiet click of the time-keeper on the mantel, marking the end of the hour.

It was late. He had to get to bed, but the thought of climbing the steps in the dark unsettled him. What if there was a knife waiting for him at the top?

He glanced over at the unfinished war hammer leaning against the anvil, but then chuckled, shaking his head at the image of himself creeping up the stairs with the heavy weapon held aloft.

No, if Wex intended to do him harm, it was because Eyck deserved it—far better to face whatever lay ahead unarmed than potentially make things worse by scaring the lad. Besides, he was probably just being paranoid.

Lifting his chin, he walked quietly up the steps, but nothing met him at the top except muffled snoring coming from the opposite end of the wide-open space. Eyes on the long dark shape of Wex sleeping on his pallet under the far window, Eyck quickly stripped down to his smallclothes and crawled into his own bed. He was so tired that sleep came easily despite his troubled mind.

Wex opened his eyes at the first raspy snore and lay watching the big blacksmith sleep, his brow deeply furrowed.

Chapter Three

Wex startled awake, chased from sleep by a strange and stressful dream, and sat up. It took him a few seconds to remember where he was.

Smoothing down the sleep-rumpled fur on his cheek, he yawned, amazed by how well rested he felt. Normally, he was anxious around new people—trust didn't come easily for him. Either Eyck's affable nature had put him at ease or the gruelling pace he'd set to South Galetsy had worn him out completely, because he hadn't woken up at all during the night. Not once.

Yawning again, he looked around. The upper floor of the smithy was just one big space with small square windows set on opposite sides and a hole in the centre of the floor for the staircase.

I'm glad I don't sleep walk, Wex thought, pulling on his trousers. He made a mental note to remember the opening in the floor in case he needed to get around in the dark. If he wasn't careful, he'd wind up with a broken neck like Eyck's late wife.

Wex quickly neatened the bedclothes over the spare pallet Eyck had found for him, then lifted his head, nostrils flaring.

Suns, that smells delicious.

He patted and tugged at his travel-worn shirt, trying to make himself more presentable, then made his way downstairs.

Eyck smiled at Wex as he came down the wooden steps. With his black hair sticking out in every direction and a sleep crease parting the fur down one side of his thick neck, Eyck looked amusingly rumpled and, despite being nearly as big as Wex, the absolute opposite of intimidating. Wex found himself smiling back without giving it a thought.

The blacksmith had six eggs cooking in a huge cast-iron pan over the coals simmering in his forge alongside what looked like potatoes and strips of . . . *something* that seemed to be the source of the wonderful smell.

"Want to grab those plates?" Eyck said, flipping the eggs with his spatula.

Wex quickly took up the stoneware plates and held them out to Eyck who loaded them up, and then the two of them sat down in their usual spots at the table.

Curious, Wex picked at the fried flat things with the end of his eating knife as Eyck carved two thick slabs of dark bread, handing one to Wex.

Wex burst the egg yolks with his bread, sopped up some of the yellow, and pushed hashed potatoes onto the bread with his knife before taking a huge bite. Then he poked at the unfamiliar brown strips again, worried.

"What's wrong?" Eyck asked around a mouthful of egg. He had crumbs of bread stuck to his lip and a bit of yolk on his chin.

Making a face, Wex pointed to the strange things on his plate.

"It's not meat, if that's what you're worried about, lad. We might be near the border, but that doesn't mean we're anything like the Oza. It's just hickory smoked wheat glutty. The miller, Ms. Tabor, makes it. Go on, you'll love it."

Skeptical, Wex cut off a small piece and tasted it. He smiled and quickly devoured the rest. It was salty and smoky and chewy with crispy edges. He'd never had anything like it.

"Yeah, Macy sure knows how to cook. Remember the bean pies you had that first time?"

Wex nodded. How could he forget? They'd been the very first taste of freedom he'd ever had.

"She made those too. Though now she puts mushrooms in them,

and I'm not sure I like the change. Ah well." Eyck sat back, wiping his face, and burped. "That hit the spot. You want more? Better fill up, lad, I'm going to work you hard today."

Wex looked at his empty plate. He could eat twice again as much but didn't want to seem greedy. He shook his head and pushed his plate away.

THREE HOURS LATER, Wex was regretting not having taken Eyck up on his offer of seconds at breakfast. He panted as he lugged the heavy quench tank full of brackish water back to its place near the anvil then quickly grabbed the bellows handle at Eyck's shout. The blacksmith might be a good-natured sort normally, but the minute he started working, he turned into an unforgiving taskmaster.

But that was fine—Wex wanted to learn the trade as quickly as he could so he could be on his way.

"Give it a few more," Eyck said, turning the workpiece with his tongs, "then get the hammer. You'll be striking."

Wex nodded and pulled down on the bellows handle again three times then hefted the huge three-weights sledgehammer with both hands. Eyck had made it look so easy that day long ago when he walked up with the hammer on his shoulder. Wex adjusted his grip on the worn handle and looked up at Eyck.

The blacksmith let out a laugh, shaking his head. "Here I thought you were the circus strongman . . . Or was it all an act? Get over here," Eyck said, lifting the red-hot metal out of the forge. He used his tongs one-handed to hold it against the top of the anvil and pulled a small metal hammer out of his apron. "Hit *here*." He tapped the glowing chunk with the little ball-peen hammer.

Wex gritted his teeth and brought the sledgehammer down hard, letting out a grunt of pain as the contact with the anvil jarred his shoulder, the hammer nearly bouncing out of his hand. His mark was way off.

"Try again," Eyck growled, tapping the same spot. "And for Suns' sake, try not to take my fucking hand off!"

By the time Wex got the hang of wielding the heavy sledgehammer with any sort of precision, both of his palms were blistered, and his right shoulder ached like a knife had been plunged into the joint. He was so sore and worn out that when Eyck held out a glass of small ale as refreshment, he could barely lift his arm to take it. Frustrated, he drank the weak beer, trying not to wince as the cup stuck to the oozing blisters. Hand shaking, he set it back on the table.

"It'll get easier. You'll see," Eyck said quietly, gone gentle again now that they were taking a breather.

Curling his lip, Wex turned his back, shrugging. Why had he assumed it would be an easy trade to learn? He couldn't read, couldn't write, and now even his muscles had failed him.

What the schatten am I going to do now?

"Hey, this is only your first day." Eyck put his hand on Wex's shoulder.

Wex tore away from the touch, fangs bared, and pressed his back against the wall, breathing heavily.

"I'm sorry. Sorry." Eyck backed away, his eyes wide and nostrils flared. "I didn't mean anything . . . I just . . . I'm sorry."

The look of horror on Eyck's face reminded Wex of what he'd overheard as he'd lay by the stairs eavesdropping on the conversation between the priest and the blacksmith the night before.

Taking a deep breath, Wex held out his hand and shook his head. *"You didn't hurt me that night,"* he signed quickly, knowing the blacksmith wouldn't understand the complex gestures. *"I was a broken thing then, not a boy, not a man, but a* thing *. . . and I barely understood what was going on or why you'd freed me. And I* hated *you for pushing me away . . . you know, I held a knife to your throat as soon as you passed out from drink, and I was going to kill you and rob you. I didn't, but now I don't regret it because you'll be useful to me . . . that is, if I can ever fucking learn how to smith. But, just because I didn't know enough* then *and wanted you to touch me doesn't mean I want you to touch me* now, *so keep your fucking hands off!"*

38

HEART SINKING, Eyck watched Wex's rapid hand signs with a mixture of bewilderment and dread. The young man seemed absolutely furious as he jabbed the air with his forefinger, pointing to Eyck with a scowl before continuing on his silent tirade, the gestures rendered ugly by the violence with which Wex formed them.

Finally, the young man ran out of steam and just stood glaring at Eyck, his chest heaving.

"Did I . . ." Eyck swallowed hard, his heart pounding. "Back then . . . Did I do something to—"

But before he could finish, Wex sliced the air with one hand and shook his head, his tail-tip flicking rapidly from side to side. Closing his eyes, Wex's expression softened as he took a few deep breaths.

He opened his eyes and once more pointed to Eyck, but this time, the gesture was calm. He followed this with the sign for *night* and the one for *talk*, ones he had taught Eyck the day before, and pointed to him again.

"That night . . . I talked?"

Wex nodded and pressed his hand to his heart, his expression going profoundly sad. He pointed and signed *talk* again.

The meaning dawned on Eyck. "I was talking about being sad. About my Manya. Yes, I remember that."

Wex pointed to himself, frowning like he was uncertain.

"You? You what?"

Wex mimed giving him something, then pointed to himself, the ghost of a smirk on his face.

"You mean . . . uh, you wanted to give yourself to me? Because I was sad?"

Wex nodded.

Eyck sat down on the edge of the table, trying to remember. "But . . . did we . . . uh . . . ?"

Wex shook his head vehemently. He pointed at Eyck and mimed a hard push.

"I . . . pushed you away?" Eyck said.

Oh, thank Suns.

Stunned relief uncoiled the dread in Eyck's belly at Wex's nod even though there was something slightly odd about the young man's expression.

You're a good man. Pash was right.

"Thank you for tell—"

Wex sliced the air again with his hand and held one finger up, a warning in his eyes.

"You don't want to talk about it." Eyck nodded. That must have been a bewildering and frightening time for the newly freed slave. Revisiting the past was obviously something Wex wanted to avoid. "I understand."

Once more, Wex pointed at Eyck, at Eyck's hand, then his own shoulder, and shook his head. The meaning was clear: *Don't touch me.*

Flustered and uncomfortable, Eyck nodded quickly. "Understood."

The smile Wex gave him didn't touch his eyes at first, but he picked up the empty cup of small ale and wrinkled his brow hopefully, his friendly mood already returning.

Chuckling a little uneasily, Eyck refilled his cup. He didn't think he'd ever met anyone as volatile as Wex. It was like being in a room with a half-tame creature—one that could bite your hand as surely as eat from it.

"All right. Drink up—don't think we're done for the day," Eyck said gruffly before finishing his own ale. He set down his cup and pulled a silver and two copper coins from his money pouch. "You're to go to the charcoal burner with a wheelbarrow and bring back some charcoal. He's on the edge of town, right near the river. Fellow by the name of Vernel. Don't worry, he'll know exactly why you're there, so you don't need to speak."

Eyck frowned, wondering whether he should put off the task until tomorrow—they had enough charcoal to last the day at the least, and Wex's palms were very obviously blistered. Clearly, the young man was frustrated and in pain. However, Wex plucked the coins out of Eyck's hand, shoving them into his pocket with a sharp nod, and left the smithy through the back.

Eyck grabbed his broom and began sweeping up, gradually pushing the pile towards the open front door to sweep it out into the street.

His mind wandered as he worked, thinking about how Wex had said he'd "offered" himself up like a gift . . . and about what might have happened had he not pushed the boy away. His face felt warm, thinking how Wex had just recoiled from his friendly touch . . .

"Still alive this morning, I see."

Startled, Eyck looked over his shoulder. The priest was wearing the cloud-white robes of high ceremony, instead of the less conspicuous ivory shirt and trousers he normally wore about town, and a flat white hat whose wide brim was peaked to either side to show the notches in his pointed ears.

"Suns, where are you off to looking like that?" he asked.

He'd only seen Pash in full priestly regalia twice before—not being of the faith himself, Eyck had gone to the service at the big church solely to support Pash when he received his deacon's collar and when his ears had been notched for priesthood. In his robes and hat, Pash looked like a stranger, and Eyck didn't like it one bit.

"We've been requested by His Excellency, the Archbessop to attend the diplomatic talks at the border," Pash said with a grimace. "The church pastor nominated three of us, and I unfortunately was one of them. Good Suns, I'm really not looking forward to it."

"Well, I'm pretty sure the king isn't looking forward to priests meddling in diplomatic affairs," Eyck replied with a grin, leaning on his broom.

"You know the Oza will bring their cultists to the table. King Enoch's going to have to put up with our presence if he's to get anywhere with those zealots . . . I just wish Pastor Deechuk had picked someone else to go."

"Hm," Eyck grunted. *You reap what you sow.* There was nothing good he could say about any of it.

Ignoring Eyck's polite disapproval, Pash glanced into the smithy. "How's your apprentice then? Where is he? Shouldn't *he* be the one sweeping?"

"Sent him to Vernel," Eyck replied, scratching the back of his neck and staring off towards the river. "Hopefully he doesn't get lost."

"I'm sure if he found his way back to South Galetsy after all these sun-cycles, he'll find his way to the charcoal mounds." Pash straightened one of the three gold belts at his waist. "So? Do you think he's got it in him to smith?"

Eyck tilted his head, wrinkling his nose in thought. "Well, he's not as strong as he looks, but I'm sure that'll change. And it took him three tries to hit the piece I was holding . . . but again, I'm sure that'll change. If he wants to be a good blacksmith, I figure he's got the raw tools, just needs to hone them. But there's one thing I'm not sure about."

"What's that?"

"Who ever heard of a mute blacksmith?"

"There's a first for everything."

"Just . . . how is he ever going to go off on his own without someone to speak for him?"

"Why don't you let him worry about that?" Pash said, turning back to Eyck with an odd look in his grey eyes. "He's just your apprentice. Teach him and let him be on his way. You don't need to get more involved than that . . . it's not like he's going to stick around."

Eyck frowned at the forced indifference in Pash's tone and wondered what was behind it, but before he could ask, Father Sprey and Father Alfert walked up.

"Father Tormil? Are you ready to depart?" asked the former, the side peaks of his hat very high to allow for his overly large ears.

"Yes. I'm coming." Pash glanced back at Eyck.

Normally, they'd clasp arms in parting, but it felt a little improper with the other priests watching.

Pash just smiled at him. "I'll see you when I get back."

"Good luck with the cultists," Eyck replied with a smirk. "And wear a pomander and breathe through your mouth."

Pash laughed. "I will."

NEARING THE SMITHY, Wex watched the three white-robed men walk away, wondering again about the relationship between the blacksmith and the priest. They were good friends, obviously, and had known each other a long time, but the fact that Eyck kept company with a priest made Wex leery.

Priests were cruel hypocrites and far more loyal to the glow of gold than to the three fabled Living Suns they supposedly worshipped. He'd experienced enough abuse at the hands of Mangley's pet priest at Stettefyr to know those who wore the white weren't averse to lust or avarice—the priests he'd seen joining the line at the darkened circus caravan had cemented that distrust.

Wex spat and pushed the wheelbarrow around the back of the smithy to begin loading the charcoal into the big wooden hopper. He'd bought a few clean rags from the surly old charcoal burner for a penny and wrapped his hands to protect them. The material was already filthy and stuck to his palms, but it was better than nothing. It would be a few days before his gloves were ready, so he had best make do.

Frowning, Wex pitched some more charcoal in the hopper, his mind on that night five cycles earlier. Eyck's hands had been blistered from pulling Mangley's blasted chariot . . . he'd forgotten about that part. Maybe Eyck still had that salve.

He dumped the rest of the charcoal in the overflow box by the door, shutting both it and the hopper tight against rain, and went into the smithy.

Eyck was standing by the table with a cup in one hand and a distracted look on his face. The light from the window caught the green of his eyes, making them brilliant against the dark fur of his face, but Wex found his gaze drawn down to the open neck of the blacksmith's grey shirt and the generous tuft of thick black fur that sprouted from it.

"Wex?"

Wex blinked, startled to realize he'd been staring, and wrinkled his brow in question at Eyck. His heart was beating fast . . . as if he'd been caught doing something wrong.

"You got all the charcoal in? Old Vernel didn't give you any trouble?"

Wex nodded then shook his head. Taking a deep breath, he stepped forward, one hand outstretched.

"What is it?" Eyck asked, coming a bit closer. He stared down at the dirty bandage as Wex peeled it away from his skin. "Ah, yes. I was wondering if you were going to want to do anything about that."

Nodding, Wex signed *salve* with the other hand and pointed to the small metal tin on the mantelpiece.

"Of course. Use all you want. Mrs. Begmard can always make more." Eyck gave Wex the tin and sat on the edge of the table, drinking from his cup.

Wex had the distinct impression that Eyck wanted to offer his help but was purposefully keeping his distance to comply with Wex's earlier request not to be touched.

As soon as Wex had the tin open, the unique scent of the salve sent his heart racing even faster than before and his mouth went bone-dry. Flaring his nostrils, he shook his head to dispel the momentary faintness, then swallowed and tried to slow his breathing.

He'd noticed before that his sense of smell seemed more closely linked to memories than any other. The first time he'd smelled cabbage soup, months after he'd run away, he'd nearly thrown up— watery cabbage soup had been the only thing fed to him the whole time he'd belonged to that bastard Mangley.

However, this wasn't nausea. It was excitement and anger and fear all wound up together into something that made him want to crawl under the table like he had five sun-cycles ago—an awful, breathless feeling that he needed to expel from his body because it was accompanied by something that was entirely unwanted: arousal.

"Are you all right?"

Eyck's voice sounded far away. Wex nodded, carefully smearing salve onto his torn palms. The smell of it had been strong on his face that night, the salve put there gently by Eyck's roughened fingers to soothe the bruises Mangley had given him.

The scent had lingered, following him like a ghost along the moonlit King's Road, confusing his anger over the blacksmith's rejection, taunting him with the idea that maybe, just *maybe* he shouldn't have left.

It had taken him a while to realize the smell was also coming from his tail and had permeated the material of his loincloth. Wex had bathed himself quickly in the icy river and thrown the loincloth away, preferring to run naked through the woods rather than be reminded that he'd offered himself to a man of his own accord.

Had he been aroused that night? It seemed unlikely . . . but Wex couldn't remember.

In a daze, Wex handed the tin back to Eyck, avoiding his eyes.

"Here." Eyck held out some clean strips of unbleached cloth.

Wex accepted them with a nod, winding them around his hands.

"You'll work the bellows for me for a bit . . . it goes faster if I can use both hands with the tongs. Then we'll break for lunch. You can learn how to prep a mould this afternoon. It's light work, but I figure your hands need a break, right? I'll run by Fagin's later and see where he's gotten with your gloves. And"—Eyck rubbed a hand over his mouth, as if not certain he wanted to speak the next words—"I . . . have something for you."

Wex lifted his eyes to meet Eyck's, but the big blacksmith had already turned away. Without another word, Eyck went upstairs, and mystified, Wex stared up at the ceiling, listening to the scraping and banging as Eyck searched for something. After a few minutes, Eyck tramped down the stairs again, his steps made heavy by his big black boots, and placed a dusty satchel on the table.

"They were my wife's. She was a schoolteacher," he said simply and crossed the room to stoke the forge.

Curious, Wex unwound the thong holding the satchel closed and peered inside, then he frowned and stepped back, bemused by the contents.

Books?

He rapped his knuckles hard on the table, and Eyck turned to look at him.

"*I can't read!*" he signed. "*You know that.*"

Is he trying *to make me feel stupid?*

"Yes, I know you can't read," Eyck replied, shaking his head. He turned back to the forge. "Those are books to learn *how*. I've decided it's going to be part of your training . . . every evening I'm going to help you learn your letters. You're going to need to read and write if you want to set up your own smithy one day."

Oh. Brow furrowed, Wex spread the books out on the tabletop. They had colourful hand-painted wooden covers. Wex recognized some letters on three of them and numbers on the fourth.

Maybe he really is *just . . . nice.*

Wex couldn't remember anyone who didn't want *something* from him. Even Red Falcorr had wanted money or liquor in return for trying to teach him to read.

Wex walked over to the blacksmith and cleared his throat. A confusing mix of emotions churned inside him, but the one at the forefront was gratitude.

Eyck turned, his eyes guarded, and Wex realized pulling out his wife's books had shaken him a bit.

"*I'm a lost cause,*" he signed. "*I don't think I can learn to read, but I appreciate it.*"

Eyck furrowed his brow. "I didn't get any of that."

Wex smiled, waving it off, suddenly in a better mood. "*Thank you,*" he signed simply.

Smiling back, Eyck nodded. "You're welcome."

Chapter Four

Eyck smiled as he eavesdropped on the conversation taking place on the other side of the smithy. After dribbling more water on the sharpening stone, Eyck slid the long chamara knife across its surface a few times, honing it, then lifted his eyes to check on Wex and his admirers.

Rammie and Esther, two young women roughly the same age as Wex, were in the smithy for the third time that week, just to watch Wex at work at the forge and anvil. They were topless in the summer heat as was the current style among the younger generation, and each wore layers of long beaded necklaces that accentuated their glossy coats and lithe bodies.

Esther wore stacks of bracelets on both wrists and a matching set around the base of her tail, the silver bright against her brown striped Grendall fur, and Rammie had jewelled golden half-moons dangling from the points of her ears.

They'd obviously dressed to beguile, and Eyck couldn't help but notice that Rammie had either rouged or pinched her nipples to make them stand out—the buds that jutted from her honey-gold Ulven fur were a curiously bright pink.

Eyck chuckled and shook his head. Such forward mating displays would have been frowned upon in his youth . . . but the world *was* changing.

The new king was young and had brought progressive ideas to the throne, like ending slavery, softening the caste system, and gradually reducing the power of the church—all things Eyck supported wholeheartedly—but sometimes he felt decorum still had its place.

Or maybe I'm just old and conventional.

He laughed ruefully to himself. Well, he wasn't *that* conventional. There *were* other things he'd like to see changed, like support for same-sex pairings, and it was frustrating not to know King Enoch's stance on it.

"Is that very heavy, Wex?" asked Esther, making her voice velvety soft as she leaned back against a stack of boxes, displaying the long lines of her svelte body to advantage.

Wex shook his head in response as he hefted the two-weight sledgehammer, bringing it down with a resounding clang on the piece of iron. The young women covered their ears and giggled as Wex began to shape a rough base for a post frame.

Eyck could see why they were willing to risk their hearing to watch Wex—under the lustrous silver fur, muscles rippled in the young man's arms as he hammered, and when he turned in place to get a better angle, they gazed longingly at his broad, powerful back and muscular backside.

Eyck blinked then averted his gaze when he realized he was staring as openly and as hungrily as the two girls. Frowning, he focused on his work.

Wex had said "Don't touch," and Eyck wouldn't dream of going against his wishes.

But . . . just because I can't touch doesn't mean I can't look, *does it?* He raised his head for another look at Wex's rump and was surprised to meet his gaze instead. The lines of Wex's face were taut, a deep furrow between his brows—he was plainly uncomfortable with the attention he was getting from the two young women.

Eyck grinned, and Wex's expression turned to pure misery as his admirers took advantage of the break in hammering to quickly ask him all sorts of things about the work he was doing, carefully phrasing their questions so that he could answer with a nod or a headshake. Neither his muteness, nor his breed for that matter, seemed to make a lick of difference, and Eyck found it heartening that the youth were leaving behind their elders' prejudices.

"*Help?*" Wex signed surreptitiously.

Eyck chuckled then sighed, putting down his work to go rescue his apprentice.

"Ladies . . . I'm sorry, but you're both such lovely distractions that poor Wex isn't getting any work done," he said. Smirking at Wex's glare, he opened the front door and gestured, his tone kind. "Please, you can come back another time."

The two looked crestfallen at being asked to leave, and for a moment, it seemed Esther would plead to stay, but she nodded and Rammie followed suit. Eyck smiled, remembering what it was like being young and so full of the urge to mate that it sometimes trounced common sense.

"Sorry, Mr. Stromsmith," they said together.

"Bye, Wex," said Rammie, her voice shy.

"See you soon, Wex," Esther added, then bit her lip and tilted her head as her gaze swept Wex from head to toe. "Sorry if we distracted you."

Wex just pressed his lips together and shrugged, the gesture ambiguous.

"Wish your parents well for me," Eyck said, ushering them out the door.

They assured him they would, apologized again, and left.

He turned to Wex. "Most lads would be delighted to have two lovely young things vying for his attention."

Snorting, Wex shook his head.

"Not to your liking, then?"

"*They ask silly questions and get in the way.*"

Eyck pondered as Wex pulled a rag out of his apron to wipe the sweat from his nape. Was Wex even attracted to females? It hadn't occurred to him that he wouldn't be. His own tastes ran to both, but that didn't mean Wex was the same way. Eyck frowned—maybe Wex didn't feel attraction towards either sex, given what he'd been through.

"But they're both very pretty, don't you think?" he asked, curious.

"If you say so."

"I think they are."

"Well, you can have them then," Wex replied without looking at him. His gestures were curt, and the muscles in his jaw bulged as he clenched his jaw. *"Now can I get back to work?"*

"Of course. Can't have my pretty face distracting you either," he joked, trying to lighten the mood.

Wex's dark-brown eyes flicked back to him. Did Wex look a little *flustered*, or was it just a trick of the light?

"I don't find you that pretty either," Wex replied at length, surprising him with a sudden, teasing grin. *"Now let me do my work, old man."*

Eyck laughed and waved him on, but once he was back at the table with the blade and sharpening stone, he thought he felt Wex's eyes on him. Sure enough, when he looked up, Wex turned quickly away.

That was . . . interesting.

LEANING BACK in the wooden chair, Eyck rested his head against the wall and closed his eyes, enjoying the warm sun on his face. He wiggled his toes in his boots, happy to be off his feet for a bit, and sighed.

From inside the shop came the sounds of Wex practicing with the whetstone. The rhythmic rasping noise was making him drowsy. It had been a very busy week, and he was glad Wex was proving himself to be more help than hindrance. The last order of short swords for the soldiers at the border had left that morning, a full day before they were due, which meant Eyck could afford to take a nice break.

He frowned, thinking about Pash—the priest had been gone for over a fortnight. By all accounts, things were tense at the border, the ongoing talks making little headway and the armies only barely adhering to the temporary truce. Fights were breaking out daily, and loss of life like this hadn't been felt in generations—not since unification of the fiefdoms under the rule of one king.

The Border War, as it had become known, was a fire that had been kindled from a land dispute. A Dankel farmer had been extending his fields into Oza territory for several seasons—either from greed or ignorance—until one day a company of Oza soldiers had arrived at his door demanding he relinquish his entire holdings in reparations. When the man refused, the Oza razed his property, seizing his wife and two young daughters. The man's family were said to have been sold as concubines to one of the Oza elders, a *Cobirati*, and were presumably being subjected to unspeakable acts.

The whole thing turned Eyck's stomach, but so little was known about the deeply xenophobic Oza, it was hard to separate hearsay from fact. Eyck had even heard whispered rumours about Oza cultists sacrificing the farmer to use his blood to temper their swords.

Which was *ludicrous*, of course. The farmer had escaped with his skin intact. Besides, Eyck couldn't imagine blood making a good quenching bath for hot steel. For one, it would take the blood of dozens of men for a single sword. Then keeping that much blood from going rancid? No . . . it was definitely a flight of fancy—

Startled, Eyck opened his eyes, suddenly aware of a presence next to him. For someone so big, it was amazing how quietly Wex could move.

"You're done?" Eyck asked, sitting up.

Wex nodded and handed him the dagger. Eyck tested the edge on his forearm, easily scraping away a copper-sized swath of fur and smiled. "Good job. That's twenty-fold steel . . . it'll keep that edge a long time." He smiled wider and gave it back to Wex. "Keep it."

Frowning Wex looked at the blade then lifted his eyes to Eyck's again, his expression wary.

"It's yours," Eyck replied with a chuckle. "Oh, don't look at me like that . . . You think I didn't see you eyeing it all week? Why did you think I had you sharpen it?"

The corner of Wex's lips quirked up in a smile, but his eyes still held suspicion in their dark depths.

Eyck sighed, shaking his head. "I consider it well earned for the time you've saved me, but if you want, I guess you can pay me back for it when you have the money. All right?"

Seemingly mollified, Wex nodded, his expression softening.

Eyck wondered if a day would come where Wex stopped scrutinizing his motives. He knew it wasn't the young man's fault;

Eyck couldn't imagine what damage a past like his had done to his spirit, but it ruffled Eyck's fur that Wex still didn't trust him.

※

WEX TURNED the beautiful blade over in his hands, the light and dark patterns in the steel seeming to shift with the sun's rays, and nodded his thanks. It was a far better knife than the chipped bronze one he'd bought himself on the road.

He'd definitely pay Eyck back—there was no way he could accept such a valuable gift, no matter what the blacksmith said.

After sliding the blade into its sheath and then into the pocket of his apron, Wex sat down on the ground next to Eyck and leaned back on the wall, eyes closed—much as Eyck had been doing when Wex came out. The late afternoon sun was warm, but the breeze was cool, and it was nice to take a break.

Wex was pretty pleased with himself. The sledgehammers were getting easier to wield every day and he could strike with precision nine times out of ten. Plus, his shoulder no longer ached like a wound. Thanks to Eyck's heated bags of seed to place against his muscles at night and his gradual adaptation to this new way of life, the pain in his arms only felt like proof of a job well done. He was even getting a real feel for how heat and pressure affected the metal he was working on . . . not that Eyck was letting him shape much on his own yet. However, Wex felt it wouldn't be long before he trusted him to handle some of the easier work himself.

He opened his eyes and glanced over at Eyck. The big blacksmith was staring in the direction of the high road leading out of town, his brow deeply furrowed. Wex knew he was worried about the priest.

He cleared his throat, catching Eyck's attention, and signed, "*No letter?*"

Eyck shook his head. "Nothing yet. I'm sure he's fine though. Pash can take care of himself. Before he became a priest, he was on his way to becoming quite the swordsman." Eyck smiled, his gaze returning to the west and his forehead still wrinkled in worry. "I'm sure he'll be all right." His tail-tip swished quickly back and forth, belying his words.

Wex surprised himself by reaching out to touch Eyck's arm.

Starting, Eyck glanced back at him, his eyes wide. The blacksmith's fur tufted up around the edge of the rolled-up sleeve. In the brief instant Wex's fingers made contact, he discovered Eyck's fur was thicker and coarser than his own.

Wex thrust his hands into his apron pocket, closing his fists loosely around the sheathed blade. Awkwardly, he shrugged, wondering why he felt so embarrassed and nervous, then he pulled out one hand and quickly signed, "*Sorry about your friend.*"

"Don't be sorry, lad. Chances are, if Pash'd steered clear of religion, he'd have joined the king's army to fight this stupid war, and I'd be sat here worrying all the same," Eyck said, smirking. He narrowed his eyes at Wex. "Say, have you ever seen one of the Oza . . . in all your travels?"

Wex slowly shook his head. He'd only heard tales about them.

"I saw some once when I was a boy. My family spent a summer in Olmtown. There's a border crossing there, and I saw two of the border guards . . . they gave me the willies." Eyck chuckled and met Wex's eyes. "Did you know the Oza all look the same?"

Wex nodded. He'd also heard they ate the flesh of animals and were deeply religious. They weren't even a breed of Kat'hoondeman— despite the physical resemblance, they were something entirely *other*.

"Yep. To a man, they've got fur the colour of bone, like they were bleached in the sun . . . and no markings at all. They're all just . . . Oza. All the same."

Wex nodded—it was hard to imagine though. No Samra to lord over them all? No Garza or Losano to school their minds or souls? No Levek or Duval merchants and tradesmen? No Dankel to farm? No Grendall hustlers and solicitors? No Ulven artists and actors? Wex looked down at his hands. *No Kirmen to enslave?*

I don't know. He thought about the nine breeds and how each were treated according to their ranks in the caste system. *Sounds kind of nice.*

"Supposedly, they have eyes that reflect red in the dark," continued Eyck.

Wex wrinkled his nose skeptically.

Eyck grinned. "Hey, I'm just telling you what I've heard. I didn't see their eyes that day—they were so far away—but they looked like, I don't know . . . wisps of white smoke, like they were only half there." He shook his head. "Creeped me out."

Smiling politely, Wex nodded, but his mind was still on the Oza. Was there really no rigid, inborn hierarchy among them? If they all looked the same, presumably any of them could rise to power. *That can't be . . . can it?*

Slapping his knees, Eyck sat straighter. "All right, we should get to your reading lessons. You ready?" He stood up with a little grunt.

"Not tonight," Wex signed quickly. He hated the lessons. They always made him feel stupid and worthless because no matter how hard he tried, the squiggles and dots that Eyck made him copy out, over and over again, never coalesced into something more meaningful. It was as if that part of his brain was just . . . missing. *"Tomorrow."*

Eyck stared at him for a moment, considering, then shook his head. "No, we should really get back to it. I feel like you were about to make a breakthrough last night . . . we should strike while the iron is hot."

"Tomorrow," repeated Wex, shaking his head. *Come on, blacksmith. You hate these stupid lessons as much as I do; I can see it in your face*, he thought, but he signed, *"Please? One night off."*

Eyck exhaled slowly, as if pondering, but Wex could tell he'd won. "Wellll," said the big blacksmith, running a hand through his thick black hair. "I *guess* that's all right." He smiled, clearly relieved not to have to struggle through another pointless lesson. "What the hell . . . let's go down to the tavern for our supper! What do you say?"

Wex lifted his brows. *The tavern? Is he serious?*

"I haven't been there in forever," Eyck said, taking off his apron, his grin widening. "Hmm . . . I wonder if Camacky still makes that molasses bread . . ."

Following the blacksmith into the shop, Wex wondered how he could get out of going without insulting Eyck. He helped put away the tools, his eyes averted as he thought.

"You're dawdling."

Wex looked up. The blacksmith had his brawny arms crossed and a look of concern on his brindled face. Obviously, Eyck could sense something was wrong.

"What is it?"

Are you that *naïve, old man?* With a sigh, Wex gestured, "*Kirmen.*"

"Oh, that doesn't bloody matter, lad," Eyck replied, laughing in relief. "Come on, hang up your apron . . . trust me, it'll be fine. I'll buy you a pint . . ."

Skeptical, Wex pulled off the heavy chamara apron and hung it on the hook next to Eyck's, and then he grabbed his cloak and threw it over his shoulders, pulling up the hood to cast his features into shadow.

Eyck watched him, a deep crease appearing above his nose, obviously thinking Wex was overreacting, but he shrugged and waved Wex out the door. "You know what?" the blacksmith said as he locked up. "We've done so well this week, I do believe I'm going to have a whiskey. How about you? Can I buy you a whiskey?"

As they walked down the cobbled road towards the river, Wex side-eyed Eyck, amused over the big man's growing enthusiasm. He nodded and signed, "*Thank you.*"

"Don't thank me yet . . . Camacky's whiskey'll burn the fur off your chest," Eyck replied with a toothy grin.

Wex chuckled agreeably, but tugged on the side of his hood, steeling himself for the inevitable.

Chapter Five

E yck sucked in his gut as he squeezed his bulk between the wooden table and bench and sat down with a satisfied grunt, looking around. Camacky's tavern hadn't changed a bit—the jar of pickled eggs still sat at the end of the bar, the lighting was just as poor as the last time he'd been, and it seemed like the same men were playing the same game of darts and daggers by the cellar stairs. He waited until Wex had settled himself on the bench opposite, the young man's back to the room, before catching the eye of the pretty Ulven barmaid.

Smiling, the diminutive, tawny-furred woman approached their table, the end of her tail tucked through the apron tie at her waist to keep it out of the way *and* out of the hands of randy patrons, and put her fists on her hips, her bright-blue eyes narrowed.

"Well, my *goodness*. Eyckmigh Stromsmith . . . as I live and breathe," Tembra said, leaning forward to swipe at the table with her rag. "When was the last time I saw you, honey? The Spring Fayre?"

There was an edge to her voice that wasn't lost on Eyck, and he scratched the back of his neck, his face warm with embarrassment. He'd completely forgotten about what had happened at the fayre.

"Uh, yeah. Yeah, I think that was the last time." Eyck regretted what'd happened with her that night. Not that she wasn't lovely to cuddle . . . quite the opposite. Tembra was plump in all the right places, her fur was soft and fragrant, and she'd been light as a feather on his lap, her warm little hands splayed against his chest as they rubbed cheeks under the big beech while the band played. However, he'd simply been caught up in the moment, in a good mood because of the warm weather. It was only when he'd gotten home that he realized she might have gotten the wrong impression.

Right . . . that's why I've been avoiding Camacky's. Because I'm a fool coward.

"Tem, I meant to come calling the next day . . . but work just, you know . . ." he said lamely.

"Mmhmm," Tembra replied, her tone heavy with skepticism. "Riiight."

Eyck looked over at Wex and frowned. The young man was smirking at him.

"I mean . . ." Eyck sighed, rubbing his coarse cheek fur up against the grain with his palm, trying to come up with something to say. "I was . . . um . . . It was . . ."

Tembra burst out laughing and delivered a stinging flick to his shoulder with her wet cloth.

"I'm only teasing, Eyck," she said, her smile mischievous. "I had fun and you did too, and that was that." Then Tembra spoke quietly, leaning towards him with her lids lowered flirtatiously. "Though I *was* hoping for a little more than just a few cuddles, hm?" She winked at him.

Eyck let out an uneasy chuckle, wondering if he really was off the hook or not.

Grinning, Tembra crossed her arms and straightened. "Now, what can I get you, honey?"

Sighing in relief at the change in subject, Eyck smiled hopefully. "Any chance you still serve that spicy lentil dish? You know, the one with the crispy spring onions on top?" At Tembra's nod, he added, "With molasses bread?"

"You got it," Tembra replied. "And what about your friend—" She turned to Wex, her eyes widening at the silver-grey fur under his hood. She glanced at Eyck and back to Wex, her lips still parted, then frowned and swallowed, looking down into the young man's upturned face. "Um." She lowered her voice, still staring at Wex. "When . . . did you get yourself a *slave*? I thought you were against—"

"I am. And he's not," Eyck said, gruff with annoyance.

Wex had averted his eyes, his nostrils quivering as he glared at the tabletop.

"Wex is my apprentice. He's a free man, Tem. Has every right to be here—same as me."

Tembra glanced over at the bar, searching for someone, then frowned at Eyck. "Camacky's not going to like it."

"Well, Camacky can go soak his tail in vinegar for all I care."

This prompted a surprised snort of amusement from Tembra. She sighed, shaking her head slowly. "I don't like this." She looked again at Wex. "I'm sorry, I hope I didn't offend you . . . I was just caught off guard. Um, *Wex*, was it?"

Wex slowly lifted his eyes, his expression guarded.

"Well . . . I'm pleased to meet you, Wex. I'm Tembra Mukenzee—Tem to my friends, and if you're a friend of Eyck's, then I guess you're a friend of mine."

With a shy, relieved smile, Wex touched his temple in greeting.

"I personally have nothing against Kirmen. And I don't believe that nonsense about you all being dirty or nothing," she said, then looked over at Eyck. "It's just . . . I don't want any trouble. If those boys over there catch sight of him"—she jerked her head in the direction of the darts and daggers players—"there's bound to be trouble. They're the ones who hunted down that runaway back a few weeks . . . strung him up—it really was something awful." She glanced nervously at Wex.

He had turned to watch the men gaming. After a moment, he stood, pulling his hood further forward with one hand while gesturing with the other, *"I'll leave."*

Tembra stared up at him wide-eyed—the top of her head only reached the lad about mid-chest.

"Sit, Wex," Eyck said. "It'll be fine."

He was almost certain Camacky would see to it that they went unmolested. Where else was the tavern owner going to get his pots repaired next time they cracked? And if he didn't . . . well, Eyck figured they could take care of any trouble. Eyck would rather fight than have Wex treated like he was something loathsome.

"Sit," he repeated.

There was at least forty weights of muscle between him and Wex, plus the dagger he'd seen Wex tuck into his shirt. Eyck slid a hand into his pocket, fingering the brass knuckles he'd started carrying with him as more and more soldiers, all strangers, arrived to convalesce outside of town—some of them didn't seem to be able to leave the battle to the battlefield.

Brow creased, Wex sat back down on his bench, his eyes locked with Eyck's. It was always hard to tell what was going through the young man's head, but Eyck thought he saw both gratitude and disapproval in his expression.

"*I told you: Kirmen not welcome,*" Wex signed.

"Can he not hear well?" Tembra asked quietly, then took a tiny step back as Wex turned his dark-eyed stare on her.

"No. He hears just fine, trust me," Eyck said. "But he's mute."

"Oh." Tembra smiled a little nervously at Wex, and then she did something that surprised Eyck almost as much as it did Wex. She approached again and slowly let her hand rest on Wex's shoulder.

Wex's eyes went comically wide, and for a second, Eyck wasn't sure how he was going to react to being touched.

However, when Tembra continued to smile and gently asked, "Honey, have you've been mute all your life?"

Wex responded with a nod after a slight pause.

"And you can talk with your hands?"

Again, Wex nodded.

"Do you think you can teach someone to do that? Someone who's deaf?"

"Well, he's already taught me quite a bit," Eyck replied at the same time as another of Wex's brief nods. "If he can teach me, I figure he can teach anyone. Why?"

"It's my brother's eldest boy. He fell ill during the last Five Cycle Sickness and survived. Barely. But it took his hearing—he talks fine, but Besdoe can't get him to understand anything without writing it down. If . . . Wex can show him how to say a few things with his hands . . . well, it would be a real help."

"I'm sure he wouldn't mind teach—"

Wex's gaze swung back to him. Eyck had the distinct impression he had intended to refuse, but the moment passed, and Wex gave Tembra a faint smile as he signed his reply.

"He says he'll do it," Eyck translated.

"Oh, thank you," Tembra replied, her cheeks deeply dimpled. "How about I bring you a bottle of Camacky's golden? On the house . . . as a thank-you?"

A whole bottle of whiskey? Well, they didn't need to drink *all* of it in one go . . . He shared a glance with Wex and said, "That'd be great. And make that two bowls of lentils and bring lots of bread."

"Sure thing, honey," Tem said, and before she turned to leave, she squeezed Wex's shoulder.

"I'm sorry," Eyck said once she'd gone. "I should have told her not to touch you."

Wex just levelled a stare at him, his eyes deeply shadowed by his hood, and Eyck understood suddenly that the no-touching policy applied only to himself. That was hard not to take personally—it made him feel like a pervert who couldn't be trusted.

Eyck looked away awkwardly. Camacky had returned to his usual post behind the bar. The potbellied Duval was wearing his signature starched apron and green hemp cap pulled low over the points of his ears—Tembra was speaking quietly to him, gesturing towards Eyck and Wex, and Camacky turned his amber eyes to Eyck, meeting his gaze without expression. After a moment, the tavern owner touched his temple in greeting.

Relieved, Eyck nodded and returned the greeting.

"Looks like Camacky's got our backs," Eyck said with a smile.

Wex wrinkled his brow.

"I *knew* he'd kick out any troublemakers before he'd kick *us* out."

"*No, you didn't*," signed Wex with a slow grin. He mimed a few jabbed punches, his meaning obvious, as he tilted his head towards the gamers.

"Fine. I wasn't *completely* sure," Eyck replied, chuckling. "But I'm a well-respected member of the community. They're a bunch of arseholes who live off bounties and odd jobs."

Tembra swooped in and placed a bottle of Camacky's good whiskey on the table, along with two of the hammered copper cups Eyck had made for the tavern keeper a few sun-cycles back—a reminder of their solid working relationship. With another wink for Eyck, the petite Ulven woman was gone again in a flash to take someone else's order, shooing a pair of scavenging white mice out of her path as she went.

"I'm sure ol' Camacky's going to try for a deep discount next time he comes by the smithy," Eyck said, carefully splitting the wax seal on the bottle. He sighed, shaking his head. "The whole thing is so fucking stupid . . . you're a free man." He looked up and smiled at Wex. "I don't know if you've heard, but the King's Council is set on pushing through that law ending slavery for good—possibly by winter's peak. The Three Suns priesthood is supposedly up in arms about it, but Pash says behind closed doors, they debate the Scrolls all the time. The younger priests are of a mind that the Scrolls were never meant to be taken literally, and the line about Kirmen having to 'shoulder the burden of beasts' was a poor translation and means something else."

"What do you mean?" Wex signed.

"Well, like the Levek and Duval breeds share the Trader's Rung, and the Garza and Losano share the Teacher's Rung . . ."

Wex nodded, looking impatient. *"Yes, yes, I know, and Grendall and Ulven share the Artist's Rung. So what?"*

Eyck scratched the back of his neck and shrugged. "Well, *maybe* Kirmen were supposed to share the Farmer's Rung with the Dankel, only more focused on animals and the Dankel doing the growing and harvesting. You know?"

Brow wrinkled, Wex looked unconvinced and signed something that Eyck only half understood.

Seeing Eyck's confusion, Wex dipped his finger in his glass of whiskey and quickly drew a chicken being followed by a man on the tabletop in front of Eyck. Then Wex did his finger signs again slowly, and the *ushering* gesture became clear.

"You think we were meant to be chicken-herders?"

Eyck laughed. "You never know."

Caste pairing, as it was known, only applied to the six majority breeds and not the aristocratic Samra at the top of the Ladder, nor the lowly Dankel farmers at the base of it—and certainly *never* to the Kirmen. In paintings of the Kat'hoondeman Caste Ladder, the Kirmen were always depicted kneeling in the dirt beneath it.

Wex shrugged as if he were humouring Eyck.

"But," Eyck said, pouring a few fingers of whiskey into each cup, "even if we're all supposed to be doing the work our breeds were *intended* to do—if you believe all that Sun Scroll hokum, anyway— well, things aren't strict like they were even five cycles back, right? Thanks to King Enoch and his amendments, folks all over are breaking with tradition and starting to do whatever they like for work—*Suns*, they have a Grendall *priest* over in New Qirtsdown, if you can believe it."

Wex smirked and picked up his cup, sniffing the contents.

Eyck sipped his own whiskey and smiled appreciatively. It was much finer than the terrible rotgut Pash used to make in the catacombs beneath the old church. *I'll have two glasses and that's it*, he thought, nodding to himself.

"Yeah," he continued, "pretty soon, slavery will be a thing of the past, the caste system will be abolished, and you know what? Maybe one day, we'll see a Levek on the throne . . . *Suns*, maybe even a Kirmen!" Eyck splashed a little more whiskey into his cup—Wex had yet to try his—but he looked amused by Eyck's words.

"All right, Wex here can stay . . . he's nice and quiet," Tembra said with a grin, appearing next to Eyck with bowls of lentil stew and a plate full of thick slabs of dark-brown bread on her tray. "But you're talking nonsense and blasphemy and scaring the nice little old ladies who tip me far better than you ever have." She set down their meal.

Eyck looked over at the nearest table. Old Mrs. Zilliam was sitting with two frail-looking Losano ladies and a woman who might have been Levek. It was hard to tell—she was so old, she was nearly bald.

Mrs. Zilliam stared at him, her golden eyes full of consternation, and Eyck touched his temple, then ducked his chin in a quick apology.

"Great. Zilliam and her church cronies," he muttered, turning back to Wex. "No doubt Pash is going to hear about this and drag me over the coals."

❖ ❖ ❖

Wex frowned at Eyck. *"Your friend is a priest, but you aren't religious?"* he signed, thinking about the bitterness in Eyck's voice the night he'd arrived back in South Galetsy. He was curious about what had happened between the blacksmith and his friend when they were young—had they been lovers? It certainly seemed like it from what he'd overheard. *"Why aren't you religious?"*

Eyck shrugged once he'd figured out the gesture for *religious.*

"My mother was a Believer, but none of it stuck with me," Eyck replied. "I've got my own theories about the Scrolls and whatnot . . . but I guess I'll wait until later, huh?" He inclined his head towards the elderly ladies' table then smiled and sipped his whiskey. A moment later, he wrinkled his brow at Wex, his grin slipping. "I'm sorry . . . I don't know why I just assumed you weren't a Believer," he said, looking anxious. "You aren't—are you?"

Curling his lip in disgust, Wex quickly shook his head. Even the smell of incense made him feel queasy, triggering memories he wished he could burn out of his brain permanently.

"Oh, good," Eyck replied, pouring himself more whiskey. "Good good."

With an eye on the diminishing contents of the bottle, Wex sniffed at his cup again. He'd never been one for drinking, but it seemed if he didn't do his part, the big blacksmith would finish it alone, and Wex didn't want to have to drag the big Levek home. Steeling himself, Wex took a sip and found the whiskey to be quite mild compared to the corn mash whiskey Red Falcorr had been fond of. He lifted his cup and nodded.

"It's good, right? But you'd better put some food in your belly," Eyck replied, his smile crooked. "It might taste smooth as satin, but it packs a mighty wallop, believe you me." He hiccupped, then spooned up a mouthful of lentils.

Wex was still mulling over what Eyck had said earlier. A Kirmen king? It was ridiculous even to consider . . . Then again, he wondered what the parishioners of New Qirtsdown thought of their Grendall priest.

The breed convention was that Grendalls were solicitors at their absolute best and outright criminals at their worst, with the rest in between, either hawking questionable tonics or setting up gambling dens or, like Chedim Bew, creating circuses that doubled as travelling freak brothels. They were also known for having a particular affinity for water and a thirst for adventure that made them particularly well suited for work aboard merchant vessels . . . or pirate ships.

Frowning, Wex tasted the lentils and, finding them excellent, ate a few big spoonfuls. He nodded at Eyck, but the Levek's attention was entirely on his food.

As he ate, Wex thought back to the first time someone had told him he was the son of a Grendall pirate. He'd believed it at the time, but he really had no idea if it was true—all he had were the stripes in his fur that pointed to a mixed lineage.

It still infuriated him that Chedim Bew had treated him so badly, considering he had been a Kirmen-Grendall mix himself. That was why all of Eyck's talk of slavery abolition didn't give Wex any real heart, not if even a slimeball pimp like Bew had felt the need to cover his Kirmen colouring. Kirmen were slaves—even when they were free, their breed was forever tainted. They became the lowest of prostitutes and beggars, sleeping in graveyards and picking through trash heaps and dying in the street because no one would deign to help them.

Scowling down into his bowl, Wex knew he was being excessively bleak about the Kirmen. On his travels, he'd seen freed Kirmen holding down proper, if undesirable, jobs, and slavery had already begun declining sharply even by the time Wex had been bought as a child. But, for every Kirmen, pure or of mixed stock that lived with some modicum of equality in society, there were a dozen "greybacks" being spat on or strung up like the poor fellow the barmaid had mentioned.

"You all right?" Eyck asked.

Wex slowly lifted his eyes, adopting a neutral expression. Here was one Levek who considered him what . . . an equal? Maybe? What was it that Eyck had said to the barmaid? *He has every right to be here—same as me . . .*

"What's wrong?" the blacksmith said, his green eyes wide.

Wex shook his head, looking back down at his stew. Then he glanced up with a smile, not wanting his troubled thoughts to weigh down their meal, and asked, *"So what happened between you and the Ulven woman?"*

"Tem?" Eyck replied, looking over to where the barmaid was making small talk with a group of old men. "Uh . . . well, things between her and me got friendlier during the Spring Fayre. Just a cuddle." He grinned.

"But you don't want it to happen again?" Wex drank some more whiskey, liking the mellow little fire it put in his belly.

"Wellll . . ." Eyck peeked over at the woman again, his fingers scratching at his nape the way they did every time he was embarrassed or uncomfortable. "I wouldn't say *no* if the opportunity presented itself—she's as sweet as a peach. But . . . I don't think it's a good idea."

Wex chewed some bread as he studied Eyck. He didn't know—and didn't *care*—if the blacksmith was handsome or not, but the man was obviously popular among the single *and* married women in town, what with all the food they kept bringing to the smithy "just in case" or their superfluous trips to repair barely dented trinkets. The doe-eyed women cooed over the Levek's brawn and skill as he flattened their bent utensils or quickly fashioned a new cloak pin to replace the one they'd lost . . . *again*. Even a few grinning Ulven lads, seemingly unbothered by the looming threat of religious recrimination, came by to butter up the big blacksmith with all sorts of stupid, fawning compliments, half of which were *clearly* innuendos. Wex tried to stay out back of the smithy when Eyck's admirers came around for fear of hurting himself by rolling his eyes too hard.

It was strange though—Eyck did flirt back, but it never seemed like he was truly interested. Wex wondered at that. With a dead wife and an ex-lover-turned-priest, the blacksmith's life seemed a very solitary one.

"Why not a good idea?" Wex signed a little awkwardly since he was

still holding bread, but he knew the blacksmith would understand him regardless—Eyck was always quick at figuring out what he meant.

Eyck blew out a slow breath as he sat back, contemplating Wex's question.

"Oh, I dunno. Tem's a nice lady, that's for sure. And the church might even bless us, were we to get married one day . . ."

"They would? Why?"

"Well," Eyck said, lowering his voice, "she's past childbearing age."

Ahhh. Wex nodded. Of *course* . . .

Though producing viable offspring between breeds was possible— he was living proof of that, after all—the church found it *problematic* to say the least. So, if Eyck and Tem couldn't mate, there would be no little "half-breeds" running around, and thus the church would play nice.

How fucking generous of them.

"But?" Wex prompted.

"But . . . oh, I don't know. I'm sure we'd have a nice life . . . it's just —call me a romantic, but if my heart's not in on it, I don't see the point."

Wex nodded again, but Eyck might as well have been speaking another language for how little Wex understood what connection there was between hearts and base physical urges like sex. Maybe that sort of thing had been bred out of Kirmen long ago.

Watching Eyck devour his meal, Wex thought the hollowness inside him felt bigger than usual, and he didn't like it. He took another sip of his whiskey and forced himself to smile.

WEX SQUINTED at the street torches, disoriented. Which way had they come? Where was the river? Why had he drunk so much? Looking up, he searched for the twinkling red Mother star that crawled across the sky every night, hoping to get his bearings by her position as he often had in the past, but it was just too cloudy.

Nearby, Eyck let out a long sigh as he pissed against one of the tavern's pilings, his stream loud in the dark. When he was done, he gave another satisfied sigh and chuckled to himself, obviously amused by his own thoughts, and then started up the road with shuffling steps, weaving drunkenly as he looked back, his eyes glinting yellow-green in the dark. "Dis way," he called, windmilling his arm. "C'mon."

Right. Uphill. The river is downhill, Wex thought, his steps steadier than the blacksmith's, but not by much. He caught up to Eyck.

"—Would have laid them out, I tell you," mumbled the big Levek, shaking his shaggy head slowly.

Wex couldn't reply—he figured the near-dark and Eyck's distraction made it nearly impossible to make his gestures understood—so he just clicked his tongue twice in disapproval.

Swerving in front of Wex, Eyck stopped walking and faced him, rocking gently from side to side. "Whu? You think I can't take 'em?" he slurred, digging into his pocket. "Fuckin' bigot should'na call you that. I'm-a show dem boys a thing or—whoops . . . *Suns!*" Eyck swore, fumbling the object he'd pulled from his trousers. It bounced twice on the cobbles with a metallic chime, landing in the tall grass by the side of the road. Leaning over, Eyck took a tumble and nearly fell on his head trying to retrieve what he'd dropped. "Crap." He laughed and turned over onto his back, rubbing his face. "Think I drank too much." He chuckled again.

Grinning, Wex shook his head. *No kidding,* he thought, crossing his arms. *How in the schatten's hell am I going to get you home?*

Eyck groaned, sitting up. He felt around in the grass for a few seconds. "There y'are," he said triumphantly, holding the brass knuckles aloft. Then he sobered, looking up at Wex. "S'not right they treat you like tha'." He slid his fingers into the knucklebusters and made a fist, letting out a low growl.

Right as they were leaving, one of the darts and daggers players had purposefully crashed into Wex. It had chafed to walk away from their taunting, but what choice did they have? Eyck was as drunk as a pirate on a double full moon, and Wex wasn't that far behind. Besides, if he was going to stay in South Galetsy for a little while, it made no sense to paint a target on his back by riling up the locals. It was best if he just kept his head down, learned his trade, and then got the fuck out of this uppity shit heap of a town.

Wex signed, "*I've been called greyback before,*" and held out his hand to Eyck.

"Doshn't make it right," the blacksmith replied, taking Wex's hand.

Wex bent down, looped Eyck's arm around the back of his neck, then slung him over his shoulders in a carry hold, the blacksmith grunting in surprise.

"W'you'doin'?"

Not able to reply, Wex just patted Eyck's back with a sigh and took a heavy, slightly unsteady step in the direction of the smithy—Eyck weighed more than a sack of bricks, and his boots knocked against Wex's thigh.

Clenching his jaw, Wex hoped the blacksmith wouldn't be sick from lying over his shoulders, but he was tired, and at the pace they'd been going, it would be nearly morning before they reached the smithy. Trudging along the cobbles, placing each foot carefully, Wex made it the rest of the way back without stumbling.

WITH ONE LAST STRAINING STEP, Wex reached the top of the stairs, wishing there was a banister to hold onto. Grimacing, he leaned over slowly to drop Eyck as gently as he could onto his pallet.

Eyck let out a groan, twitching awake.

The motion caused Wex to momentarily lose his balance. He went down hard on one knee, nearly falling on top of Eyck. Chuckling, he pushed himself back onto his ass but then got his tail caught between his calf and thigh.

He let out a grunt of pain. *Suns, do I need to sleep this off . . .*

"You . . . just made a noise," Eyck mumbled, turning his head on the pillow, his eyes only half-open.

Wex stared blearily at Eyck, not knowing how to reply. Sure . . . sometimes he made sounds, sometimes he didn't, but it was outside his control. Wex's voice was lost somewhere inside him, down deep where the hollowness was cold and dark, and there was nothing he could do about it.

"Thanks . . . f'the lift home," the blacksmith said, closing his eyes. "Yr'a good kid, Wex. Glad y'r . . . here. I . . . um . . ." Eyck snorted, then took a deep, snoring breath.

Wex was surprised to find himself smiling. A good kid? It might be drunken praise, but it felt nice regardless.

Chewing thoughtfully on the corner of his lip, Wex sat there for a bit, then crawled quietly to Eyck's feet and pulled off his boots. He covered the sleeping Levek with the blanket and sat back down near his head, wondering what he'd been about to say before he drifted off.

Frowning, Wex reached out to tug the blanket higher, then froze with a sharp intake of breath when Eyck's hand suddenly covered his.

Wex was startled by the unexpected contact, and his eyes grew wide as Eyck patted the back of his hand twice then resumed snoring.

With a breathy little laugh from being caught off guard, Wex started to draw his hand away. But he changed his mind and lightly placed it atop Eyck's, letting it rest there. After a second, he gently traced the contour of Eyck's big knuckles, the fur rough and short, then ran his fingers down the back of his hand and over the burn scars that crisscrossed his wrist.

Wex felt a bit guilty and nervous about touching the blacksmith without his knowledge, but he was . . . curious?

Holding his breath, Wex followed the line of buttons up the front of Eyck's shirt with the tip of his finger, then skimmed over the thatch of fur that sprung thick and unkempt above the collar.

Then slowly, *very* slowly, his shaking finger touched Eyck's bottom lip.

Wex breathed out hard, startling himself. His pulse was racing, his face warm with the blood rushing into it.

When Eyck twitched, Wex almost fell backwards and down the stairs. Trying to silence his panting, he stayed on all fours, afraid to move until he was sure Eyck was really asleep.

He quickly crossed the room and lay down on his own pallet, his heart still beating a frantic rhythm. Squeezing his eyes shut, Wex swallowed, his throat dry, and touched his own bottom lip.

What the fuck did you do that for? he thought, feeling jittery and weird.

He'd never done anything like that before.

It has to be the whiskey. No more drinking, he swore and turned over to face the wall, pulling the blanket over his shoulder. He forced himself to breathe normally and tried to summon sleep. The sooner this bizarre day was over, the better.

Chapter Six

Eyck winced and pressed his fingers into the hollows above his eyes, breathing slowly through his nose. His skull felt too small to contain the swollen, pulsing mass within.

Good Suns, how much did I have to drink? It had been a very long time since he'd had a hangover. Grimacing, he massaged his temples. Actually, he *knew* how long: just about five sun-cycles.

He frowned, turning to look at the pallet across the room. It was empty with the blanket neatly folded at the foot of it. The scrape of metal came from downstairs just as Eyck's nose registered the smell of eggs frying. Normally, that would have made his mouth water, but right then, it was hard not to retch. Eyck covered his nose with his hand and squinted, wondering what time it was. The light had a midmorning quality to it.

Come on, old man. Out of bed. You can do this.

He struggled to a sitting position and instantly regretted it as his stomach roiled in protest. Groaning, he rubbed his face and sat as still as possible until the nausea passed.

Downstairs, Wex was whistling something cheerful as he cooked. The sound of the spatula on cast iron made Eyck shiver, and he let out another small moan. It dawned on him then that he had no idea how he'd gotten home.

His pulse surged as hazy, panicky thoughts started bouncing

around in his aching head. Breathing heavily, Eyck tried to recall the end of the evening, but he couldn't even remember leaving the tavern.

He groaned—the last time he'd been so drunk, things had gone . . . *weird* with Wex. What if something had happened again?

He's cooking breakfast, Eyck reasoned. *If I'd acted inappropriately, he'd be long gone.*

Not unless he enjoyed *it,* whispered a sly little voice in response.

Eyck shook his head, wiping his mouth with the back of his hand. No, the *last* thing Wex wanted was Eyck getting too friendly—he'd been painfully clear about what he thought of being touched by him—but maybe his stupid, drunken self had done something stupid.

Fuck.

Don't jump to conclusions, you idiot.

But . . . what if . . . ? He had to admit to himself that it was more than just worry making his pulse soar. The thought of Wex and him . . . together . . .

Clenching his jaw, Eyck listened to Wex for a few more minutes, trying to quiet his thoughts. He wasn't going to find out what happened by sitting there like a lump on his bed. No, he needed to get up and go downstairs, make amends if needed, and if not . . . Eyck swallowed and scratched the back of his head, his thick fur tangled and greasy feeling.

What *if* something *had* happened and Wex didn't want an apology? The memory of Wex's tail, warm in his hand, swam before his eyes. Eyck shook his head again to clear it, making himself lightheaded in the process, his head throbbing miserably.

Eyck slowly got to his feet, his eyes squeezed shut as he stood there swaying for a second, feeling jittery and ashamed and muddled.

"No more drinking," he muttered softly. He squared his shoulders and exhaled hard, shaking his head again to clear his thoughts.

No more fucking drinking.

***

WEX LOOKED up as Eyck descended the stairs looking like he'd lost a battle with his bedding. His fur was sticking up in clumps everywhere, the hair atop his head wild like a black scribble of ink, and his shirt was heavily creased and hung on him like a tattered sail. Eyck's green eyes were bloodshot and rheumy, and he squinted against the sunlight pouring in through the big window by the table.

Shaking his head, Wex lifted the cast-iron pan with his gloved hand, using the spatula to push the potatoes onto the plates that sat warming by the fire. Then he quickly set the plates on the table, skirting around Eyck who stood blinking blearily in the middle of the room, and sat down. He looked up at the blacksmith expectantly.

Swaying, Eyck opened his mouth to speak, then suddenly turned away and pushed the front door open, rushing outside. A moment later, retching came from the alley next to the smithy.

Poking at his fried eggs, Wex sighed, waiting for him to return. He couldn't understand why folks enjoyed drinking to excess if all it did was destroy you the next morning. His own head was a little tender and his stomach wasn't happy with him, and he'd only had a *third* of what Eyck had consumed. Wex couldn't imagine how much pain Eyck was in, but that didn't mean he pitied him. If anything, he was annoyed because of the late start on their work today.

After a few minutes, Eyck came back inside, his shirt balled up in one big fist, wearing a sheepish expression. His fur was dripping wet —Wex guessed he'd gone to the pump on the corner to pour water over his head.

"Thanks for making breakfast, lad," Eyck said in a hoarse voice as he chucked his soiled shirt under the bench near the front door. "I'm, ah . . ." He frowned, staring down at the floor, then raised his head to meet Wex's gaze. "I'm sorry for last night. I hope I didn't make too much of an arse of myself. And uh," he mumbled, looking back down as he scratched his neck, "I hope I didn't do anything . . . you know . . ." He lifted his green eyes again and gestured to the space between them in a vague way, but his meaning was crystal clear to Wex.

Wex frowned and gave a firm headshake, quickly dropping his gaze to concentrate on the food in front of him. His heart was beating too fast, his face uncomfortably hot—all he could think of was how Eyck's hand had felt on top of his last night and how warm and smooth the blacksmith's bottom lip had been against the tip of his finger. No matter how hard he tried to shove that memory down deep with all the other things he longed to forget, it kept crawling back into his thoughts, confusing him.

Grimacing as he pushed his eggs around his plate, Wex tried to clear his mind, but then Eyck sat down across from him, still shirtless, and Wex found it even harder to breathe normally. It wasn't because of the stink of old liquor and wet fur—Wex's nostrils flared of their own accord, eagerly scenting for Eyck's unique smell, and it made him angry and hungry and helplessly cornered by his own instincts. He ground his teeth together, shoulders hunched, trying to ignore the blacksmith.

"Are you all right, lad?" Eyck asked.

Wex tried hard to make himself believe the Levek's voice was roughened only by last night's excess . . . but all he could hear was genuine, heartfelt concern.

Stomach in knots, Wex slowly raised his head, trying not to look directly at the solid, furry body in front of him, the dark nipples jutting from swirls of black and brown, the strong, sloping shoulders, and thick, corded neck. Wex swallowed, staring at Eyck's jutting jaw and wide mouth for a moment, then forced himself to meet Eyck's gaze, his quick pulse making him woozy.

"*I'm fine*," he signed, forcing his mouth into a smile, but he was so far from fine, he felt like he was going to be sick. "*Too much whiskey.*"

Reassured by the lie, Eyck chuckled and nodded in sympathy before digging into his breakfast, leaving Wex free to drop his smile and exhale a shaky breath as he averted his eyes.

He'd been lying to himself about his complete indifference towards the blacksmith, and it felt like a knife in his guts now that he was faced with the blatant truth—he was attracted to Eyck and not only was he attracted to him, it seemed he *desired* the man with a hunger that bordered on panic.

Dragging another smile across his face when Eyck asked him for the pepper sauce, Wex braced himself, trying not to flinch when their fingers touched.

His first real taste of desire . . . and he *hated* it.

EYCK MADE a face as he quickly drank the ginger and willow bark tea down to the dregs. He'd probably need a second one later to get through the day. Wiping his mouth with the back of his wrist, Eyck turned around to see what Wex was doing and found him laying out some tongs. However, he had the distinct impression Wex had just looked away, as if he'd been staring at him. Again.

Frowning, Eyck pointed to the set of punches in their wooden box and watched Wex fetch them. Something was wrong with the lad, that much was certain, and he'd bet his fangs that it had nothing to do with too much whiskey.

Wex set the punches down next to the half-formed door to Mr. Yesper's stove, the piece they were finishing that day, then just stood there with the same hunched posture he'd been adopting all morning, his eyes barely straying to Eyck for more than a second. Well, when Eyck was looking anyway.

"Are you going to tell me what's wrong?" Eyck said. Crossing his arms, he stared hard at Wex.

Wex's head jerked up, and he just stared back at Eyck for a second before replying with a terse gesture. *"I'm fine."*

"You're obviously not. What's eating at you, lad? You can tell me."

This time Wex's eyes narrowed menacingly as he cut the air between them with a violent *"I'm fine."*

Sighing, Eyck decided to drop it. However, as they worked side by side, taking turns beating the new door of the stove into shape, whatever it was that was troubling Wex seemed to make him angrier with every passing minute until he was visibly trembling and wild-eyed, wielding the fuller like he was attacking the iron instead of spreading it.

"Ok, that's enough for now," Eyck said.

Wex continued striking the metal with resounding *clangs*, ignoring him.

Thinking Wex hadn't heard him, Eyck raised his voice and barked, "Enough!" loud enough to startle Wex into losing his grasp on the hammer.

The fuller flew back from his hand and struck the wall before falling onto a box of nails, knocking it off the shelf and spilling the contents all over the floor.

Eyck stared down at the mess with annoyance, shaking his head. "Well?" he said, glaring at the lad when he hadn't moved. "Get cleaning."

"It's your fault," Wex signed angrily.

"How's that?"

"You yelled in my ear."

"I didn't *yell* in your ear," Eyck replied, reaching for the broom. He held it out to Wex who made no move to take it. "Listen, if you'd been paying attention, I wouldn't have had to speak so loud."

*"I was *paying attention*.* Wex bared his fangs, his dark eyes locked on Eyck, and his tail swished fast from side to side.

"No, you were about to make a hole in Mr. Yesper's door."

*"I *was* not. I *was fixing your mess*.*

Eyck held his tongue, not wanting to be pulled into such a childish argument. He sighed, shrugging. "Why don't you just tell me what's bothering you? It's obviously distracting you."

"I told you there's nothing wrong, you Levek—" Wex replied, his lip curling as he made a gesture Eyck didn't recognize.

Eyck guessed it was an insult.

"Will you just relax, Wex? Listen . . . give me a hand in cleaning this up," he said in a gentle voice, hoping to placate the young man. "Then we'll take a good long break and have some lunch."

He held the broom out again, and this time, Wex grabbed it to begin sweeping the floor with the same vehemence with which he'd been striking the iron door. As such, he was sending nails flying with every pass, and after watching him for only a few more seconds, Eyck yanked the broom from his grasp.

"Ok, you need to take a walk and cool your head," Eyck growled.

Wex just stood there, blinking at him.

"Out. Now," Eyck said, pointing to the door. "Don't make me throw you out."

"Fine. Clean your own schatten mess," Wex signed, then turned tail and tramped out the door, leaving it to slam in his wake.

Eyck cursed under his breath, counted to ten to calm himself, then began to sweep up the scattered nails. A moment later, the bell above the door jingled, and he turned.

"What did you forg—oh!" Eyck exclaimed, grinning wide at Pash. "You're back!"

They met in the middle of the room, and Eyck threw his arms around the priest, squeezing him tight with relief. Then he stepped back and looked his friend up and down, finding him to be in one piece, albeit travel-stained and weary-looking, and gestured to the table. "Sit, sit . . . I'll make you some tea."

"I can't stay. I just stopped by to say I'd returned. Figured you'd be beside yourself with worry," Pash replied with a crooked smile. He jerked his thumb over his shoulder. "Ran into your apprentice down the street. I said hello, and he *growled* at me. He looked fit to be tied . . . did you two get into a fight?" There was something odd about Pash's expression.

"Ah . . . we're fine," Eyck replied. "I think maybe neither of us got enough sleep last night."

"Oh." A wrinkle appeared on Pash's high forehead, and he looked away, his grey eyes distant. "I see."

"You *see* what?"

Pash turned back to him, searching his expression. "You know I have no issues with it, but you understand that from a church standpoint, I can't publicly be seen condoning anything. Are you being discreet, at least?"

"*Suns!* We're not doing *that*, you idiot," Eyck said, scratching the back of his neck, his face warm with embarrassment. "We stayed out late at Camacky's having supper and some drinks, Pash." He shook his head. "Sheesh . . . I can't believe you."

"I'm sorry I assumed," Pash replied, reaching for Eyck's shoulder to give it a warm squeeze. "I misunderstood, is all." His thumb brushed the side of Eyck's neck, a tender little touch.

Eyck's eyes widened.

It was unmistakable—Pash was relieved, but not because of some bullshit church intolerance. No, that was *jealousy* he'd heard in the priest's voice, pure and simple. It prickled his fur, and not in a good way.

So, he only wants me when he thinks someone else does?

He shrugged out of Pash's hold under the guise of resumed sweeping and gave him a smile that hopefully looked sincere. "Did everything go well then? At the border?"

The priest scrubbed his face with one hand, looking even more haggard. "A complete waste of time," he muttered. "It was doomed right from the beginning, I think. The Oza had an endless list of ridiculous demands that they *had* to have known we couldn't—or *wouldn't* meet. It's like they're just itching to go to full-fledged war with us. And they've got all these rituals . . . they're so quick to take offence to absolutely *every*thing." Pash let out a laugh devoid of any humour. "Supposedly, they beheaded their first interpreter because he used the wrong word for something."

"*What?*" Eyck froze mid-sweep and stared at Pash, aghast.

"They took him away so quickly, no one had time to react. Suns, Eyck . . . I don't even have the words to describe how awful these people are. I've been walking on eggs for weeks . . . I'm completely exhausted."

"Go home. Get some rest," Eyck said gently. "We'll talk tomorrow."

"Before I can sleep, I need a bath," Pash replied. "The stench of their cooking . . . I don't know if I'll ever be rid of it."

Eyck felt a little nauseous. He'd heard tales of the Oza boiling the flesh of strange, legless desert animals—huge carrion-filled cauldrons that bubbled and belched day and night making unholy stew to feed the Oza hordes. "That bad?"

"Worse," said the priest with another somber chuckle. "I think it'll haunt my dreams."

Grimacing, Eyck clapped him on the shoulder. "Well . . . I'm glad you're home," he said. "Come see me tomorrow, and I'll feed you some of Macy's black bean soup."

"She still cooking for you, *hm*?" Pash replied with the shadow of a smirk on his spotted face. "She hasn't given up yet?"

"What do you mean?"

"Why do you *think* she brings you all that food?"

"Because she makes too much . . ." Saying it out loud made him realize that her excuse *did* sound a little fishy. "Huh. You think Macy's sweet on me?"

"You're only realizing that now? I swear to the Three Suns, you're unbelievably dense sometimes." The priest shook his head, laughing, then held out his hand to clasp arms with Eyck before turning to leave. Pash started pushing open the door, but he paused and looked over his shoulder at Eyck, his expression pensive.

"Another thing you should know . . . there are Kirmen with the Oza," Pash said.

"What do you mean?"

"Just that: there are Kirmen living across the border. Free . . . and some with high-ranking positions, as far as I could tell."

"Ok, but why are you telling me that?"

"You've got a Kirmen under your roof . . ."

"Half-Kirmen. And? What *about* him?"

"I'm just saying," Pash replied with a shrug as he looked away. *"Be careful."*

Eyck closed the door after the priest and frowned.

BY THE TIME Wex reached the river, his anger had simmered down enough that he was beginning to feel sheepish over how he'd acted, but he knew it was going to be a problem if he couldn't get himself under control around the Levek blacksmith.

Wex kicked some rocks into the water, watching the ripples sway the riverweed in their wake. He chewed the inside of his cheek, his eyes following a flash of silver beneath the surface—a hungry dace or perch probably—but his mind was on the ridiculous attraction he couldn't seem to shake. Maybe it would just fade away eventually.

It has to, right? He kicked a clump of dirt into the river where it dissolved into an opaque brown cloud. *I just have to stop* thinking *about it.*

Wex crushed his eyes closed, his fists balled at his sides. Eyck was just a big dumb sucker who was willing to train him up, nothing more. Wex was only feeling the way he was because Eyck was nice to him—that's all. Just a simple, stupid reaction to kindness.

But Red Falcorr had been nice to him too, and Wex couldn't remember ever feeling like . . . *this*.

It was like a crawling itch he couldn't scratch, and it was making him antsy and angry and uncomfortable. He cupped the bulge in the front of his pants and gave himself a hard squeeze, painful enough that a little moan actually escaped his lips. He stood there trembling, nauseous with self-loathing.

Raised voices startled him out of his daze—Wex dropped his hand in alarm and looked around, but it was only a couple of sailors coming off the boardwalk to take the road up to town. The shorter slight one was definitely Ulven—he was tawny without markings—but the tall woman walking next to him, while mostly Duval-black, had ginger spots sprinkled across the sable fur on her cheeks. She looked to have some Dankel in her.

"What'choo starin' at, fella?" growled the tall sailor, a sneer on her interesting face. Her fangs were capped in gold.

Wex quickly looked down, not wanting to provoke a fight, and shook his head, relieved when they passed him by. When he could no longer hear their footfalls, he looked up again and headed towards the boardwalk. He'd only been once before to fetch barrels of saltwater for the smithy and hadn't really taken a look around. He was curious.

His boots clomped loudly on the warped wooden planks as he made his way to the sailor's market with its ever-changing array of goods procured from all over—but he didn't stop at any of the stalls. In his haste to leave, Wex had forgotten his hooded cloak, and people were staring at him.

This was a mistake.

Turning around on his heel, he ran smack into a wiry little Kirmen in a long ragged tunic and torn trousers, and quickly grabbed the man before he fell to the ground.

The Kirmen looked up at him with a smile—his grey face was deeply lined, and his teeth were yellow and blunt with age, but his brown eyes were bright and clear.

"My, you're even bigger from a-close," the old man said with a chuckle. "You've the blood of a Titan in you, no doubt."

Wex had heard the same thing probably fifty times—even Eyck had compared him to these mythical beings who had supposedly roamed the world over a thousand cycles ago. According to the Sun Scrolls, the Three Living Suns had birthed the Titans, enormous god-creatures tasked with the creation of the Kat'hoondeman race, moulding their forms and purpose to the rungs of the Caste Ladder. As such, Wex had only bitter contempt for the Titans, real or not.

Releasing the old man's arm, Wex curtly touched his temple in farewell and started walking away.

"Hold on, young man," said the spritely old Kirmen, jogging beside him. "I have something for you."

Wex stopped and looked over, shaking his head at the sheet of paper the old man held out to him.

"Here. Please. Take this. It might be of interest to you."

Shaking his head again, Wex signed, *"I can't read,"* even though the man wouldn't understand him.

The stranger wouldn't take no for an answer so Wex finally accepted the paper with a sigh, then watched the old man disappear down the boardwalk. He looked down at the sheet in his hand. It was thin and cheap-feeling and the wood-block letters on it were smudged and not too straight . . . and Wex couldn't make heads or tails of it. He folded the leaflet up and jammed it into his pants pocket. Maybe Eyck could tell him what it was.

"Lands, you're the blacksmith's apprentice, ain'tcha?" called out a deep voice.

Wex glanced around. A ship's captain waved to him from the gangplank of a two-masted vessel. Curious, he nodded as the man approached. The man was Levek and only a little shorter than Eyck was, but where the blacksmith was broad-shouldered and solidly built, this man was shaped like a large pear. He peered up at Wex with eyes the colour of new spring leaves.

"I'm Captain Rupern. I've got something for Stromsmith in my hold—iron ore and some ingots from Tuksbury. Be a while before it'll unload though."

Frowning, Wex stared at the man for a second, then shook his head.

"What's that?" Captain Rupern replied, tilting his black hemp cap back to scratch his head. A swath of fur was missing right above his brow ridge, the skin below mottled pink and grey and shiny with scar tissue. Being a sailor was dangerous business—the Grendall Wex had shared a jail cell with for a time at Hange had been a merchant sailor. He'd been missing a leg and half his tail as well as one of his eyes, and he'd told endless stories of pirates and deadly, horned sea creatures so big they could swallow a sailing ship whole. It had quashed any notion Wex had held about perhaps becoming a sailor himself.

Wex shrugged and shook his head at the man again. *"He gave me no money to pay for goods,"* he signed, exasperated.

"It's already paid for, lad," the captain replied, surprising Wex with his knowledge of signing language. "Why don't you go have a drink at the pub. I'll have one of the boys come get you when it's ready?"

Wrinkling his brow, Wex stared at the man. *"The tavern in town?"* he signed, thinking he meant Camacky's. Wex wasn't sure he wanted to go back there on his own after what had happened with the darts and daggers players.

"No . . . down yonder there's a pub. End of the boardwalk . . . called the Giddy Dankel. You can't miss it—Dama Sunshine's brothel is right next to it."

A brothel, eh? Maybe South Galetsy wasn't the pious little town he'd assumed. Then again, it probably shouldn't have surprised him, given that every port town he'd been to had had either a whorehouse or pub house or both that catered to the sailors that passed through daily.

Wex nodded. *"Yes, I'll wait there. Thank you."*

Captain Rupern smiled and held out his hand, and Wex clasped arms with him, bewildered by the man's friendliness. Aboard Rupern's ship, some young men were handling barrels—they were Kirmen or of mixed Kirmen stock.

Heartened, Wex continued east along the boardwalk, towards the tavern, and this time when the hawkers stared at him, he met their eyes and realized they were only looking for a sale . . . not judging him for the colour of his fur. Wex lifted his chin a little higher and smiled.

THE PUBLIC HOUSE was downstairs from a small inn, and even before Wex sat down at the bar, he already felt far more comfortable than he had at Camacky's in town. Only a few others were seated around the small dark room, mostly Grendall or Ulven from the looks of it, and they paid no attention to Wex at all. The bartender, a beefy Duval with a thick golden ring through his broad nose, gave him a friendly smile.

"What can I get ya?" he said, sliding a bowl of mixed nuts and dried fruit in front of Wex.

Suddenly, Wex was unsure. He didn't really want anything very alcoholic, not after the night he'd had, but at the same time asking for water seemed a bit . . . boring. Here he was, sitting at a pub unmolested and free from judgment—at least for the moment—with a couple of coins to spend in his pocket. He frowned, wondering what he could ask for and how he could ask for it. Pointing to his throat, he shook his head.

"Can't speak? Oh, that's all right," replied the bartender with a shrug. "Let's see . . . Do you want whiskey?"

Wex shook his head.

"Rum? Apple Brandy? Beer? Barley wine? Water? None of those, eh? Hmm . . ." the man said, rubbing his chin. He seemed to be enjoying the challenge of finding Wex something to drink. "What about . . . some honey wine?"

Honey wine? Wex tilted his head inquisitively.

"Make it myself. It's a bit sweet, not too heavy, and you can have a glass or two and not have it go to your head. It's no stronger than small ale."

Nodding, Wex smiled. *Perfect.*

For the next half hour, Loomis the bartender kept up a steady, one-sided conversation which suited Wex perfectly. He nodded and listened, the gossip from across the river keeping his mind from revisiting his problem with the blacksmith as he surreptitiously watched the people coming and going from his stool at the bar.

It took him a while to realize that someone was watching him too —at the far end of the room, a lanky Grendall sailor was sitting on his own, drinking a tall glass of something amber, and looking at Wex whenever he thought Wex wasn't watching. Wex stared at him, wondering what the man wanted.

Loomis noticed Wex scrutinizing the sailor and leaned forward on his elbows, speaking in a low voice. "That's Stilig. He sails on a merchant ship called the *Sparkshade*." He shifted his gaze to Wex. "If you're looking to make a few silver, Stilig isn't the type to look down on Kirmen—don't you worry about that. Though you should know . . . I hear him and his crewmates can be rough . . ."

Wex stared at Loomis, bewildered. *Rough?* What was being offered?

The bartender held Wex's stare for a moment, now looking uncertain, and Wex glanced at the sailor again. This time, Stilig met his gaze, his amber eyes full of amusement and . . . *interest*. Then the Grendall grinned and winked. Startled, Wex looked away, focusing on the nearly empty glass he was clasping in both hands and gave a jerky little headshake.

"Oh. *Ah.* My mistake," Loomis said. "Dama's brothel only has women, so some lads come here to find what they're looking for. And that's all right with me. I hope I didn't offend." He reached for the bottle of honey mead to refill Wex's glass.

Again, Wex shook his head, getting hastily to his feet. "*I have to go,*" he signed, forcing a smile to show Loomis he wasn't offended. He touched his temple and nodded in thanks. Feeling extremely conspicuous in the small space, as though every movement were stiff and awkward, Wex thought he could sense Stilig's luminous amber stare boring into him as he made his way to the door.

He quickly traced his steps back to Rupern's ship, and when the captain told him the shipment wasn't quite ready yet, Wex replied that he'd wait by the gangplank.

"*It's not a problem,*" he signed, seating himself on a nearby wooden bollard. "*I like the sun and fresh air.*"

Captain Rupern just shrugged and went back to directing the men emptying the ship's hold. A few minutes later, Wex heard the sound of boots on the boardwalk, the strides long and purposeful. When he saw it was the winking Grendall from the pub, he quickly looked away, his face warm. Clenching his jaw, Wex surreptitiously watched Stilig climb the gangplank, the sailor ignoring him completely until he reached the top. Then he turned and gave Wex a sly grin, touching his temple in parting as he stepped out of sight.

EYCK HELPED Wex place the heavy crates of raw metal into the storage shed behind the smithy, then went out to pay the wagonman. Wex had returned in a much calmer mood, bringing with him a load of supplies from Tuksbury that Eyck had only been expecting later that week, and apologized for his earlier behaviour.

Although Eyck had assured Wex everything was forgiven, he couldn't help but feel like something was still troubling him. But there was no point in poking at the hornet's nest again . . . he just hoped that Wex would confide in him before too long. Maybe he could help with whatever it was.

The rest of the day passed without any more drama, and the two of them, still hungover, turned in early for the night. There was a lot to do the next day, and Eyck was looking forward to finishing the rest of the wrought-iron fence he was making for the Vanbecks. He thought he would let Wex help—maybe the lad had blown up at him earlier because he needed something more creative to do. He nodded to himself and turned over, wearily closing his eyes.

Eyck was just drifting off when a noise from the other side of the room shook him out of sleep.

Holding his breath, he listened, wondering if his ears were playing tricks on him. No, there it was again. Quiet sounds of furtive, rhythmic movement . . . short, hoarse breaths. And then a tiny moan. Eyck swallowed, his eyes trained on the dark blotch across the room, and lay there motionless, just listening to Wex. Soon the lad's ragged breathing became more audible, and Eyck silently moved his hand down his own body to where his cock was beginning to harden, the smooth head already poking out of its furry sheath. Feeling a little ashamed of himself, Eyck nevertheless strained to hear Wex better.

Soon Wex's breathing became a quiet panting . . . then suddenly it stopped, followed by a suppressed grunt, and silence again. A few seconds later, Wex let out a shuddering sigh. His breathing resumed, but it was staccato, as if he were struggling to catch his breath quietly.

Eyck's erection throbbed impatiently in his grasp, but he didn't dare do more than squeeze it. What would Wex do if he heard him? He would obviously realize Eyck had been listening.

Well, maybe Wex wouldn't mind . . .

The thought pulled a skeptical snort out of Eyck, and across the room, Wex fell completely silent.

Schatten. Eyck let out another snort, turning it into a little snore, as if he were just making noises in his sleep.

After a moment, Wex began breathing again, but Eyck had the feeling the young man was on high alert. Eyck stifled a sigh and relinquished his hold on his cock, closing his eyes as he tried to ignore the persistent pulsing in his groin.

He seemed to always be feeling ruttish as of late, taking care of his needs on the sly whenever he could. It was because of Wex's presence, of that he was certain. However, he couldn't very well do anything now—even if he waited for Wex to fall asleep, how could he be certain he wasn't just pretending? Might as well just try to go to sleep unfulfilled.

It felt like it took forever.

Chapter Seven

Try as he might, Wex could not focus on the task at hand, which was sorting hundreds of metal rings into different boxes. The rings needed to be sorted by size before they were sent to the metalworkers to be made into chainmail. However, Wex kept putting the rings in the wrong boxes, and a few times, he belatedly saw he had missed bent or rusted rings, which forced him to sift through what he had sorted before he could continue.

The problem was that Eyck was right in his line of vision, and because of the day's heat, the blacksmith had taken off his shirt to work bare-chested as he cleaned and repaired his various tools. Normally, even when it was stifling hot within the smithy, Eyck wore his apron and a shirt to keep from burning himself . . . but he hadn't lit the fire today as it wasn't needed.

Wex frowned, trying to pay attention to the little metal rings in his palm, but soon found his gaze wandering again to watch the way Eyck's muscles moved under the short fur of his back, his eyes straying to the long tail that reached nearly to the floor behind him, the tufted end twitching in time to his low humming. Gritting his teeth, Wex flared his nostrils when Eyck lifted a hand to idly scratch a broad shoulder, and he realized he was unconsciously sniffing the air for the big Levek's scent.

Suns. It was getting ridiculous.

Wex growled, surprising himself like he always did when he managed to pull his voice out of the pit where it normally languished beyond his reach.

"Hm?" Eyck looked over his shoulder, his eyes wide. "Did you . . . uh, say something?"

There was something terribly alluring about those pale-green eyes, so often full of warmth and good humour . . . tenderness . . .

Wex shook his head, bending again to his task, but felt Eyck's gaze linger on him a while longer before the blacksmith turned back to his own work.

Miserable, Wex hunched his shoulders, wishing he could cure himself of whatever this bizarre obsession was.

Desire for the big Levek was a creature that hounded him all night in his dreams, but even when he was awake, he couldn't escape it. Wex refused to give into it, no matter that Eyck had given zero indication of interest on his part.

He just needed something to help purge his system and calm him down so he could think clearly. Wex didn't intend on staying in South Galetsy for even one day past his apprenticeship, and all this mooning about, making mistakes, was wasting precious time.

"Wex?"

Wex lifted his head, meeting Eyck's eyes. *"What?"* he gestured impatiently.

"Uh . . . I was just going to ask if you could drop those off at Dugan's yourself. Are you all right?"

"I'm fine," Wex replied curtly. *"I'm just bored. This is stupid work."*

Eyck gave him a wry grin. "Yes, I know. But it's necessary."

"Why don't you just keep the rings according to size when you're making them, instead of making extra work later on?" Wex signed, curling his lip at Eyck.

"Because I accidentally put those together in one box. Now, can you take them to Dugan's workshop or not?" Eyck looked annoyed.

Wex knew if he kept complaining, Eyck would just send him on a walk to cool off. It happened almost daily now.

"Yes, fine," he signed. *"When I'm done."*

"Thank you," Eyck replied brusquely and went back to his tools.

Not a minute passed before Wex found himself staring at Eyck's broad back again. Disgusted with himself, he stood and grabbed the boxes he'd finished, then stomped out of the smithy, slamming the door behind him.

He'd drop off the rings . . . then he'd pay a visit to the wharfside pub.

WEX SAT on his stool and sipped at his honey wine, nodding in the right places when Loomis paused in his monologue. He'd been there an hour and the sole patron in all that time.

He was about to give up when the door banged open, and a group of men entered, their boots thudding on the floorboards and voices raised in a cacophony of lively debate. Wex ducked his head and peered slowly to the side, trying to see whether the lanky Grendall sailor was among their number, and was annoyed when he wasn't.

The men, all sailors it seemed, settled at two tables and continued their loud conversation, calling for ale and whiskey and including the bartender in their good-natured argument when he went to serve them.

Then Wex noticed a familiar figure lounging in a seat by the end of the bar, the corners of his amber eyes once again creased in playful amusement, as though he and Wex were sharing a secret. The man must have come in while Wex was distracted by the others—he wondered how long he had been watching him.

He turned away, scanning the bottles behind the bar to distract his jitters. He'd whored himself before . . . but never like *this*. The previous times had been for shelter, food, protection—was he really going to go through with it now just to sort his head out? Surely, he was able to do that on his own.

I don't need to do this . . .

Wex sighed and put his hands on the bar but didn't push himself off his stool. The bartender's words kept coming back to him: *I hear him and his crewmates can be rough.* Rough was exactly what he needed —the rougher the better to remind him how humiliating and uncomfortable the act was. He needed to teach his body a lesson . . . maybe then it would stop seething in lust every time Eyck took his schatten shirt off.

Gritting his teeth, he folded his forearms on the bar and looked over his shoulder at Stilig. The Grendall cocked his head, the beginnings of a sly smile on his lean face, and sat back, crossing his arms over his chest. *You have my attention,* the pose said.

Wex felt his face grow hot with embarrassment over what he was doing. He looked away but swayed his tail slowly, the tufted end sweeping the floor, then flexed and lifted it at the base. Then, with another look towards the sailor, he flicked his tail to the side suggestively, signalling his interest.

One of Stilig's white fangs teased at the corner of his lip, his grin spreading. He nodded then jerked his head towards the front door as he stood, one hand nonchalantly adjusting the noticeable bulge in the front of his loose trousers.

With a sigh, Wex stood and followed the Grendall sailor out of the tavern. The sun was low, and only a few merchants were left, most packing up for the night.

Halfway down the boardwalk, Stilig stopped and shoved Wex into the space between two buildings where the shadows were deep.

He forced himself not to flinch as Stilig leaned close, peering up at Wex as he slipped a hand up his shirt to fondle his chest. The Grendall grabbed Wex's nipple between thumb and forefinger and squeezed hard.

"I'll give ya one silver," the man said quietly.

Wex blinked in surprise, having forgotten that money would be exchanged. It was a very fair sum—Loomis had been right about Stilig's treatment of Kirmen—but Wex hesitated. He hadn't expected to simply be done quick in an alley and felt—oddly—a little let down.

"Fine. One silver and two copper," Stilig said with a shrug.

Wex shook his head, wondering how he could make himself understood.

"What's that?" Stilig asked. His fur smelled faintly of burning wood and sweat, but it wasn't unpleasant, and his expression was still friendly, though guarded.

Grimacing, Wex pointed to his throat and shook his head.

"I know ya can't speak, fella. I asked Loomis about ya. That's all right. I can understand a bit of signing."

Wex remembered then that the captain of the *Sparkshade* had understood his gestures, and he smiled with relief.

"We do this here?" he gestured, using the simplest signs.

"On the ship if ya don't mind. And it'll be me and my brother. Ya good with that, fella?"

Frowning, Wex nodded a bit hesitantly.

"How about a silver and three for ya. That enough?"

When Wex nodded, Stilig pinched his nipple even harder, causing him to wince.

"Good. But I want to know if ya can take a bit of a beating. My brother and I have appetites that may seem downright bestial . . . to some. Yer not soft, are ya?"

Wex quickly shook his head, his heart racing.

Yes. This is more like it.

"Good good," the Grendall said, releasing Wex and stepping back.

He was a head shorter than Wex and probably weighed half of what he did—if anything went wrong, Wex could overpower Stilig without a problem. But what about the brother?

Squaring his shoulders, Wex gestured. *"Are we going?"*

"Eager. I like that," Stilig replied with a toothy grin, then he led him out of the shadows towards the ship.

STILIG'S BROTHER Klok looked *exactly* like him, which surprised Wex. Kat'hoondeman females rarely birthed more than one pup at a time.

Maybe not actually twins. Maybe just close in age.

Wex had a hard time telling them apart once they'd thrown their shirts to the deck. He looked down into a matched pair of amber eyes and twin cocky smiles. It was a little disorienting.

The brothers quickly took control of the situation. Four hands began to grope him all over, and Wex tried to maintain his balance. One of the brothers smacked Wex's pecs with both hands, then squeezed them like he was testing ripe melons. He looked over at the other Grendall with a broad smile.

"What a big beauty ya found us," the man said, revealing himself to be the brother, Klok. "Can I have his arse first?"

"We flip on it."

"*Suns*, Stilig . . . just this once?"

Stilig laughed, then reached into his trousers for a silver coin. "I'm Suns; you're King's Head," he said, flipping the coin high into the air.

Wex watched in a state of detached curiosity and mild amusement as Stilig declared himself the winner.

So that's how they do things, is it? He couldn't remember ever having been in a similar situation.

"All right, fella . . . ya come this way?" Stilig said, motioning for Wex to follow.

Wex nodded but was surprised when they didn't go belowdecks. The Grendall brothers led him out of the lamplight to the other side of a stack of crates where they couldn't be seen from the boardwalk. However, they were very much out in the open.

Uncomfortable, Wex frowned at Stilig.

"Oh, don't worry, fella," the Grendall said with a smile. "We do this all the time. It's pitchy enough no one'll see . . . and no one cares, really. Trust me, will ya?"

Wex looked around. *"Where are the others?"*

"You mean the crew? Out and about," Stilig replied, shaking out a big blanket.

Klok helped him drape it over a single crate on the deck. "There. That'll do for it, eh? Come here."

Wex took a step towards the man, feeling jittery and uncertain

Klok's hands came around his waist from behind, tackling the fastenings on his trousers as Stilig pulled Wex's shirt up. In no time at all, he was stripped bare. The cool night air ruffling his fur triggered an unwelcome memory of running through the woods naked.

He closed his eyes, breathing deep. *No. Don't think about that.*

"Fella?"

Wex's eyes snapped open, and he looked over at the sailors. Each had a hand down the front of his trousers, obviously eager to begin. Slowly, Wex nodded, swallowing hard.

"On your back," Stilig said, pointing to the covered crate. "Knees up."

Wex did as he was told, lying back on the crate and grabbing the backs of his thighs.

"Open those knees nice and wide," Stilig said, slapping the inside of Wex's thigh. "Yeah, just like that." The sailor grabbed Wex by the hips and slid him a little closer.

Something wet touched Wex's pucker, and he flinched involuntarily.

Wex was so distracted by what was going on between his thighs that he started when a hard cock smacked him in the cheek. He looked up at Klok's grinning face.

"Say *ahhh*," Klok said, then slid his cock into Wex's mouth when he opened it. "Oh, *Suns*."

The Grendall didn't have a lot of girth, but he made up for that in length. Wex gagged when his throat was probed. Reaching back, he pushed at Klok and coughed, his eyes full of tears.

"Can ya take it or no?" Stilig asked as he yanked lightly on Wex's tail.

Nodding quickly, Wex opened his lips again, trying not to choke when Klok plunged his cock deep again. Wex struggled to breathe around Klok's slow rhythm, and each time, Klok seemed to be waiting for him to gag again before pulling back.

Wex wondered what Stilig was doing—the man's hand was still around the base of his tail but nothing else had happened. Listening hard, he made out the sound of Stilig stroking himself. The man was just standing there watching his brother get his cock sucked.

For some reason, that made Wex's pulse soar. He was getting aroused.

Damnit. Why?

"That's good. That's good," Klok kept murmuring to himself. He leaned forward, grabbed hold of Wex's pecs, and pushed his cock deep into Wex's throat.

Wex couldn't stop himself from choking, and he frantically shoved back at Klok's thighs to dislodge him.

The Grendall just leaned into Wex harder.

As Wex's body convulsed, his muscles tight with panic, Stilig shoved his cock into his ass.

The pain was shocking in its intensity.

The breath torn out of him by Klok's cock popping free was more like a soundless cry. Shaking and panting, Wex turned his head and spat as Stilig's cock slammed into him again.

Laughing, Klok slapped Wex's face. "Having fun?"

Wex's throat was raw, and it felt like Stilig's dick was halfway up to his stomach. He was in pain and miserable . . . and every shred of arousal he might have felt earlier had evaporated.

Perfect.

Eyes closed, Wex nodded and opened his mouth again.

Chapter Eight

Wex sat down gingerly and leaned over his bowl of tomato soup, scooping it into his mouth mechanically. He'd gone down to the wharf three more times that week, and his backside felt like it would never recover.

The Grendall brothers were a curious mix of brutal and courteous in their treatment of him. As long as he kept nodding when they checked in on him, they had no qualms with fucking him nearly senseless. Wex's nipples felt swollen and tender from Stilig gnawing on them, and he was sure there were bruises under his fur where Klok had nearly strangled him—it was painful to swallow his soup, but he refused to show any sign of it. Eyck would only ask more questions he had no intention of answering.

"When we finish with those rods for Gandy's cart, do you want to continue with your reading lessons?" Eyck asked quietly.

Wex grimaced. Without looking up, he shook his head.

Eyck sighed. "You agreed this was part of your training."

Curling his lip, Wex shook his head again more forcefully.

"Suns, Wex . . . You *have* to learn to read."

"*Later*," Wex signed with his free hand.

"What's going on with you?"

"*Nothing.*"

EYCK SAT BACK, watching the young man eat his supper seemingly without any enjoyment. During the day while they worked, Wex was polite and reserved, and there had been no more outbursts, but something was very wrong with him. He'd been staying out after dark by himself, coming home late, and acting peculiar.

Eyck almost missed the simmering anger that had provoked arguments between them—at least that had felt real. This cold civility was like a wall between them.

Scratching the back of his neck, Eyck sighed. He wished he could figure out what had happened. Was this his fault? They'd been on friendly terms only a week ago.

Eyck pushed the basket of bread towards Wex, thinking the gesture might make him warm up a bit, but Wex just shook his head and stood, leaving his soup half-eaten.

"I'm going out."

"Why don't you stay home for one night? I was thinking you could teach me that card game you mentioned you liked playing . . ." Eyck said, keeping his tone light.

Wex pointed to the time-keeper. The metal bead was rolling slowly down the coil. A moment later, it fell into the receptacle at the bottom with a faint click.

"The agreement was to keep the same hours as you. I've kept them. The day is done, and I am free to go," Wex signed, his jaw visibly clenched.

"I don't mean to keep you here against your will, Wex. That's not what I meant," Eyck said with a helpless shrug. "I just thought . . ."

"You thought wrong." Wex looked impatient to leave, but he stayed where he was for a moment, staring down at Eyck.

"You're not getting up to any trouble, are you?" Eyck asked. What was going on behind those dark eyes? He'd heard a disturbing rumour about Wex, but Wex was a grown man . . . it was none of his business what his apprentice got up to in his free time. He only wished he knew whether what he'd heard was true—it didn't make any sense to him.

To his surprise, Wex actually gave him a reassuring smile. *"No. No trouble. Don't worry,"* he signed. *"See you tomorrow."*

Eyck nodded and watched Wex leave, his gait strangely stiff.

WEX FROWNED to himself as he took the road south to the river. He wished Eyck would stop looking at him with those big green eyes full of worry . . . it certainly wasn't helping. However, he'd never intended to cause any problems for the blacksmith. He *was* thankful for Eyck's help, when it came right down to it—he was learning a valuable skill from a patient teacher after all—and though Wex wasn't going to stick around, he didn't want to damage Eyck's reputation. He owed the man that much.

All at once, Wex couldn't breathe. The blow had come out of nowhere.

At first, he had no idea who or what had hit him. Doubled over, he fought for breath, and when it finally came, he heard laughter.

A group of unkempt soldiers, a mix of Levek and Duval men and one Losano, were loitering by the side of the road, their armour dented and spotted with rust, and their blunted swords piled by their feet. It was a common sight these days—strangers coming to take part in the fighting—and most of them up to no good. From the edge of mania in their laughter, Wex guessed the men were drunk.

As they hooted and pointed at him, he glanced down and saw the rock. No doubt one of their number had thrown it. For a moment, Wex could only stand there, fists at his side. There were seven of them and only one of him. Even if he got in a few good punches, they would no doubt beat the crap out of him . . . maybe even kill him. It wasn't worth it.

Teeth clenched, he kept walking, ignoring both the pain in his middle and the slurs they continued to toss at his back—words that pelted him where hurled stones couldn't reach.

Suddenly, Wex was no longer in the mood for Stilig and Klok's specifically tailored abuse. A quiet evening with Eyck playing cards didn't sound half-bad . . . but he'd have to walk past the soldiers again. Wex slowed on the steps up to the boardwalk, considering again going back to the smithy, but . . . even if the soldiers weren't there, he knew he *couldn't*. Just being around the blacksmith made him tense and miserable, and when they argued, it was even worse.

What in the Three Suns is happening to me? he thought, continuing on to where the *Sparkshade* was still moored.

It was still light out, but the shadows were getting longer, and Wex waved at the first sailor he saw. The man was a roly-poly little Dankel named Hoody with bright-orange fur and a missing left ear. He grinned wide and waved back, pointing in the direction of the pub, and Wex touched his temple in thanks.

Wex pulled open the door to Loomis's pub. Stilig and Klok were seated with some of their shipmates. The *Sparkshade*'s skinny Ulven first mate grinned wide at Wex.

"Oh hey, boys, your Kirmen's come lookin' for you," she said, then leaned over and spat a stream of brown baccy juice into the bronze spittoon. *"Again."*

The lanky Grendalls glanced back at him. Wex still couldn't easily tell the brothers apart, but when the one on the left spoke, Wex knew it was Stilig—he always took the lead in everything the brothers did.

"Fella?" Stilig said, furrowing his brow. He looked at the group of grinning sailors before getting to his feet and leading Wex away a few steps. "Listen, fella . . ." He rubbed his furry jaw, shaking his head slowly. He looked sheepish. "I don't know what to tell ya, friend, but I'm skint. Sorry, but I can't pay . . . not today."

Wex shrugged and signed, *"No money. Free."*

Stilig straightened, silently staring up into Wex's eyes with uncharacteristic gravity for long enough that Wex had to avert his gaze.

"That what you *really* want, fella?" the man said very quietly.

Clenching his jaw, Wex felt a surge of irritation. He frowned down at the Grendall.

"It's my business," he signed tersely.

Stilig studied Wex for another few seconds, something like concern on his lean face, then he shrugged one-shouldered and grinned.

"Alrighty. If that's what ya want. Go wait up yonder by the *Spark*. Klok and me'll be with ya when we're done here, eh?"

Nodding, Wex left. As he passed the stairs leading up to Dama Sunshine's, he thought he saw a familiar figure entering the brothel. Frowning, he shook his head. He must be imagining things.

Wex walked back to the *Sparkshade* and settled himself on one of the wooden bolsters to wait.

It was dark by the time the brothers came sauntering up the boardwalk alone. Without a word to Wex, they dismissed the grizzled old Levek who guarded the ship and walked up the gangplank, Wex following close behind.

This time, there was no crate to lie atop, just the old blanket, but that didn't matter to Wex. On his knees, he huffed out a few quick breaths, wincing as Stilig, who was once again the winner of the coin toss, hilted his cock solidly into him. Klok crouched over Wex, holding him by the throat as he fed his long shaft into his mouth, chuckling quietly when Wex gagged and bucked back.

"Want to see how long you can hold your breath, mate?" Klok murmured, grabbing the back of Wex's head to force him to stay put.

Wex's eyes streamed as he choked, fighting against the panic of not being able to breathe. He barely noticed Stilig adding a finger next to the cock in his ass, but when the sailor tugged hard on his tail, one of Wex's knees gave out from under him.

Wex barely managed to turn his head to keep from biting down as the three of them fell in a heap. Klok started laughing, and Stilig slapped Wex across the rump.

"All right, fella, on your back then?" Stilig said, helping Wex to turn over.

Bracing his backside with his hands, Wex parted his knees and steeled himself to continue—but, as soon as he was impaled again from both ends, he heard footfalls.

"Oh, hullo there," said the stranger, stopping near Wex's shoulder.

Wex's pulse surged, but he couldn't move his head—Klok was

holding him fast, still probing his mouth with shallow thrusts—but out of the corner of his eye, he could see a pair of scuffed brown boots.

"Modig!" Stilig said jovially. "Back already?"

"*Suns*, Drunsworth is a fucking hole . . . I would'a been back yesterday, but we ran into some trouble on the road. Soldiers are gettin' to be thick as ticks, eh?" The stranger laughed. "So, who's this then? Will ya look at the size of him . . . And that fur! Yeah, that's right pretty, it is. Like fresh-minted silver."

"He's our new friend," Stilig said, squeezing Wex's thighs in an oddly affectionate way.

"Looks like yer havin' yerselves a nice time . . ." said the stranger a little wistfully.

"Hey, fella?" Stilig said, patting Wex's belly. "Do ya mind if our brother Modig joins in?"

Brother? How many brothers are there?

Wex started pulling his hand out from under him to gesture, but Stilig said, "Hey, will ya take yer cock out of his mouth for *one* bloody second so's he can answer?"

"It's not like he can talk," Klok pointed out, clearly reluctant to stop.

"And it's not like he can nod with yer knob lodged in his throat, now can he?"

Klok pulled out, and Wex closed his mouth, swallowing. His jaw was getting sore.

"Right. Sorry, Stilig," Klok said. He patted Wex's cheek. "So? What d'ya say?"

Wex stared wide-eyed at Modig. He looked just like the other two —the only difference was that he wore a patch over one eye, a thin pink scar curling out from the bottom of the black material. It was as if all three had come from the same litter, which in itself was amazing, but what made it even *more* exceptional was that all three had been spared by the Five Cycle Sickness. A religious man would call them blessed; Wex thought them very lucky. He looked at Modig's eyepatch again, wondering what had happened to him.

At least I can tell him apart from the others, I suppose, he thought as he nodded. *The more the merrier?*

"That's a good mate," Stilig said. "What'll it be, brother o' mine? Would ya like to sample his arse?"

"But I was going to go next—" Klok started, but Stilig cut him off with a sharp growl.

"This is our brother's first taste of our treat . . . be unselfish, now Klok."

Klok nodded and sighed so woefully that Wex almost felt sorry for the Grendall. Wex opened his mouth helpfully, and Klok gave him a wide smile, stroking his cheek as he fed his flagging cock back into his mouth. Wex closed his eyes and tried to relax.

"His arse is always a bit pinched at the beginning, not what ya'd expect from who's been incarcerated as has our dear silver-pelted friend here."

"Incarcerated, ya say?"

"Hange."

"Good Suns," Modig said, sounding impressed.

"But I've opened him up a fair bit . . . his hole's like a sweet, sucking kiss—a true delight for the pecker. I think with more of a warmup, he could accommodate two . . ."

Wex's eyes popped open, his pulse racing.

"That's all right," Modig replied with a chuckle. His belt buckle hit the deck with a loud crack, startling Wex. "You know what I like."

At that moment, Klok decided he needed more attention and began to push himself further down Wex's throat again, causing him to choke, and Wex thought Modig said something about being more careful.

Wex was so distracted by what Stilig and Klok were doing, that the reason Modig straddled his waist, facing away, wasn't evident at first. Then Modig grasped the furry sheath covering Wex's limp cock and Wex started, his thighs trembling.

He couldn't pull his hands out from under him because of Modig's weight, so he lay there, blinking in alarm, mouth and ass in vigorous service as Modig began to stretch his sheath open. It wasn't painful, only a bit uncomfortable, but he didn't like it at all . . . less even when Modig spat on the end of his own cock and docked the entire length of it into Wex's sheath like it was a sleeve, the

Grendall's cockhead butting up against Wex's soft member nestled within.

With a pleased sigh, Modig grasped himself through the thin furry skin, and began thrusting quickly, his buttocks rocking against Wex's abdomen as he pleasured himself.

Wex stared upside-down between Klok's thighs and saw a white mouse against the side of the ship. It was sitting up on its haunches, pink paws clutched to its furry white chest as it stared at him with red eyes, whiskers twitching. Then it was gone in a blink, evidently uninterested in what the three Kat'hoondemen were doing to Wex.

Wishing he could escape just as easily, Wex crushed his eyes closed and waited for the brothers to be done with him.

WEX SWISHED the water in his mouth and spat it out, then wrung the cloth again and hung it up on the brass hook.

There was a small looking glass over the basin, but Wex avoided it. He felt so degraded.

Sighing, he buttoned up his trousers over his still-damp fur, thankful that the sailors always let him wash up after their encounters. The way he was feeling wasn't their fault. For all their strange ways and bizarre tastes, they were good men when it came down to it. No, it was all his own damn fault.

I have to stop doing this to myself.

He stepped out of the tiny cupboard-like space and slid the door closed behind him, taking the stairs to the upper deck. Klok and Stilig were sitting on the far gunwale, sharing a pipe, and Modig was regaling them with some tale.

When he heard Wex, he turned around with a broad smile. "That was mighty fine, it was," Modig said with a chuckle. He shook his head and sighed. "Yer a beaut, fella. I want to thank ya . . ." He must have seen something in Wex's expression, because he paused, brow wrinkled. "I didn't hurt ya none, did I?"

Wex shook his head and forced a polite smile.

Modig nodded, then dug into his pants pocket. He held out a gold coin. "Here, for your trouble, friend. My brother says he didn't pay ya . . . can't have that, can we now?"

Touching his temple in thanks, Wex accepted the *extremely* generous payment, and Modig nodded again.

"Well, this is farewell, friend," said Stilig, approaching. He gently laid a hand on Wex's shoulder with a smile. "Don't know when we'll be back this a-ways, what with the war . . . dangerous times and all that."

Farewell?

It hadn't really occurred to Wex that they would leave, but why would they stay? This was a merchant ship, not a permanent fixture. *"Of course,"* he signed. *"Safe journey."*

Klok just waved, but Stilig clasped arms with him like they were friends.

Wex turned to leave, feeling strangely conflicted. He'd already decided on his own not to visit the brothers again, but now that they were leaving, he didn't know what he would do without them.

Before he got to the gangplank, Stilig stopped him, coming in close. "Don't know what it is yer running from, Wex," Stilig said, surprising him by using his name for the first time. Wex wondered where he had learned it. Smiling, Stilig shook his head. "I hope ya find peace. I do. And can I offer one bit of advice?"

Wex nodded and was surprised when Stilig took his arm, lifting his sleeve to bear the prison brand.

"Yer a blacksmith, and blacksmiths sometimes get nasty burns," he said, tapping the letter on his forearm. "No one will question a burn scar on a blacksmith."

Lifting his brows, Wex nodded slowly, catching the sailor's meaning. He tapped his temple and smiled.

Chapter Nine

E yck whistled an old shanty as he hammered a twist into the piece of iron he was working on. Wex was out for the afternoon, finally visiting Tembra's brother to teach him and his son a bit of signing language, and Eyck wondered how it was going. Wex had come home late the previous evening in an oddly subdued mood, looking disheveled and smelling of wet fur and tobacco . . . and something *else*.

He frowned, pushing the metal back into the fire as he reached up to pull the bellows. Was Wex really selling himself to men on the wharf? The rumours made little sense to Eyck, but he couldn't help thinking about the rangy Grendall sailor who had come by a few days earlier when Wex was out delivering a stove pipe. The sailor hadn't purchased or commissioned anything—he'd just stood there with an easy smile, asking all sorts of questions about Wex before cheerfully bidding Eyck a good day.

The encounter had left Eyck unsettled, not because the sailor had said anything overtly inappropriate, but because the piqued interest had brought out a strange feeling in Eyck. Was it resentment? Did he *resent* Wex for not confiding in him? For seeking out others?

Eyck snorted and shook his head, hammering the iron piece into shape. Why was his fur so ruffled over the thought of Wex being touched by strange men? Was he jealous because Wex was willing to lift his tail for them but wouldn't even let Eyck so much as pat him on the shoulder?

Truth was, he'd revisited the memory of Wex offering himself to him so many times that it had worn a groove in his thoughts—he fell easily into the fantasy of *what if*, every time his mind strayed.

It was stupid.

"*Suns*, I need to get laid," he muttered, straightening. He started when a board creaked behind him, and he turned.

"What was that?" asked Pash, setting his basket down on the table.

"Oh, hey," Eyck said, face warm. "I was just . . . I didn't hear you come in."

"It's a wonder you hear anyone come in over that infernal clanging. I'm amazed you're not stone deaf."

Eyck chuckled and put the piece of iron into the cooling bath, setting aside his hammer. "I hear just fine."

"Speaking of hearing—I ran into Mrs. Begmard just now. She says you've got Wex teaching Besdoe's boy?"

"Yeah." Eyck dipped his cup into the pail of well water and drank deep, then wiped his mouth. "Did you bring lunch?" he asked, pointing to the priest's basket. He was starving.

"Unfortunately not," Pash said, lifting the corner of the checkered cloth. There was a jumble of small pots within. "Taking some more medical supplies out to the old mill. Another dozen men arrived this morning, all badly wounded."

"Ah." Eyck sighed, wondering if he had any bread left.

"Do you think it's a good idea?"

"Think what's a good idea?"

"Letting Wex around children."

Confused, Eyck shook his head slowly. "Why would that matter?"

"You know . . . considering what he's been . . . *doing*," Pash said, giving Eyck a pointed look.

"How's that any of your business?" Eyck replied, his tone sharp with annoyance. "And what does it matter? It's not like he's going to recruit young Gawen into whoredom."

"But what if they're left together alone . . ."

"Ludicrous."

"I'm just saying Wex could corrupt that young boy. Maybe by accident," Pash said, his nostrils flaring. "What if, through his lessons, he plants immoral ideas . . . somehow alludes to men lying with men."

"I strongly doubt that. But what if he does?"

"An innocent young mind could be led down a sinful path . . ." Pash trailed off suggestively.

Eyck growled, losing patience with his old friend. "And what sinful path is *that*, Pash? What happened to *'There was no sin in what we did'*? Are you telling me now that you believe I somehow 'corrupted' your young mind, because I sure as *Suns* remember it was *you* that led me into the storeroom that day . . . and it was *you* that said 'Fuck me harder, Eyck, give—' "

"Stop!" Pash growled.

"And it was *you* that climbed through my window all those nights because you couldn't get eno—"

"I said stop!" Pash swung his fist and hit Eyck in the face. It was a clumsy punch and not a particularly hard one, but Pash's thick gold Suns ring caught the corner of Eyck's lip.

He tasted blood and wiped his mouth, glaring at the priest.

"I . . . I'm sorry," Pash said, looking aghast. "I didn't . . ." He picked up the basket of medical supplies and took a step back. "I should go."

"Yes, you should," Eyck replied, crossing his arms over his chest.

Pash and he had fought throughout the sun-cycles of their long friendship, but it had never come to blows before. He was both shocked and furious that the priest would come here spewing garbage about Wex. Then he remembered how Pash had been so relieved when Eyck had told him there was nothing going on with Wex. Jealousy was such a spiteful emotion.

At that moment, the bells above the door gave a jingle, and Wex strode into the smithy, a smile on his face. However, it only took one glance at Eyck and his bloodied lip for his expression to go dark.

He snarled and turned on the priest, grabbing him by the neck to slam him back against the wall hard enough that the window rattled. The basket fell to the floor, its contents tumbling out.

"Call your . . . guard dog . . . off," Pash said in a strangled voice. "Eyck . . ."

A low, menacing growl was coming from deep in Wex's huge chest, and his tail whipped back and forth. It was frankly terrifying.

"Wex! It's all right. Stop. It was an accident. Put Pash down," Eyck said, gingerly placing a hand on Wex's muscular shoulder. "Please. It's all right. I'm all right."

The growling stopped, but Wex kept his hand on the priest's throat. He stared daggers at Pash, his fangs bared and nose wrinkled up in fury. It was a fearsome display, one that Eyck hoped never to be on the wrong side of.

"Wex?" Eyck's pulse was speeding, worried that the lad would kill the priest.

Wex just gave Pash's neck one final squeeze then stepped back, releasing him.

Pash sagged in relief, coughing. "Suns . . . you're a menace. An *animal*."

Feeling Wex's shoulder tense under his touch, Eyck stepped between them before he could pounce again. "Just take your things and go, Pash. Don't make it worse." His lip felt puffy, but he was certain that Pash's throat bore the worst of the exchange.

Still coughing, Pash bent and scooped everything back into the basket. He left without a backwards glance.

"*Suns* . . ." Eyck swore, sitting down on the bench. "He's my best friend, Wex."

"*Is he?*" Wex's mouth was set in a hard line as he stared down at Eyck. "*Why would a friend hit you?*" he signed.

Eyck scratched the back of his neck. "It was just a small argument. I goaded him on . . . Pash is . . . well, uh . . . you make him *nervous*," he said, opting to use nervousness instead of jealousy—he had no idea how Wex would react to the truth.

Wex blinked, his forehead creasing. *You were arguing about me?*

Schatten. "Not directly, no," Eyck replied, then tried to pivot the conversation by asking, "Haven't you ever fought with a friend over something stupid?" He smiled.

Wex just stared at him, his expression stony, before turning away.

Eyck frowned. "What is it?"

"What friend?"

"Oh, come on. You've had friends. What about this Red fella you talk about?"

With a snort, Wex pulled something wrapped in paper out of his shoulder bag and set it down on the table. Eyck's stomach grumbled comically loud as the smell of hickory-smoked wheat glutty wafted to his nose. Wex had obviously stopped by Macy's mill-house on the way home. Eyck's mouth watered, wishing he'd had the foresight to ask Wex to bring him something to eat.

"Red was an asshole," Wex signed, smirking. *"Not a friend."*

"Well," Eyck said, eyeing the wrapped sandwich. *"We're* friends . . . aren't we?"

Narrowing his eyes, Wex stared at Eyck for a few moments. Then he pulled a second sandwich from his bag and smirked again, setting it in front of Eyck.

"Oh . . . *thank* Suns," Eyck said, fumbling at the wrapping. "I was ready to start chewing a table leg."

Wex hadn't answered his question, which bothered him some, though the lad *had* thought to bring him lunch . . . and who else but a friend would spring to someone's defence so quickly? That was curious, the way he'd reacted to Pash hitting him.

Eyck took a big bite, closing his eyes as he savoured it. "Well, as far as I'm concerned, you're my friend whether you like it or not," he said, once he'd swallowed.

Wex stopped chewing, his expression unreadable. Then he shrugged, looking away.

"And . . . I'm sorry I touched you earlier," Eyck added. "I was just afraid that you were going to reach in and pull Pash's spine right out of him."

This time, Wex smiled wide, then started chuckling and shaking his head, obviously amused at the imagery Eyck had conjured.

Grinning, Eyck sat back. "I'd like his spine to stay where it is. Got it?"

"Yes, boss," Wex signed one-handed, still laughing. *"And touch ok."*

Eyck was startled for a moment, but Wex was concentrating on his lunch and hadn't noticed his reaction.

Touch ok? The abridged signs forced simplicity, so was he just forgiving him? Or was that permission to . . . ?

Wex looked up from his sandwich.

Eyck averted his gaze, not wanting the lad to read anything into his expression. "Boy, does Macy sure know how to cook, eh?" he said awkwardly.

Wex just nodded his enthusiasm, thankfully not picking up on what direction Eyck's mind had started running, yet again.

Chapter Ten

Wex jolted awake at the touch, his heart pounding.

"You all right? You were making noises in your sleep," the big Levek said, peering down at Wex on his cot. "Sounded like you were having a nightmare."

Breathing out a shaky breath, Wex nodded.

"Well, if you want to talk about it . . ." Eyck gestured to himself, but Wex quickly shook his head. "Yeah . . . ok." The blacksmith yawned, showing his long curved fangs, slightly yellowed from age, then ran a hand over the top of his head, trying to tame his thick mop of hair. "Well . . . it's early, but we might as well get up. Right?"

Wex nodded again, wishing Eyck would hurry up and leave him alone. Thankfully, the blacksmith only stayed long enough to tidy his bed before going downstairs.

"I'm making pancakes," he said as his head disappeared down the stairwell. "Don't dawdle or I'll eat the lot myself."

Sighing in relief, Wex rolled onto his back. It was a damn good thing he slept on his side or else Eyck would have realized it was no nightmare he was having. He lifted his blanket and stared down at the stiff pink cock jutting from his furry grey sheath.

A small drip fell from the tip of it, landing on the short fur of his belly, and he grimaced, willing his erection to go away. It didn't work

—the dream was still too vivid in his mind—so he wrapped his hand around his shaft, stroking it quickly.

He and Eyck had been naked, curled up together in the soft grass of a sunny meadow. No real touching, nothing overtly sexual . . . *yet*. Mostly it was just the *feeling* of being there . . .

Wex's breath was coming in short gasps, and he hoped Eyck couldn't hear him from downstairs, but he had to take care of it quickly. He gritted his teeth, frustrated and on edge.

Oh, come on, he thought clasping his furry balls with the other hand as he worked his cock faster. It wasn't enough so he closed his eyes and let himself think about Eyck. He pictured them together, like in the dream, only this time Eyck ran his hand up the inside of Wex's thigh.

Yes.

He imagined Eyck's big rough hand moving higher to squeeze his balls.

Yes.

Wex panted, arching his neck and head back on the pillow. Now, Eyck's hand closing around his cock . . .

YES.

The cum burst out of him in two huge surges, the release so intense he didn't register the creak of the stairs until he was twitching and sighing through the smaller aftershocks of his orgasm. He looked over at the stairwell, his heart pounding as he tried to get his breathing under control.

No one was there. Had he just imagined it?

Fuck.

EYCK SAT down on the bench, his knees a bit weak. He'd heard a moan and, not thinking, had gone upstairs to see if Wex had fallen back to sleep and into his nightmare again. He hadn't been prepared for the sight of the young man with the blanket down around his knees, hand stroking his cock, eyes crushed closed and completely oblivious to anything but the pleasure he was feeling.

Stunned, Eyck had frozen in place and watched hungrily as Wex gasped and sent a thick spurt of cum onto his chest—it was enough to shake him out of his trance, so he bolted down the stairs before he was caught peeping.

Fuck. Eyck closed his eyes and breathed in slowly. *Suns.*

He couldn't remember the last time he'd wanted anyone as much as he wanted Wex. Not even his teenage lust for Pash could compare. No, this was a deep, primal *need*. He let out a groan no louder than a sigh.

Schatten's hell.

The tread on the stair jerked him to his feet, and he nearly leapt to the forge where the pancakes had started to burn. With his back to the stairs, Eyck forced his expression into something he hoped looked nonchalant.

"Almost ready," he said cheerfully and glanced over his shoulder. Wex peered at him suspiciously for a moment but said nothing and seated himself at the table.

Feeling guilty and flustered, Eyck flipped the pancakes onto a plate, burnt side down, and set the plate in front of Wex. "Sap-syrup or honey?"

Hunched over, Wex looked miserable and angry, but Eyck suspected that the anger was directed at himself. But why?

"Wex?"

The lad continued to stare at nothing.

"Hello, Wex?"

Wex jolted out of his daze. *"What?"* he signed curtly.

"I said, sap-syrup or honey? For your pancakes."

"Either is fine."

Eyck frowned, wondering what was going through Wex's head. Would he ever know? He wanted to ask but knew he'd be rebuffed. Sighing, he placed both the sap-syrup and honey jars in front of Wex and went back to the forge to make his own pancakes.

. . .

THE AFTERNOON WAS NO BETTER than the morning. Wex had gone from sullen to downright impertinent, and Eyck was getting to the end of his very last nerve.

"Is it *me*?" he asked, exasperated when Wex called him an imbecile for the third time. "Did I do something to you? Did I say something? What is going on with you?"

Wex frowned, glancing up from the cuirass he was repairing.

"Well? What's going through that moody head of yours?"

"*Mind your own business, Levek,*" Wex signed curtly before going back to the broken shoulder hinge in the armour.

Eyck gritted his teeth and counted silently to ten, resisting the urge to give Wex a good smack to the back of the head. "Wex . . . talk to me, lad." He slowly reached out and put a hand gently on his shoulder.

Wex froze, then slowly looked up, his eyes very wide.

Eyck couldn't tell if Wex was furious or shocked, but the taught muscle under his hand vibrated softly, the way a metal spring did when it was being compressed, and his tail had begun thrashing from side to side.

Discomfited by the lad's reaction, Eyck cleared his throat and stepped quickly back before he was attacked.

"For Suns' sake, Wex," he said, his heart thumping hard in his chest making it hard to breathe. "Sort your fucking head out." He rubbed his face, weary and stressed out at the same time. "Right now, I have half a mind to kick your ungrateful ass out for all the strife you're causing me. I can't go on like this. So, sort out whatever in *schatten's* hell has your back up all tetchy-like because I can't keep creeping on eggs."

The second Eyck mentioned ending the apprenticeship, Wex's expression flashed to one of open-mouthed surprise, then onto unmistakable contrition.

"*Please. I'm sorry,*" Wex signed. "*I want to stay.*"

"Do you want to talk about whatever it is that—"

Wex shook his head quickly, but this time, something in his eyes gave Eyck pause. Was it fear?

"Well, if you're not going to talk to me, you have to talk to *someone* about it. What about that Grendall fella you were palling around with?"

* * *

Wᴇx sᴛᴀʀᴇᴅ at Eyck in shock.

"How do you know about that?" he asked, a sick feeling in the pit of his stomach.

"I don't think there's a soul in South Galetsy that hasn't heard about your nightly doings."

Anger and embarrassment hit Wex like twin cannon blasts to the chest, and he shot to his feet, taking a step towards Eyck. *"That's my business,"* he gestured furiously.

The big blacksmith stood his ground. "You could try being a little more discreet about it, then maybe I won't have to keep hearing about what you've been up to."

Snorting, Wex curled his lip. *"Why . . . are you jealous?"* he signed, then froze. That's not what he had meant to say. The last thing in the world he wanted was to make any allusion, no matter how small, to the two of them doing . . . *that.*

Eyck was staring at him, a confused look on his brindled face, then Wex realized he'd never taught him the sign for the word *jealousy*. Relieved, he scowled and signed, *"Never mind. I don't care."*

In the tense silence that followed, the click of the time-keeper was very loud—the workday was finished.

"I'm going out," Wex signed, then hung up his apron.

"Fine. Go. But if you don't change your attitude, you're out. I mean it," Eyck called after him.

When Wex looked back, the big Levek was on the front porch, one hand scratching the back of his neck, a puzzled look on his face.

Pᴏɪɴᴛɪɴɢ to the cask of honey wine, Wex sat down at his usual stool at the end of the bar. Loomis nodded and poured out a mug, setting it down in front of him with a smile.

"Haven't seen you 'round lately. How you been keeping?" the bartender asked, putting some nuts and dried fruit in a bowl for Wex.

Wex shrugged, taking a sip of the mead. He wanted to ask Loomis whether he'd seen the *Sparkshade*, but he doubted whether he could make himself understood. Besides, hadn't Stilig said they might not come back to South Galetsy because of the war?

Sighing, Wex looked over his shoulder at the motley collection of sailors seated at the far side of the tavern. They were all strangers, mostly women, and none of them seemed the least bit interested in his presence.

Why did Eyck have to bring up Stilig?

What if he is actually jealous?

Why should that concern me? I don't care.

Do I care? Groaning inwardly, he rested his head on his forearm, feeling deeply uncomfortable with himself. *I wish I could turn my brain off.*

"You all right there?" Loomis asked, concern in his voice.

Wex sat up, nodding. *Sure, I'm all right*, he thought. *I just need something to get my mind off that stupid, fat-headed old pushover . . .*

Would it be so bad? The thought popped into his head uninvited, and he grimaced. *Yes. I don't belong to anyone. I am in control. I will* never *be someone's slave again.*

Wex downed the rest of the mead and stared down at his glass. *That* was one way of distracting his thoughts. He caught Loomis's attention by rapping softly on the bar, then pointed to his glass. The bartender went to refill it with mead, but Wex shook his head, making the gesture for *stronger*. Loomis just stared at him, blinking dumbly. Sighing, Wex tried the sign for *bigger*, hoping that the garrulous Duval would catch his meaning.

"I'm sorry, fella . . . I'm not sure what you're trying to say."

"He wants something stronger," a voice said over Wex's shoulder.

Surprised, Wex turned. It was a sailor with brown-striped fur and, for a split second, thought it was Stilig. However, this Grendall was shorter and thickly muscled unlike the lanky brothers. The sailor smiled, and Wex saw he was missing an upper fang.

"Give him some black rum," the stranger said, taking the stool next to Wex. "And pour me some too while you're at it."

"Sure thing, fella," Loomis replied, reaching for a bottle on the highest shelf. When he set the two glasses of black rum in front of them, the Grendall slapped down a few silver on the bar.

"I've got this."

Wex frowned but touched his temple in thanks. He lifted the glass to his lips, and even before he'd taken a sip, he began feeling a little lightheaded from the fumes. The first swallow burned going down, and he gasped and coughed.

"Strong enough for ya?" asked the sailor.

Wheezing, Wex nodded and set down his glass.

"The name's Klav, by the by," said the man, grinning again.

Something about his expression made Wex a bit uncomfortable, but he couldn't put a finger on what it was.

Wex pulled up his medallion to show Klav the saint.

"Oh, I know who you are, puppy," Klav said, leaning towards him. He lowered his voice. "You're the Kirmen who likes a little . . . *fun*." He winked and nonchalantly placed his hand on Wex's forearm.

Wex was so shocked he didn't know how to react. He stared down at the Grendall's hand, his heart pounding. Eyck was right—he'd been carelessly indiscreet.

"*I'm sorry. I'm not interested,*" he signed quickly, hoping the man could understand him. "*You've got the wrong idea.*"

"*Do* I, though?" Klav said, squeezing his arm. "I've a room hired upstairs and a big ol' cock that needs seein' to."

Appalled, Wex pulled his arm out of the sailor's grasp. "*No.*"

Klav's expression went dark, his nostrils flaring, and Wex tensed, bracing himself for violence, but the moment passed and Klav smiled wide again.

"My mistake," he said, thumping Wex chummily on the back of the shoulder. "Enjoy your rum." He lifted his glass, toasting Wex, before walking away.

Pulse still flying wild, Wex stared after the man.

What in Suns' hell?

He reached for his glass and took another sip of the black rum. It burned his throat again, and he winced. Wex hadn't noticed the flowery taste before, but it did help the rum go down. He looked over his shoulder again—Klav had taken a seat with a group of newcomers, but his eyes were on Wex. He grinned, lifting his glass to Wex again.

What a creep, thought Wex. He yawned.

✦ ✦ ✦

EYCK JERKED out of his sleep, startled by pounding on the door. Groggily, he peered across the room and saw Wex hadn't returned home yet. He sat up, groaning.

"I'm coming, I'm coming," he said as he trudged down the stairs in the dark. He unlocked the door, pulling it open. "Did you forget your key?"

"We're going to the river," Pash said, pushing past him. He looked Eyck up and down. "Where's your shirt?"

"My shirt?" Eyck asked, puzzled.

"Put a shirt on and grab your hammer."

"What's going on?" He rubbed his face, still half-asleep. He saw Pash had his basket of medical supplies with him. "Is someone hurt?"

"Wex is in trouble. The bartender from the Giddy Dankel's been locked out. Put your boots on."

"What? Wex? Giddy *what*?" Eyck slipped his feet into his boots. "*Where* are we going?"

Pash found one of Eyck's shirts on a hook and threw it at him. "Snap out of it. The wharfside pub. Loomis, the bartender, is pretty badly beaten."

Tugging on the shirt, Eyck followed Pash out of the smithy, pausing to grab his three-weights hammer next to the door. He was so confused.

"Suns, slow down," Eyck complained, breathing hard as he jogged to catch up with the priest, his tail tangling in his legs. "Ok, tell me one more time. We're going to get Wex because he beat up some bartender? I'm confused."

Pash turned to Eyck, his expression bleak. "No. The bartender tried to break up what was happening and got thrown out. He sent for the City Guard, but we're closer . . . we have to—"

"What *was* happening? Pash, what's going on? Is it a fight? What are we talking about here?"

"It's not good. Either Wex got too drunk, or something was put in his drink . . . He's in trouble, Eyck." Pash's eyes were wide. "Some soldiers have him . . ."

It was obvious from the priest's expression what that meant. All remnants of Eyck's stupor evaporated in the flash of anger. He started running, barely feeling the earth pounding beneath his feet.

I'm coming, lad.

HIS BODY WAS MADE of lead, and his mind was somewhere between asleep and awake.

Wex was aware of what was happening to him, but it seemed like it was happening to someone else. The laughter around him sounded like buzzhawks picking at a corpse. There was pain, but it waxed and waned as he drifted in and out of consciousness—he tasted vomit, blood, and seed.

Chapter Eleven

Eyck was drenched with sweat and panting hard by the time they arrived at the pub. Sitting by the steps, cradling his arm, was a stout Duval with a gold hoop through his nose. As Eyck got closer, he saw the man's eye was swollen shut, and there was blood down the front of his shirt.

"In there?" growled Eyck, pointing to the door of the tavern.

The bartender nodded.

Eyck roared, swinging the hammer with all his might. It only took one hit for the wooden door to split, and he kicked the broken pieces aside as he stumbled into the tavern.

The scene before him was bewildering and shocking. A dozen or so soldiers in various states of undress were crowded at the back of the pub, all of them frozen in place, staring at him.

Right at the center of the group, atop two tables pushed together, was Wex. He was naked, legs akimbo.

A muscular Grendall slowly backed away from Wex, his eyes on Eyck. The man's penis, red and erect, still poked from its furry sheath.

"Wex!" Eyck bellowed, shoving past two Garza soldiers.

Someone grabbed his arm. He turned and slammed his hammer into the man's startled face. Bone crunched and the soldier fell to the ground, senseless.

Pash yelled behind him, trying to clear the room, but the men had already started fleeing. Judging by how some of them were stumbling and weaving, many were dead-drunk.

Eyck landed another blow to the shoulder of a Grendall scrabbling to get out of his way.

"Wex! Wex, can you hear me?" he leaned over the young man, looking for signs of life, and sighed with relief when Wex's chest rose and fell.

When his fingers came into contact with something cold and slimy in Wex's fur he recoiled in disgust, casting around for someone else to smash with his hammer.

Vile schatten animals.

Pash came up beside him, his grey eyes narrowed in concern. He stepped over a small puddle of vomit and lifted one of Wex's eyelids. The eye rolled in its socket, finding Eyck, and a plaintive little moan escaped his slack lips.

Eyck's fury was a red-hot ingot, sizzling in his belly and choking him with dark smoke. He'd kill every last one of them. Eyck threw back his head and roared again.

The muscular Grendall who'd been raping Wex when Eyck had come crashing through the door stood with his back to the wall, edging slowly sideways, obviously set on fleeing the scene.

"Oh no, you fucking don't," Eyck snarled and threw his hammer.

The three-weights head caught the man right in the sternum, knocking him to the floor where he gasped and gagged. Eyck bent down and grabbed the man by the throat, lifting him off the ground before slamming him back into the wall. And again.

The Grendall clawed at Eyck's wrist, and he coughed, the spittle white on his dark-brown lips.

"Eyck! Stop it!" Pash yelled through the murderous fog in Eyck's head. "You're going to kill him."

"*Good*," Eyck said, his voice hoarse. He would drag the man back to the smithy and rip his cock off with a pair of tongs. Then he would—

The sound of a sword being drawn startled him, and he looked over at the priest.

"I said stop, Eyck. *You're not the law.*" Pash held the sword easily at his side, and from the expression on his face, Eyck knew their friendship wouldn't stop him from using it.

"Did you *see* him? Did you see what he was doing to Wex?" he said, his tone pleading.

The Grendall's eyes bulged in his striped face as Eyck continued to squeeze.

"I did. And now we need to take care of Wex. Put him down," Pash said gently. "Come on. Wex *needs* you."

Pash's words finally broke through Eyck's anger.

He sighed, reluctantly dropping the Grendall to the floor where he slumped over on his side.

"That there is the ringleader, Father," said the bartender, glaring down at the man on the floor. He clutched his arm against his chest, his nostrils flaring in anger.

Nodding, Pash looked around. Only a few men were left in the tavern—those that Eyck's hammer had taken down and some who had evidently passed out from drink. "Loomis, do you know where Wex's clothes have gone?"

"No, sorry, Father, but I got a blanket you can use."

"Thank you, that will do. Do you have any idea what they gave him? Was it just drink? Or maybe a powder to make him sleepy?"

"I don't know," Loomis replied, looking uncomfortable. "See, that one there was trying to purchase your friend's services . . . uh . . . beggin' your pardon, Father. This isn't really that sort of—"

"That's all right. What happened then?"

"I was across the room, but I guess Wex turned him down. That could've been when he slipped him something. I wasn't watching. I'm sorry, Father."

The sound of boots and chainmail heralded the arrival of the City Guard. From the shouting, it sounded like they were rounding up the men outside.

Pash pushed up Wex's eyelid again, peered at his pupil, then touched Wex's neck. "His heart is still beating strong. That's good at least." He sighed, turning to Eyck. "Let's get him back to the smithy."

Eyck clenched his jaw, his fury melting into horror. He felt like he was going to be sick.

"Come on . . . give me a hand," Pash said, taking the blanket from Loomis.

"Ok," Eyck whispered, his hands shaking and clumsy as he helped Pash cover up the young man.

"Take the barrel cart," said the fat bartender, jerking his head towards the back. His eyes were bloodshot. "Please. It's the least I can do, and I'll tell the Guard all what happened, I swear it."

WITH A STRAINED GROAN, Eyck helped Pash move Wex onto the table they'd pushed into the middle of the smithy. There was no way they could carry him upstairs—he was just too big and heavy—so the table would have to do for now.

While Pash examined a lump on the side of Wex's head, Eyck began washing the worst of the filth out of his fur with a cloth. The lad was covered in doubloon-sized bumps, some of them crusted over with blood—it took Eyck a minute to realize he was looking at bite marks, dozens of bite marks all over Wex's body.

Hot bile rose up in his throat. He took a step back, shaking his head. "Should have let me kill him."

Pash straightened and fixed Eyck with narrowed grey eyes. "They would have hanged you for it."

"Not if the Guard weren't wise to it," swore Eyck, baring his fangs. "Would you have told them?"

The priest just sighed and went back to his work, checking Wex's injuries from his head down.

"*Schatten*," Pash swore quietly when he saw the mess between his thighs.

Jaw clenched, Eyck took one of Wex's big hands between his own, wishing he could start the evening over, back before the argument. Surely, if he'd been more patient, more understanding . . .

Suns, why did I have to bring up the Grendall sailor? If he hadn't, would Wex have stormed off the way he had? Maybe if he hadn't been such a thick-headed lout, Wex wouldn't be lying here on the table, broken and abused. He let out a shuddering breath, squeezing Wex's hand.

Wake up, lad.

Eyck looked up and saw Pash staring at him with a strange expression; when the priest resumed his ministrations, his mouth was set in a tight line and his hands seemed less gentle than before.

OVERALL, Wex didn't seem to be gravely injured. But, before he left, Pash had voiced some concern about the lad being damaged somewhere inside where they couldn't see—they'd only know that when he woke up, and that could take minutes or hours. Without knowing what the men had given Wex, it was impossible to guess when he'd come out of it.

Eyck hummed to himself as he dabbed more salve on one of the many bite marks on Wex's chest. Wex's nipple had also suffered some damage—poking up through the silver fur, the pink nipple was puffy, and a bruise was forming under the thin skin. It was like it had been chewed on . . . like a soft, pink candy . . .

Clearing his throat, Eyck straightened up self-consciously, feeling ashamed of the image that had popped into his head—of sucking that plump pink bud.

Schatten . . .

Wex was lying there unconscious, the victim of grievous assault—now was *not* the time for lustful fantasies. Mortified, he muttered a soft sorry as he covered Wex up with the blanket.

Then he sighed and scratched the back of his neck. It was the middle of the night, but he wasn't tired. Also, he didn't want to risk being asleep when Wex finally awoke. With another deep sigh, Eyck took up his whetstone and strop and grabbed an unsharpened sword out of the pile. He pulled up a chair and sat down to his work.

LIGHT WAS the first thing Wex noticed—soft, flickering candlelight. Next was the foul taste in his mouth.

Swallowing, he tried to open his eyes wider, but his eyelids felt like lead . . . too heavy to lift. Then, the pain came. Pain *everywhere*—

throbbing in some places, sharp in others. Had he been in a fight? Wex couldn't remember anything.

Suns . . . it even hurt to breathe.

It seemed impossible to sit up, but he could move his hands. His fingers encountered stiff, crusted peaks in his fur, swollen tissues tender to the touch . . . and his nakedness under the thick blanket. Alarmed, he tried again to lift his head but only managed a few fingerwidths before his muscles gave out. The surface beneath him was hard and unyielding, hurting his head when it landed with a *thud*.

Am I on the floor? Where am I?

Mind racing, he tried to focus on the last thing he could remember.

The Giddy Dankel . . . the Grendall creep . . . Oh, Suns.

There it was, the shadow of a wisp of a foggy memory only half remembered . . . of rough men mounting him one after the other, like he was a carnival ride. He took a few rapid breaths, his jaw clenched, fighting back nausea and fear. Wex was thankful he could only remember the little he could.

Don't think, he told himself. *Don't think. Block it out.*

He didn't need more nightmares to join the ones already committed to memory—it was getting crowded in there.

But where am I? he thought, panic mounting again. *How did I get here?*

A moment later, his questions were answered in the form of a familiar snore.

Wex turned his head gingerly. The big blacksmith was fast asleep in a nearby chair, his head hanging back and mouth wide-open in sleep. Balanced on one knee was a soldier's falchion and clutched loosely in a big scarred hand was a whetstone.

Knowing he was home safe and sound, Wex closed his eyes, his strength completely sapped.

Home? he thought in wry amusement before sleep snatched all other thought away.

Chapter Twelve

E yck carried the heavy pails of heated water to the stool where Wex sat, naked as the day he was born. The lad shivered, his eyes bleak as soapy water dripped from his nose to fall in the growing patch of mud at his feet.

"Almost done," Eyck said. "I'm sorry."

Wex just nodded and closed his eyes as Eyck poured a pail of water over him, rinsing away the last of the soap and filth from his fur.

Across the small yard, the back door to the glassworks opened, and Ormerod stepped out to shake a rug. The potbellied Duval wrinkled his brow in curiosity at the sight of Eyck and Wex, but only touched his temple in greeting before going back into his shop. However, Eyck saw movement in the small window set into the door.

"Up, lad," Eyck said gruffly, moving so he was shielding Wex from his nosy neighbour's prying eyes. "You'll, uh . . . want to wash your backside."

Wex stood slowly, his expression blank.

"I can give you a ha—" Eyck started.

Wex cut him off with a curt "*No, thank you.*"

"All right." Eyck cleared his throat and turned around to give the lad some privacy.

He could see Ormerod in the window again. Crossing his arms

over his chest, Eyck glared at the man until he retreated into the glassworks. He could hear Wex soaping himself, a few soft sighs, then the splash of water.

A tap on his shoulder surprised him.

"All done?" he asked, turning back around.

Wex looked miserable. He stood trembling in the early morning sun, his thick arms wrapped around his torso, his fur plastered to him, highlighting his generous musculature.

Eyes averted, Eyck pulled the bath sheet off his shoulder and spread it out between his hands, stepping forward to envelop the wet young man.

It was only as Eyck was wrapping the cloth around Wex did he realize he was more or less embracing him. Face warm, he cleared his throat and went to step back.

But then Wex did something unexpected—he leaned into Eyck.

It was only for a few seconds and the motion so slight that, had Eyck not been so keenly aware of the effect Wex's proximity had on him, he might not have even noticed.

Wex quickly turned away, clutching the bath sheet to himself, and headed into the smithy leaving Eyck scratching the back of his neck.

Well . . . I'll be.

WEX FROWNED AT EYCK.

"*I'm fine,*" he said, pulling his apron off the hook.

"You're *not* fine, lad," Eyck said. "You've just been through a—"

"*I don't want to talk about it,*" Wex replied, his signs quick and terse. He tied the apron around his waist. He just wanted to get back to work. There were just a few more things he needed to learn, and then he could get out of South Galetsy for good—and never look back.

"Take a day, at least," Eyck said in a soft voice.

"*No.*"

"Well, I guess I'm not lighting the forge today."

Stubborn old fool. Wex glared. "*Fine, I'll finish riveting the chest plate.*"

"It's already done. And all the swords are sharpened." Eyck crossed his arms.

Wex knew he was testing the big Levek's patience. And the blacksmith had been in *such* a jovial mood all morning.

Jaw clenched, Wex yanked his apron off and jammed it back on its hook.

"Shall I sweep, then?" he signed angrily.

"You can sweep. You can sort nails. You can go to Penermann's farm and get eggs," Eyck conceded. His brow creased up, jade-green eyes wide with worry. "I just don't want you to *strain* yourself. You need to heal up from what hap—"

"Don't want to talk about it," Wex said again, his fingers and hands slicing the air like knives. *"Ever."*

"All right, lad. All right."

An hour later, Wex had to admit to himself that Eyck had been right. He *was* feeling poorly. His head still ached from the potion they had slipped in his drink, and his body just felt *wrong*. Sighing, he rapped loudly at the gate again, waiting for someone to let him in. After a minute and no sign of the Penermanns, he decided he'd just take some eggs and leave money behind. Eyck had assured him that the elderly couple wouldn't mind.

He reached up over the gate and unlocked it, letting himself into the side yard where the Penermanns kept their chickens. He was immediately surrounded by the curious flock.

Smiling, he thought, *Sorry, should have brought you some dried peas to eat.*

One of the more ambitious chickens tried to climb his leg, its four clawed feet grappling at his boot. Laughing to himself, he reached down and dislodged the creature, its scaly green body warm and deceptively soft.

"Silly, I'm not a tree," he signed at it, grinning. One of his responsibilities while traveling with Bew's circus had been tending to the troupe's small flock of chickens—he'd become fond of the little beasts.

"Hey! What are you doing here?"

Startled, Wex straightened and turned around, taking a step back from the tines pointed at his face. A plump little Dankel the colour of dull copper bared his yellowed fangs and jabbed the pitchfork forward again. Wex recognized him—Farmer Penermann.

Wex lifted his hands, shaking his head. The farmer had seen him before at the smithy. He could only hope the man would figure out who he was before he stuck him with the pitchfork; he might tower over the little Dankel, but those tines looked sharp. Feeling stupid for not bringing something in writing with him—and Eyck should have known better than to send him without a note—he slowly lowered one hand and pointed to his pocket.

"Eh? What's that?" the old Dankel said, squinting.

With a smile he hoped looked innocuous, Wex reached into his pants pocket and pulled out the copper pieces Eyck had given him for the eggs.

Penermann looked down at Wex's palm and lowered the pitchfork. When he glanced back up, his eyes held recognition in them.

"Oh! You're Stromsmith's dumb Kirmen!" the old Dankel said, suddenly friendly.

Wex caught the glower before it reached his face, then nodded and forced himself to grin wider—he *hated* the term *dumb*.

Pointing with one hand to the chickens still crowding around his ankles, he put the thumb and forefinger of the other hand together to form an oval shape. Then he held up five fingers twice, followed by two fingers.

Penermann just looked confused for a few moments, and Wex repeated the gestures, wondering if the old Dankel was going senile.

"Oh. Yeah, yeah . . ." muttered the farmer, finally catching on. He leaned the pitchfork against the side of the house. "Come on, come on." He gestured broadly for Wex to follow.

When they reached the back porch, Penermann held his hands up. "You. Stop. Here," he said loudly while pointing to the ground.

Wex flared his nostrils but nodded. "*I can hear just fine, you old coot,*" he signed while giving the man a toothy smile.

The Dankel farmer frowned, puzzled by Wex's hand signs, then turned, shaking his head as he ascended the stairs. "Can't imagine keeping a defective greyback mutt around for Suns know what . . ." Penermann's words trailed off as he went further into the house.

Wex stood there, fists balled at his sides, breathing deep as he waited. *Defective?* He wasn't schatten "defective." He wasn't even completely mute, given that his voice broke through every once in a while. And *"greyback mutt"* . . .

Wex looked up at the sky, trying to shove his anger into the pit of his stomach where it wouldn't get him into trouble.

In the bigger cities, they cared much less about the caste breeds intermingling, so there was less stigma to being a—

Wex shook his head, refusing to use the word again, even in his thoughts—of *mixed stock.* A memory came back to him, so sharp and bright that it startled him.

THE HUGE LEVEK *stared down at him as Mangley explained his supposed parentage. There was curiosity in the man's green eyes and . . . pity? No . . . it was . . . compassion. At least he hoped so. Whatever it was, it was better than the loathing and contempt he got every day from Mangley and his ilk.*

"So he's of mixed stock?" asked the Levek, nodding and furrowing his brow.

The little glimmer of hope got brighter inside him. Maybe this Levek was a good man.

"Mixed stock? That's dainty. He's a schatten greyback mutt," Mangley said with an oily sneer.

"Turn around for me," the brindled stranger said to him in a quiet voice after frowning at Mangley.

It was that frown, that obvious distaste for the way Mangley described him, that made him decide to drop the charade and obey the request. He turned his back to the Levek, hoping he wasn't making a mistake.

"ARE YOU ALL RIGHT, SON?" Penermann said, staring up at Wex.

Wex started, quickly nodding as the memory faded into the background. His heart pounding and mouth dry, he accepted the small hay-lined box full of eggs. He touched his temple in thanks and quickly left.

The memory of Mangley and Eyck that day long ago had rattled him, and in his daze, he nearly tripped. Catching himself at the last second, he managed to save the eggs but only barely. He shook his head, carrying the delicate parcel carefully in both hands.

The more he thought about the way Eyck had freed him five sun-cycles ago, the more certain he grew of one thing: he had to leave South Galetsy as *soon as possible*. It made sense now to him that it was his *gratitude* that somehow amplified this terrible, relentless attraction. It was lust born of thanks, nothing more, and he knew the suffocating, frantic feeling in his chest that accompanied that misplaced lust would only subside once he was far, far away from the blacksmith.

He'd leave the next morning, but first, there was something that needed taking care of.

Chapter Thirteen

The huge flames surrounding Eyck began to lose colour, becoming vague, no longer hot by the time they had disappeared into darkness. Blinking, Eyck realized he could make out a pale square in the gloom. The window across the room.

He had been asleep and dreaming of a terrible fire. Disoriented, he turned over onto his back and then frowned.

If I'm awake, why can I still smell burning fur? He sniffed the air, trying to make sense of it, and bolted upright when he heard the rhythmic creak and *whoosh* coming from downstairs.

The bellows? A dim orange glow came from the stairwell.

What in the Three Living Suns?

He threw his covers off and ran down the stairs in his smallclothes, his heart in his throat.

Seeing it was just Wex, Eyck heaved a sigh of relief but then gasped when the lad pulled a red-hot piece of metal from the forge and pressed it to his own forearm. The sizzling sound and the shuddering, voiceless, breathy yell coming from Wex spurred Eyck forward as if pushed. He snatched the metal rod from Wex's hand and threw it in the quenching barrel where it hissed and steamed.

"What are you *doing*?" he said in a strangled voice.

Wex stared at him through pain-narrowed eyes, his fangs bared and chest heaving. "*Nothing*," he finally signed, one-handed. His other arm he held rigid at his side, a little smoke wafting up from his singed fur. *"Go away."*

"Like schatten I will." Eyck grabbed Wex's wrist, pulling his arm closer to the lantern. Even in the dim light, he could make out a number of blistering burns and charred fur. Then he saw the familiar swoop of the stylized H and realized what Wex was trying to accomplish. "Why are you doing this? Have you lost your mind?"

"Go away," Wex repeated, his hand trembling through the simple gesture. His eyes closed in a grimace of pain. *"None of your business."* However, he didn't try to pull his injured arm out of the blacksmith's grasp.

"Removing a prison brand is a *death* sentence." Eyck grabbed the jar of salve and scooped some out. He spread it liberally over the burns, not being particularly gentle.

Wex gasped but stood still.

"Why would you do this, lad? Most folks *know* you were at Hange. No one cares, and if they do . . . well, they can go soak their tails in vinegar for all I care." He ground his teeth together, shaking his head. He was angry, but it was an anger born entirely of worry for the young man.

Eyck grabbed a few clean linen rags and wrapped them around Wex's forearm. Wex's eyes remained shut until Eyck released him.

"Now you tell me what's going through that fool head of yours, or I'll send you packing. I mean it." He didn't, but what else could he threaten?

"That's fine," Wex signed wearily, looking away. *"I was planning on leaving once this was done."* His mouth twisted up at the corner, a sardonic grin. *"And it's done, so I'm leaving."*

Eyck stood there, completely dumbfounded. Hadn't Wex pleaded to stay just a few days ago? He rubbed the back of his neck slowly. "Is it because of me? Did I do something wrong?" he asked in a soft voice.

Maybe it was the tone of his voice, or his words, but Wex's gaze snapped back to him, his eyes wide.

"It's just . . . I'd hoped you would stay." Eyck shrugged weakly. "Maybe for a while—a long while."

Searching Eyck's face, Wex's confused expression shifted quickly to anger. He bared his fangs, his nose crinkling. *"I am no man's slave,"* he signed quickly, his gestures sharp. His tail whipped from side to side.

Eyck frowned, his bewilderment deepening. "I don't know what you me—"

Wex cut him off with a swift slice through the air accompanied by a harsh noise from the back of his throat. *"I can't stay here. Not anymore. I won't be your slave. I must be my own man."*

"No one is trying to ma—"

Again, he was cut off, but this time, it was because Wex took a menacing step towards him.

Eyck could take care of himself in a fight, but Wex had size and youth on his side, not to mention what looked like absolute fury.

"Listen, Wex," he said, putting his hands up in a gesture he hoped would pacify the lad. "I don't know where you got the idea that you would be—no, *listen* to me. I hoped you would stay. I'm getting on in age, and I haven't anyone to pass this smithy on to. Never had children." He sighed. "Do you understand?"

"You want to make me your child?" Wex asked, his brow deeply furrowed.

"No!" Eyck chuckled, albeit nervously.

Wex still loomed over him, the embodiment of danger.

"Not my child, *obviously*—I mean . . . er . . . as partners. And, in time, if you wanted to stay, I could petition to give you my family name."

Taking a step back, Wex stared at Eyck like he'd gone mad. *"Partners?"* he signed.

"Yes. Partners."

"Business partners?"

And maybe something more, one day, if you want, Eyck thought, but just nodded.

Wex's shoulders slumped, and he blinked rapidly, averting his gaze. When he turned his eyes back to Eyck, they were full of pain.

Though he hadn't expected Wex to jump for joy, this was definitely *not* the reaction he'd expected at all. He swallowed back his disappointment.

"I . . . thought you would like that."

"No. I can't stay. I can't." Wex's gestures were strangely limp, like his hands had gone numb.

"Why?" Eyck asked, his chest tight. "Will you please tell me what's going on?"

"Because." Wex breathed out hard, his nostrils flaring. *"Because."* His fingers made the same hooking motion a few more times, like he was a broken wooden stick-puppet. *"Because, I would be a slave. Of my doing. Something is not right. With me. I am already half your slave, and I—"*

The last two signs were ones Eyck didn't recognize.

"Explain."

Gasping for breath, Wex looked like he would collapse any second, but when Eyck reached for him, he took a step back. And another.

"I look at you and it makes me your slave. I smell you and it makes me your slave. I have to go. I have to."

Eyck felt a ripple up his back as his fur rose with excitement, Wex's words finally hitting home.

The lad is taken with me.

Pulse racing, Eyck licked his lips and cleared his throat. "Bear with me here—we Levek aren't the brightest bunch, you know, and I don't want to jump to conclusions . . . but are you saying you *like* me?"

Ignoring his question, Wex stepped forward again, his gestures turning more violent with every word. *"You are no dumb Levek, for Suns' sake. You're smart. And"*—Wex bared his fangs again—*"kind. You're kind."*

"And you like me."

"And I like you," Wex conceded angrily.

This was not the right moment to smile, so Eyck schooled his features and crossed his arms. "I don't understand why that would make you a slave."

"Because it is out of my control!" Wex exhaled hard, his exasperation tangible.

"So, you don't *want* to like me."

"Yes."

"What if I told you I liked you? That I liked you an awful lot?"

Wex's eyes widened, and he shook his head rapidly. *"I have to go."*

"What if I told you I haven't liked someone like this in a long time?"

It seemed like Wex was going to bolt for the door, so Eyck grabbed his arm before he could flee. He struggled with the lad for a moment, trying to wrap his arms around him.

"No!" The raspy word burst out of Wex.

Eyck closed his eyes, feeling guilty. The poor lad had been forced to do things against his will for most of his life—how was subjecting him to a hug any different? He started to let go but was surprised when Wex suddenly threw his arms around him.

"Oh, lad," Eyck murmured, stroking his hand slowly down Wex's broad back.

Wex was shaking like a leaf, panting and holding on to him like he was terrified to let go.

"It's all right. It's all right," Eyck said.

It took a long time before Wex calmed, long enough that the forge's fire was but glittering embers.

Eyck could feel Wex's heart slow, their breaths gradually syncing as they held onto each other in the near dark.

When it seemed the worst had finally passed, Eyck cracked a smile. "This is called a hug," he said, making his tone light. He was extremely conscious of the fact that he was wearing next to nothing, his body pressed up tight to Wex's. Eyck didn't want to spook the lad if his body started to react to the proximity.

Wex let out something that sounded like a breathless chuckle and drew back out of the embrace.

"I know what a hug is, you idiot," he signed, a wry smile on his face.

Eyck committed the new sign to memory. He was getting better and better at understanding Wex's signing language—it helped that the lad had a natural talent for pantomime and could sketch as well as any Ulven street artist.

"You *just* said I wasn't dumb," Eyck joked. He reached out and cuffed Wex playfully on the shoulder.

The lad didn't flinch for once.

Eyck gestured towards the stairs. "Let's go to bed."

Wex's eyes narrowed, and he licked his lips, his posture stiffening.

"Separately, I mean," Eyck said, his grin sheepish. "Let's go to our *separate* beds. To sleep. I don't know about you, but I'm bloody exhausted. And we'll talk more in the morning. About the business. And about . . . us . . . if you want to."

Wex's shoulders relaxed, and after a long pause, he nodded.

Without another gesture, he turned and climbed the steps, leaving Eyck to turn down the lantern. It barely made a change—the light from the windows heralded the coming morning. Frowning, he scratched the back of his neck and sighed, making a decision. He scribbled a few words on a piece of brown paper and stuck it to the windowpane in the front door.

Upstairs, Wex had dragged his pallet over to Eyck's side of the room. They weren't exactly side by side—a few footlengths separated the beds—but he was surprised. Wex stared up at him in the gloom, his eyes guarded, then turned onto his side, facing away.

Smiling to himself, Eyck slid back into his rumpled bedding. After a few minutes, he sighed.

This could go two ways, he realized. Maybe this was the start of something wonderful but challenging, given the wounds of Wex's past. Or maybe Wex would murder him in his sleep for what Eyck had just put him through. Eyck closed his eyes. He sure hoped it was the former.

WEX TURNED AROUND AS SOON as he heard Eyck start to snore. It was bright enough now that he could see Eyck's greying, brindled face clearly.

He likes me. And I like him.

Seemed simple enough, but it was terrifying. Escape was no longer an option—Eyck's words had as good as shackled him here.

Now what? Isn't this what normal folks do? Find a mate and live in harmony, happily ever after? he thought, watching Eyck sleep.

At least that's what happened in the faeries' tales the circus troupe sometimes performed. Except nothing was normal about him, or the situation. They were both males. He was Kirmen and Eyck was Levek. He was a broken ex-slave, and Eyck was . . . Wex frowned.

Eyck is broken from his wife's death.

Nowhere near as broken as he was—Eyck still had his voice, after all—but maybe that was where they intersected. Wex pondered this new realization, remembering the way Eyck's voice had been ragged and choked as he poured his heartbreak out that long, confusing night so long ago.

What if I told you I haven't liked someone like this in a long time? That's what Eyck had said. Wex worried his bottom lip with a fang. No, not a normal situation . . . but maybe one they both needed.

Chapter Fourteen

I t was almost midday by the time Eyck finally opened his eyes. He glanced over at Wex's neatly made-up bed and frowned, but he could hear movement downstairs.

Eyck hadn't been murdered in his sleep, and Wex was still there— now the only question was whether it would be awkward when he went downstairs or *very* awkward.

He debated staying in bed a while longer, but his bladder was full to bursting. He sighed and dug through the small pile of clothing in the wicker basket, looking for something halfway clean. The last few days had been so stressful, he'd completely forgotten to send out their laundry. Patting down the creased brown shirt, he descended the stairs barefoot, his claws clicking on the wood.

Wex was seated at the table with the metal punch set in front of him, cleaning the pieces with an oily rag. He didn't look up when Eyck quickly ducked out for a piss, but when Eyck came back in and sat across from him, he lifted his head. His expression was . . . cautiously friendly.

"I wondered why no clients," Wex signed. *"Then I saw you put a sign on the door. Are we closed?"*

"I figured we needed a little vacation. I haven't closed the shop in . . ." Eyck thought about the seaside vacation he and Manya had taken. No, that wasn't right. The smithy had been closed for six days after his wife's death. "Well, it's been long time," he finished quietly.

From Wex's expression, it seemed he'd guessed where Eyck's thoughts had taken him.

"I thought you'd like sleeping in."

"Yes. Thanks, lad." Eyck scratched the back of his neck. "Look, we should probably talk about what happened last night, *but* we don't have to do that now. I understand if you need a few—"

"No, I don't want to talk about it," Wex signed quickly. Then he gave Eyck a nervous smile. *"But I will."*

"Oh, good." Eyck let out a long sigh, scrubbing a hand across his face.

"When you said you like me, you meant more than friends?" Wex studied his face intently.

Eyck groped for the right words. What did Wex want to hear?

Just tell the truth.

"I meant friends . . . and maybe more. Eventually. Or . . ." Eyck laughed self-consciously. "I don't know. I'm willing to try anything you are."

"What if I want nothing but friendship?"

"I think I might be disappointed, but I'd get over it."

Eventually?

Eyck had no idea how deep his feelings actually ran. There was a desire to be friends, and there was a desire to bed the lad, but would that lead to something more profound?

Wex slid the metal punches aside and rapped the tabletop softly a few times, his eyes lowered like he was deep in thought. Then his hands started moving, slowly and gracefully.

"When I look at you, I feel strange. I feel grateful that you rescued me." Wex glanced up with a small grin. *"Twice, now."*

"I couldn't let you—"

"I'm not finished." Wex sighed, frowning. *"When I look at you, I also feel cheated. The kindness you've shown me reminds me of the not-kindness I was shown my whole life. The more I see the good, the more I'm aware of the bad. Do you understand?"*

Eyck nodded but stayed silent, waiting for Wex to continue. He was amazed the lad was opening up to him like this. It gave him a bit of hope.

"And when I look at you I feel—"

The gesture was one Eyck hadn't seen before. "What was that?"

A deep crease formed on Wex's brow. He looked embarrassed, making the gesture again slowly. Then he added, *"Hungry, but for mating."*

"Oh. Lustful?" Eyck's pulse kicked up in reaction.

Wex nodded. *"Lustful. And lustful makes me angry."*

"Why would that make you angry of all things?"

"I don't want it." Wex shrugged nonchalantly, but something in his eyes spoke of confusion and doubt and shame. *"I don't like it."*

Eyck nodded again, sitting up. "I can understand that."

"No. You can't."

WEX STARED HARD AT EYCK, and the big Levek nodded after a moment.

"You're right." Eyck's forehead wrinkled up, his jade-green eyes sad. "You're completely right. I mean, how could I possibly understand what you've been through . . . and *still* going through, I guess. I'm sorry. I'm here if you ever want to talk about it. How's that?"

Scoffing, Wex shook his head. *"Telling is living it again. No, thank you."* Then he quickly added, *"But, thank you."*

Eyck seemed amused when he nodded in reply.

Wex scowled at him, his hackles raising. The end of his tail twitched. *"What is funny?"*

"I'm sorry. I'm just . . . I'm adjusting to this new, polite Wex. Forgive me."

Narrowing his eyes at the blacksmith, Wex decided he was being sincere. Had he really been so rude to Eyck this whole time?

What is this feeling? Guilt?

Eyck leaned towards him. "I'd like to ask you to do something for me, if that's all right."

Wex tilted his head, his fur ruffling again in response to Eyck's words.

"If you *do* decide to leave . . . just, please don't go without saying goodbye. That's my request. That's it."

It was a simple request, but for some reason, it felt . . . significant. *"Fine,"* Wex promised.

Something was happening inside him that he didn't like. His heart was beating too fast, and his stomach felt a bit queasy. He breathed deep, trying to shake the feeling, but it only made him lightheaded.

Eyck was watching him with concern. "Wex?"

Wex shook his head. Sweat trickled down his spine.

Eyck lifted his hands and slowly executed three simple hand signs: *You want hug?*

Breathing out hard, Wex quickly nodded before he could change his mind.

He lurched to his feet and dove into Eyck's arms, his eyes squeezed shut, and buried his face in the side of the blacksmith's thick neck.

Eyck stank of stale sweat and iron, but it wasn't coming from the man himself.

Wex pulled back and yanked Eyck's dirty shirt out of his trousers and over his head. Then, because it seemed right, he tore his own shirt off and fell back into the hug, pressing his furry chest tight to Eyck's.

He pushed his nose into the crook of Eyck's neck, sniffing deep. Now all he could smell was the Levek's unique scent. It took him a few seconds to notice Eyck had gone rigid in his arms.

Cheeks warm, Wex realized what he had just done.

He drew back a bit to make sure it was all right.

Eyck looked comically stunned, his eyes wide and lips parted. Talking and hugging at the same time was almost impossible, so Wex just gave him a wide embarrassed smile.

Eyck let out a deep belly laugh and pulled him back into a tight hug. "Yes, you definitely know what a hug is," he said, still chuckling.

THERE WAS something so deeply satisfying about embracing someone his own size.

Eyck sighed out softly as Wex snuffled his neck again, his fur lifting with excitement. He wasn't going to be able to hide his erection if Wex kept it up, and he wasn't sure how the lad would react. In fact, he wasn't exactly sure what their embrace even meant, but it felt good and he didn't want it to stop.

He slid his hand down, resting it in the crook of Wex's back, testing. When Wex didn't object, he closed his eyes and wondered how he would react if he let his hand wander lower . . . maybe to cup his bum. Or wrap it around the base of his tail.

Just as he was contemplating an attempt the lock clicked, and the door of the smithy swung open with a *bang* and a jangle of chimes.

For a few seconds, the three of them were a motionless tableau.

Pash stared in shock at their shirtless embrace. Eyck hastily stepped back. The priest's expression went stony, his grey eyes averted.

"Pash . . . what is it?" Eyck asked, crossing his arms over his chest.

"You were closed. You're *never* closed. I was worried there was sickness or"—Pash glanced over at Wex—"worse."

Eyck could see the comment stiffen Wex's spine, but to his credit, the lad did nothing more than flare his nostrils at the implication.

Then, he did something that Eyck would have never seen coming in a hundred sun-cycles.

Wex stepped towards Pash and bowed his head, his hands quickly signing.

"He says thank you for rescuing him and treating his wounds," Eyck said, jumping in to translate. "He says he's indebted to you, and if there's anything he can do to repay the kindness, you can ask it of him."

Pash looked uncomfortable. "You're welcome. There's no need." He clasped his hands behind his back and cleared his throat. "I take it you're staying a little while longer then?"

Wex looked over at Eyck.

"I've asked him to stay on indefinitely. As a partner," Eyck told Pash. "He's mulling it over."

However, something in Wex's expression told him he'd already made up his mind. Eyck smiled at the lad, growing even more annoyed that Pash had interrupted them.

"Ah. I see. I just . . . assumed after what happened, he'd want to leave as soon as he could," Pash said, addressing him instead of Wex.

Eyck stared at the priest, a horrible suspicion building in his guts.

"He's not deaf," Eyck growled softly.

"Ah. Right. Yes." Pash's eyes flicked to Wex, but no apology was forthcoming.

Was that guilt in his friend's expression?

"Actually, Wex could you please excuse us?" Eyck said as mildly as he could. No need to include Wex if he was wrong about Pash.

The young man stared at him for a long moment, concern plain on his furry silver face, but he nodded, giving Eyck the benefit of the doubt, and went out the back door. Something told him Wex would stay within shouting distance.

"Does he really say all that with those—" Pash fluttered his fingers in the air in a mockery of signing language.

Eyck stepped up to the priest, looming over him even unshod, and asked, "Did you do it?"

Pash's mouth hung open for a moment, his eyes wide. "Did I . . . what? Do what?" He backed up.

Eyck followed, trapping him against the wall.

"What are you talking about?"

"Tell me you had nothing to do with what happened to that boy. So, help me, *Suns* . . ."

"I had nothing to do with what happened, Eyck. Why would you even—"

"You haven't liked him since day *one*. Don't think I don't see the way you mope and gripe when he's around, like some sort of jilted lover."

The priest parted his lips to talk, but Eyck grabbed him by the back of the neck, gripping it tight enough that Pash winced.

"You don't want him around, you're *burning* with jealousy, so you hand some potion to those animals, tell them to give it to him rough so he'll tuck tail and run away? *Is that it?*" Eyck bared his fangs, digging his claws into Pash's nape. "No wonder you were so quick to find and *help* him."

"What in the Three Suns are you talking about? Stop it . . . Eyck, you're hurting me." Pash reached back and clasped Eyck's arm but couldn't dislodge him. "Please . . . I can't believe what you're accusing me of."

"You can't, *hm*? If I look in your medicines, will I find something that could make Wex docile? Make him sleep through being ravished by a dozen drunks?" He squeezed harder.

"Eyck . . . calm down." Pash gasped. "Listen—just . . . listen to me. I didn't do anything. Yes, you'd find a few potions and powders in my bag to make someone sleepy the way we found him, but whatever it was that incapacitated him, it didn't come from me. I would never do that. *Ever*."

Eyck studied Pash's wide-set eyes for a moment longer . . . and could find no guilt. With a growl, he released Pash and backed away, his fists balled.

Rubbing his neck, Pash scowled at Eyck. "Why would you even accuse me of that? *Suns* . . . do you really know me so little?"

"I feel like I *don't* know you, Pash. Not anymore. Not since . . ." He gestured at Pash's priestly attire.

"I wish you would stop that. I haven't changed."

"Haven't you? You abandoned *me*, Pash. You left *me*. Not the other way around."

"I swear to the Three Suns, Eyck . . . You're going to have to let that go one day. I wish to *schatten* you'd get it through that thick Levek skull of yours that Walking in the Suns' Light was the best and most important decision of my life, and I didn't make it lightly. Do you think it was an easy decision for me? Because it wasn't. Trust me. But if I had to do it all over again, I would."

Eyck looked away, teeth clenched and heart pounding.

"And I'm not jealous, I'm *worried*," Pash continued.

When Eyck turned back to him with a snort, the priest shrugged and sighed.

"All right, fine. I'll concede there might be the smallest bit of jealousy . . . but even if I *was* 'burning' with it, as you said, I would *never* put another Kat'hoondeman in harm's way, whatever breed he was. I swear it by the Sun Scrolls."

His anger fizzling out, Eyck sighed and nodded. "Fine. But . . . there's just one thing that bothers me still about what happened."

"And what's that?"

"What were you doing around the wharf so late at night?"

"Oh." Pash looked down at his boots. He took a deep breath. "I was next door. At Dama Sunshine's."

Eyck's head jerked back with surprise. "What were you doing at a brothel?"

Pash lifted his eyes. "I minister to the ladies who work there. Soul and body . . . that's why I had my basket with me that night."

Something about the way Pash shifted on his feet, averting his eyes, made Eyck frown.

"That's *all* you were doing?"

The priest's eyes snapped back to Eyck's, and he said nothing for the span of a few breaths, betraying his half-truth. Then his shoulders sagged, and his smile became small and sheepish.

"Sometimes . . . the ladies pay with, ah . . . a *kindness*."

"Bloody Suns, Pash."

"Some things"—the priest gestured vaguely—"are permitted to us. I did nothing wrong."

"As long as it's with a female."

"Yes," Pash said quietly. "Exactly."

Eyck couldn't bring himself to be angry. All he felt was disappointment and fatigue. "Just go, Pash." He held the door of the smithy open.

Pash looked startled at the abrupt dismissal but kept his thoughts to himself. He stepped towards the door.

Eyck touched his shoulder, stopping him.

"I'd like my key back."

Brow creased and lips pressed together, Pash gave a tight nod and dropped the key into Eyck's waiting palm.

Eyck realized he was punishing the man for what amounted to nothing, but he really didn't want Pash to walk in on him and Wex again.

He cleared his throat. "Listen, I'm sorry I accused you, and I'm sorry I hurt you. I just think a little space will do us good right now."

The Losano priest looked up at him, and his handsome spotted bronze face creased into a sad smile. "I understand, Eyck. No hard feelings." He touched Eyck's forearm softly, then he turned and left.

Eyck watched him walk up the block towards the clergy house. Pash never looked back.

Eyck wondered if he'd just caused irreparable damage to their friendship.

With a deep sigh, he closed the door and turned, abruptly coming face to face with Wex.

"How much did you hear?" Eyck asked.

"Just some," replied Wex with a shrug. *"Enough. You didn't tell me when to come back."*

Eyck chuckled tiredly. "True."

"He's telling the truth. About the—" Here he made a sign Eyck didn't know. *"The place next to the pub,"* he added helpfully.

"Yeah? The brothel?"

Wex nodded. *"I saw him go in once."*

"And you didn't feel like sharing that?"

"None of my business. None of yours."

Eyck rubbed his face wearily. "I suppose you're right."

"And he's right too."

"About what?"

"About the past. You're holding on too tight."

"Hm" was all Eyck replied. He put his arms around Wex and drew him in for another hug.

Chapter Fifteen

"Your fur is so much softer than mine," Eyck said, stroking Wex's arm. "I don't think mine was ever this soft, even when I was a pup."

"*I like how thick yours is. How dark.*" Wex smiled. "*I like how it makes your eyes greener.*" He ruffled the black-and-brown-streaked fur on Eyck's chest, making it stand up in unruly spikes, then smoothed it down again.

They had retreated upstairs after a quick breakfast of toast, sharp mustard, and mushrooms, pushing the bed pallets together to make one so they could lounge comfortably in the warm sunshine and cool breeze coming from the open window.

Wex had surprised himself by choosing to curl up close to the big blacksmith, using his broad shoulder as a pillow.

It was so easy to feel pleasure in their closeness once he'd allowed himself to—he couldn't get enough of it.

Eyck's fingers meandered their way further down Wex's arm, giving him delicious little chills. Then he touched the bandage on his forearm. "Does it hurt?"

"*Not much.*" Wex was signing one-handed which made for less-nuanced conversation, but Eyck always seemed to pick up on the subtleties of the gestures, no matter how abridged.

"I'll change the bandage and add more salve later."

"Yes. Later."

Wex placed his hand gently back in the centre of the Levek's chest and stared at the dark nipple protruding from the brindled fur, so close to his fingers that he would barely have to move his hand to touch it. And he *wanted* to touch it.

Clenching his jaw, he closed his eyes and breathed deep, trying to ride through the surge of lust that swelled throughout his body. He felt a stiffening in his groin and moved his pelvis back a tiny bit, hoping Eyck hadn't noticed.

"Are you comfortable?"

Wex nodded, liking the gruff kindness in Eyck's voice. He couldn't remember ever being this comfortable.

"You?"

This time, when he lowered his hand after signing, he placed it even closer to the jutting brownish-purple nub.

Ugh. He shifted his lower half further back.

"I am. I just . . ."

Waiting for Eyck to continue, Wex decided to lightly scratch the blacksmith's chest, his claws gentle.

"Oh, *Suns.* Lad, you have no idea what you're doing to me." Eyck swallowed audibly.

Curious, Wex lifted his head to see Eyck's face. The big Levek's eyes were half-closed, his expression dreamy and vague. *"Good?"*

"It's good . . . trust me. It's just . . ." Eyck replied, his words husky and quiet. "You're driving me crazy, lad."

Frowning, Wex chewed the inside of his cheek.

"And," the blacksmith continued, "I don't want to do anything that will . . . scare you."

"You don't scare me." Wex smirked.

"You know what I mean," Eyck said, cuffing him gently on the chin, just a brush of his knuckles, really.

Wex's hackles rose . . . not in fear, but in excitement.

Wex nodded and laid his head back down on Eyck's furry shoulder. Closing his eyes, he lifted his hand, the gestures rendered abrupt by nervousness. *"Do whatever you want."*

He felt, rather than heard, Eyck's quick intake of breath.

After a few seconds with no movement or reply from Eyck, Wex opened his eyes again, confused. A snippet of memory flashed through his mind, of Eyck pushing him away, rejecting him. Wex ground his teeth together hard before lifting his head again.

Eyck was gazing up at him, his expression guarded.

"I give you permission," he signed, in case Eyck hadn't fully understood. *"Do what you want to me."*

"Oh, lad," rumbled Eyck, a deep crease on his brow. "I'd love to *do* things to you, don't get me wrong. But I'd rather do things *with* you. And I want you to enjoy yourself."

Wex scoffed. *"Won't enjoy it. Never have."*

Eyck pushed him aside as he struggled to a sitting position, his pale-green eyes sorrowful. "Have you *never* enjoyed yourself with another person?"

Wex also sat up, moving his tail so it curled around his knee instead of under it. He shook his head.

"Schatten, that breaks my heart, Wex."

Brows knit, Wex looked down at his hands. Twisting some strands from the brown tuft at the end of his tail, he worried he had ruined the moment. *"I'm just being honest,"* he signed quickly.

"What about that Grendall sailor you were seeing in the evenings? Surely . . ."

Wex shook his head.

"Bloody Suns . . . *why* would you go to him, then?" Eyck seemed completely mystified. "Do you need the money?"

"No. And I don't want to talk about it."

"All right. Well, I know you've enjoyed yourself . . . by yourself."

It took a second for Wex to register what he meant, and he lifted his head, shocked. *"You saw me?"* His face was as hot as when he worked forge-side.

"Heard once. Saw another. Didn't mean to." Eyck gave him a crooked grin. "I'm sorry."

"So, what if I did that? What does it matter?"

"It's just . . . are you so certain that you won't enjoy it now?"

Eyes narrowed, Wex sat up straighter. Didn't Eyck realize he was irreparably damaged?

"*Yes. Certain.*"

"Can you see my dilemma, Wex? See, I only want to do things you enjoy. The last thing I want is permission to *use* you like others have used you. If you're so certain I can't please you . . ." Eyck exhaled hard. "Do you see where I'm coming from?"

"*You do please me,*" Wex signed tersely. "*I like hugs.*"

"So do I. But you have such an effect on me . . . I'd like more."

"*So do more.*"

"Not unless you like it."

Exasperated, Wex bared his fangs. "*I feel like you're . . . manipulating me.*"

"That I'm *what*?"

"*Reforging me to suit your needs.*" He did the sign for *manipulate* again. Wex hoped Eyck would pick up on the need he was clumsily trying to convey. "*Like you want to . . . force me . . . to try something.*"

A flicker of understanding flashed in Eyck's eyes.

Yes, that's it.

"Well, maybe you've a head like an anvil, thinking you can't enjoy something without trying it!" Eyck said, his voice getting louder.

They sat, glaring at each other.

"*Trying what, exactly?*"

Eyck's frown deepened, the muscles moving in his jaw. "Oh, I'll *show* you," he growled.

"*Fine!*" Wex replied angrily.

However, when Eyck reached for him, Wex shied back, suddenly anxious. "*Wait. Wait.*"

The blacksmith's scowl melted into a sympathetic smile. "All right. But, do you want me to keep pretending to bully you into something? Because that's what you were hinting at, right?"

Heart beating hard, Wex nodded. "*But one thing I don't want,*" he signed, his hands trembling. "*Don't go inside me. Please.*"

Eyck's forehead became a landscape of creases. "Oh, I wouldn't dream of it, lad. I know you're still hurting from . . . the other night. I wouldn't do that to you."

"*What if I never want that again?*" Wex signed, his heart in his throat.

"Then that is something we will never do. It's not important, I promise. I'm taking your lead here, all the way." Eyck smiled. "There are plenty of other things we can do. Do you trust me?"

Drawing a few quick breaths, Wex nodded.

❋

EYCK LET his grin drop and reassumed his surly expression.

From the outside, it probably looked like a silly game they were playing, but it seemed important to Wex that he be "bullied" into complying—he was actively consenting to be forced. It didn't really make a whole lot of sense to Eyck, but if that's what Wex wanted, that's what he would get. Maybe this was the only way Wex thought he could allow himself to enjoy sex: by being *forced* to enjoy it.

Eyck planned to talk about it with him afterwards, to make sure he was doing everything to make him feel safe throughout, but for now, he forged ahead.

He pushed Wex back onto the bedding and had to stop for a moment, just to admire the young man. The fur on his bare chest was glossy and sleek over his hard muscles, silver with just a hint of the darker-grey stripes that ran down his back and arms.

He was beautiful, that was certain, but Eyck couldn't help seeing the small patches where he was missing fur—old scars and new injuries—and that made it all the more important to him that this go well.

He reached out and ran his palm down Wex's front, avoiding the injured nipple and landing on the laces that held his trousers shut. Swiftly, he untied them, glancing up to see Wex's reaction. The lad had gone still, his eyes crushed closed, just waiting.

Shaking his head, Eyck pulled down Wex's trousers, finding him without smallclothes beneath. That discovery startled him into pausing again—he'd planned to tease out the moment of nakedness longer—but Eyck just shrugged and leaned forward.

He pressed his face against Wex's stomach, ruffling the fur there with his nose, going lower until his cheek rested on Wex's thigh, his lips against his small protruding sheath. He could hear Wex breathing heavily, and a glance showed the young man held onto the edges of the pallet, his knuckles in high relief with the force of his grip.

Eyck rubbed his mouth against the soft furry pouch that held Wex's limp cock hidden within, but when that didn't elicit the reaction he'd hoped for, he decided on a different route. Removing Wex's pants completely, Eyck pulled up on his legs so they hooked over Eyck's shoulders, then he crouched forward, lying down on his stomach to bury his face beneath Wex's balls. Extending his tongue, he touched it to the smooth, hairless rim of Wex's pucker.

He felt a slap to the back of his head and rose up on one elbow. Wex was panting, his eyes wide and wild.

"Relax," Eyck said with a grin. "Just lie back and let me take care of you."

Blinking rapidly, Wex stared at him.

"I promise this will feel good. Lie back."

Wex flared his nostrils, the edges visibly trembling, then closed his eyes and lay back down.

Eyck once again made himself comfortable before resuming. With his arms looped around Wex's raised thighs, he licked Wex's hole with a flat tongue a few times, working gently but deliberately.

Wex squirmed a bit, his breathing ragged, so Eyck rewarded him with a slow sucking kiss to the sphincter as the tip of his tongue slid over the puckered opening.

Wex's thighs tensed, so he did it again, this time letting his tongue run along the base of Wex's tail first, over his pucker, and ending at his testicles, teasing them with nibbles and caresses from his seeking lips.

Carefully, he uncurled his hand from around Wex's leg and began stroking upwards from the back of his thigh, to his hip, to just below his ribcage with his fingers. Wex's abdomen tightened under Eyck's palm when he reached it, so he paused, lapping at his slick, quivering sphincter, enjoying himself immensely. The languid pace was the perfect tease—Eyck's hard cock pulsed, trapped against his stomach as he grinded against the bedding, lavishing Wex's hole with continuous flat-tongue kisses.

Wex sighed and panted, tensed and shuddered as Eyck gradually worked just the very tip of his tongue inside him. Not enough to break his promise, but to tease the sensitive nerve endings as his hand crept down Wex's belly . . . and there it was. Hot and hard against his searching fingers, Wex's cock protruded from its furry cover, the pointed tip covered in a silky warm dollop of precum.

Grinning to himself, he took hold of Wex very carefully, but what he encountered gave him pause. He stopped lapping at Wex's pucker to lift his head, inspecting the raised lines under his fingers. It was obvious someone had tried to mutilate the young man—a long time ago judging by the healed scars that ran along the side of his dark pink shaft. He gently stroked the maimed skin, moving forward to kiss the wet tip of Wex's cock.

With a loud gasp, Wex lifted his head to stare down at Eyck. The lad's dark eyes were mere slits, his expression tortured. He jerkily signed out two words: *Don't stop.*

Ignoring the scars, Eyck shifted forward and quickly engulfed Wex's cock with his mouth, grasping it at the root with his free hand. A single moan tore its way out of Wex's chest, spurring Eyck on.

He slurped and bobbed, trying to take in as much of Wex's shaft as he could, working his tongue over the dribbling slit on the return, until the lad was panting and so tense the muscles under his free hand felt like steel. Then Wex let out a harsh, staccato exhale, grabbed the sides of Eyck's head, hands rough and clinging, and filled Eyck's mouth with his seed.

Eyck swallowed twice to keep from choking and tried to ignore the claws digging into his scalp as Wex jerked his pelvis again, his whole body trembling.

Finally, the last pulse of cum dribbled over Eyck's tongue, and Wex's body became suddenly soft as putty. The lad let out a long sigh and released Eyck's head, folding his hands over the middle of his chest, his eyes shut.

Grinning a bit smugly, Eyck sat up, ignoring his own neglected erection, and squeezed Wex's thigh. "So," he asked, "did you enjoy yourself?"

Wex's eyes slid open a crack, and he stared at Eyck for a few seconds before nodding. Then he lifted his hands and gestured.

"Never again."

Stunned and confused, Eyck sat up straight. "What? Why? Did I do something wrong? Was it too much?"

Wex turned his head to look out the window. *"No. It's fine. I just don't want to do any of that again."*

"All right," Eyck replied slowly. Disappointment didn't begin to cover what he felt. Definitely some anger . . . which he knew was *completely* uncalled for. Schooling his face in an attempt to belie the bemusement he felt, he asked, "Can I do something to help?"

"No." Then Wex glanced at him. *"Yes. Some cold water? I'm thirsty."* His stiff gestures paused before he added, *"I'll come get it downstairs."* Another pause, coupled with a small frown. *"I need a moment alone."*

"Sure thing," Eyck replied with a forced smile. "I'll go do that now, lad. Take all the time you need."

As he walked down the stairs, out of the corner of his eye, he saw Wex turn on his side, his arms hugging himself—any and all bitterness Eyck felt immediately evaporated, and he chided himself for his kneejerk reaction. The horrors Wex had been through were *unfathomable*. Suns, the worst abuse Eyck had ever suffered was being called a fatherless bastard by a schoolyard bully when he a was pup.

It was unfair of him to have assumed that Wex would be ready for anything so soon. Maybe he would *never* be ready.

Eyck picked up his discarded shirt and threw it over his head before he went outside, water bucket in hand.

If Wex never wants to go further than a simple hug, will that be enough for me? he pondered as he pumped. By the time the bucket was filled, he believed he had his answer.

Wex nervously waited for Eyck's return, his fingers fidgeting with the buttons on his shirt as he stood by the window on still-wobbly legs.

He had no idea what to expect. Would Eyck pretend like nothing had happened between them? Even so, if he managed to do that for a short while, Wex was certain that everything was ruined. Eyck, having had a taste of Wex, would either eventually lose patience and *actually* force himself on him, or Eyck's resentment would make him grow cold.

Clenching his jaw, Wex shook his head.

The briefest of brief moments of joy, lost forever because of a stupid mistake—Wex had never experienced shame like this before.

I should leave before he has a chance to send me away.

He thought about the anger that had flashed momentarily across Eyck's face, and stopped fidgeting. Yes, he would leave.

Fuck the blacksmith and fuck his conditional affections—I don't need any of it, he thought, riling himself up. He scowled, turning to the stairs, intent on grabbing his belongings before Eyck returned, but was startled by the jingle of the bells above the door.

"Sorry it took so long," Eyck said, grinning as he swept past Wex. He grabbed a clean, beaten-copper cup and filled it to the brim with the bucket's ladle, placing on the corner of the table nearest to Wex. "Say, I was thinking, since we have the rest of the day off and all, you can finally teach me that game you told me about. The card game you played when you were with the circus? I have a deck of cards here . . . some*where* . . ." He scratched the top of his head, looking around. "Hm."

Wex blinked, watching the blacksmith rummage through the wooden crates that took up so much of the smithy's floor space. He lifted the cup of cold water but didn't bring it to his lips. Suspicious of the Levek's nonchalance, Wex scrutinized his expression, wishing he could believe it was authentic.

"Ah! I think they're upstairs," Eyck said and straightened. He gasped, grimacing, and grabbed his back with both hands, stretching backwards for a few seconds. "Getting old is a blight." The blacksmith sighed then shrugged. "Thank Suns, you're staying on with me, lad." He chuckled. "You know, soon you'll take over, and it'll be *me* doing safe, boring chores." Pausing at the bottom step, he looked over at Wex. "You *are* staying, aren't you?" His green eyes were wide and hopeful.

Wex pressed his lips together. He realized he was clutching the cup so hard he was afraid he might dent it, so he set it down.

"You still want me to stay?" he signed.

"Of course, I do," Eyck replied.

Wex could see nothing but gentle affection in the big Levek's brindled face.

"Even after what happened?"

"What *did* happen?" the blacksmith replied, lifting up one shoulder. "We tried something, and it didn't work out the way we thought it would. I don't care."

"You don't care if it never happens again?"

"Nope." Eyck smiled.

Wex tilted his head, appraising the blacksmith.

Eyck's expression sobered the longer Wex stared at him. "Please, lad. Stay with me." His voice was just a low rumble.

The words caused Wex's fur to lift all along his spine. He swallowed hard against the fluttery feeling in his stomach. *"And if it doesn't work out?"*

He didn't know why he was drawing this out—he'd already made up his mind.

"It'll work out, lad. I know it."

Wex snorted, allowing himself a grin. *"How can you be so sure?"*

"I dunno. I've got a good feeling about this," Eyck replied, smiling back. "About you and me, I mean, whatever form it takes. Something just feels right about it."

Wex made a show of mulling it over, even though he felt . . . giddy. *"Maybe it does."*

They stood wordless, eye to eye, until Eyck reached out. Wex gladly let himself be pulled into Eyck's embrace, and he closed his eyes, leaning his temple against Eyck's for a moment. When Wex stepped back, Eyck winced and grabbed his back again.

"Now," Eyck said with a sharp exhale, "if you don't mind . . . can you go look for the cards? I need to sit."

"Fine . . . old man." He flashed Eyck a cocky grin, but on the inside, he felt . . . tender, like newly healed skin. *"Where are they?"*

THE REST of the day was spent just enjoying each other's company. Wex lit the fire only long enough to make tea and heat up a seed-bag for Eyck's aching back, the two of them opting for fresh tomato sandwiches to fill their bellies at dinnertime. Eyck picked up the game of Big Two with the same ease and enthusiasm with which he learned the signing language Wex used—after only three games, Wex found himself sorely outmatched.

"It took me weeks to learn this," Wex grumbled, signing one-handed. *"Not fair."*

"Beginner's luck," replied Eyck with a shrug.

"It's not *beginner's luck,"* Wex signed, baring his fangs. *"You're just smarter than I am."*

Eyck frowned, rubbing the back of his neck. "I'm really not. But we can stop if you want to. Do something else."

"You are." Wex put his cards facedown on the table and leaned back with his arms crossed, staring hard at Eyck. After a moment, he signed, *"Why don't you see that?"*

"See what?" Eyck replied with another shrug. "I'm just a big dumb—"

"If you say you're a big dumb Levek one more time, I'm going to bite you."

Eyck let out a startled bark of laughter. "You will, eh?"

"I'm serious, blacksmith. Why do you pretend you're some bullheaded lout, only as smart as the lies we are told of our breeds?"

"I'm sorry?"

"You say we are the same, you and I. That I'm not less because of my Kirmen blood, yet you insist on upholding the breed conventions."

"I do?" Eyck's forehead creased.

"Do you really think all Dankels are superstitious and stubborn? That all Grendalls are natural schemers and liars? Do you think Ulvens are always overemotional? Or that every Losano and Garza is wise and patient? What about the Samra? Do you really believe they are born leaders, full of courage and dignity just because of the colour of their coat and the blood in their veins? And Kirmen . . . am I really that submissive and weak-willed?"

"Of course not, lad."

"Then why do you think Duvals and Leveks are stupid?"

Eyck pondered for a moment, scratching his chin. "I don't know.

It's hard to get away from something you're taught from birth, I guess. Didn't realize I was doing it."

"Plus, you can't say that you and I are the same and then call yourself dumb," Wex pointed out with a small grin. *"That would make me an idiot, and I'm not."*

"No, you're not. It's true. I'm sorry." Eyck looked embarrassed.

Wex found the expression on the big Levek's face endearing, so he reached out and clasped the man's hand briefly before continuing.

"Not only are you one of the smartest Kat'hoondemen I've met, you're also one of the kindest and most giving. I'm sorry I've been such a burr in your coat."

Eyck looked like he was in great pain as he stared at Wex, then he sighed, chuckled, and shook his head. "That's fine, lad." He patted Wex's hand. "That's fine. And I'm sorry I pushed you this morning to do something you weren't comfortable with, I shouldn't have."

Wex stared at the big hand on top of his, the black-and-brown fur scored and scarred from working with hot metal all day, the black claws blunt and dull from age. He felt like his heart was going to split into shards.

"Come." Wex stood and beckoned Eyck to follow him up the stairs. *"Come."*

As soon as he'd reached the room above, Wex pulled off his shirt and doffed his pants, sinking to his knees on one of the sleeping pallets. Eyck stood on the second-to-top step, staring, his expression one of deep confusion.

"Come." Wex gestured again, then went down on all fours, facing away from the blacksmith. Closing his eyes, he twitched his tail to the side, winking his desire to mate.

"Wex," Eyck rasped. "You can't mean this. I don't need this. I—"

Wex looked over his shoulder and repeated the tail flick, lifting his tail high at the base to give Eyck a good view of his pink pucker, before hiding it again.

"You're still hurt . . . from those soldiers."

Impatient, Wex signed one-handed. *"I'm fine. Come."* What he'd suffered through in the pub was nothing compared to his past, but Eyck didn't need to know that.

Wex turned away again and once more shut his eyes, waiting. He heard Eyck's step and the sound of cloth hitting the floor, then he braced himself, wondering nervously what was taking the blacksmith so long.

Would he be gentle? Restrained? His own body was reacting with a mind of its own, his cock poking free of its sheath. His hate of desire and lust was born of his fear, something he fought even now as he widened his knees further.

"Wex." Eyck's voice was very quiet, and his breathing had quickened.

Curious, he looked back at the blacksmith again. Eyck was kneeling, his eyes wide. "This morning . . . you said you didn't want—"

Wex rose up and sat on his heels. *"I changed my mind. I might change my mind tomorrow,"* Wex signed, his nerves making his fingers clumsy. *"It's my mind to make up,"* he pointed out, feeling on edge now, defensive.

"Of course, it is. I just want to make sure this is something you really want. After what happened earlier . . ." Eyck replied. "Well . . . you lead, and I'll follow."

Wex frowned. What an odd thing to say.

"I have a request though," Eyck said with a wince. "Can you be on top?"

On top? Wex blinked, his heart pounding loud in his ears. *"What do you mean?"*

Eyck didn't answer at first, simply crawling forward to lie down faceup next to Wex. "Like this. Straddle my hips." He smiled. "Better for my back."

Oh.

Wex stared at Eyck's thick dark-red cock jutting proudly from the furry black sheath for a moment before nodding. He'd not often been in this position, maybe twice, and only because he'd been servicing two at once. Carefully, Wex put a leg over Eyck and settled himself so that the Levek's erection rested between his cheeks, the head of it peeping past the silver-furred sack of Wex's testicles.

"Am I too heavy?" Wex signed, seeing a grimace cross Eyck's face

and realized that in this position, he was free to use his hands to speak. He liked that.

"No. You just feel nice." Eyck closed his eyes for a few seconds, then cleared his throat. "We don't have to do more than this, you know. I don't need anything else."

Brows furrowed, Wex rose up on his knees and spat into his hand, causing Eyck's eyes to snap open. Breathing gone shallow and quick, Wex reached back and stroked Eyck's dick to wet it, then propped it against his sphincter, shifting on his knees to make the angle better before letting himself settle back down again.

Wex was still sore from the abuse he'd suffered, but it wasn't really that painful when Eyck's cock slid into him, opening him up. Eyck was big, but not uncomfortably so, and when Wex rested his whole weight, forcing Eyck in deep, he stayed there for a few moments, not moving. Partly, it was because Eyck let out such a groan that Wex was afraid he'd already spent himself, but also because he was shocked by how different it felt to be the one taking control. He'd always been passive, used—was this what Eyck meant by leading and following?

Eyck let out a low, happy grumble deep in his chest when Wex began to move a little, Wex's body growing accustomed to the hard length inside him.

Reaching out, the blacksmith went to grasp Wex's erection, but Wex stopped him by smacking his hand away.

"Sorry," Eyck said. "No touching?"

"*No touching,*" Wex replied. He wasn't quite ready for that again.

"All right. You're the boss." Eyck smiled blissfully and folded his hands behind his head.

"*Why do you say that?*"

"Say what?"

"*That I'm the boss. That I'm leading.*"

"Because it's the truth."

Oh.

It was like a spark had suddenly gone off in his head, illuminating all the cracks that had formed in his towering walls. Cracks that had begun to let in concepts like . . . trust.

"*No touch unless I say so,*" he signed.

"My hands will not move from this spot," Eyck promised, then he moaned loudly as Wex began to move again. "Though, next time, maybe you should tie them together to make certain."

Wex tilted his head, his breath caught in his lungs. *Oh?*

For some reason, the thought of tying up the blacksmith made his dick even harder. He grinned.

● ۞ ●

EYCK PANTED, straining up to feel more of Wex, teetering on the edge once again only to be denied when Wex took to his knees, letting Eyck's dick slide out of him completely to smack down on his belly.

"You're cruel," he said, his voice hoarse and mouth dry.

Wex had been teasing Eyck with enthusiasm for Suns knew how long—long enough that his fur was soaked through with sweat, and his balls ached for release. However, as tortuous as Wex's treatment of him might be, Eyck was actually pleased and a little amazed by how much the lad seemed to be enjoying himself.

Wex gazed down at him, his dark-brown eyes half-lidded and his chest heaving as he stroked his own cock, dribbling precum all over Eyck's tormented erection. Well, perhaps Eyck wasn't the only one being teased.

He longed to touch Wex—certainly he wanted to take his length in hand, but also just to feel the silky fur against his palms—but he kept his promise, locking his fingers behind his head so they wouldn't wander of their own volition. Finally, Wex lowered himself back down on his dick, his insides so slick and hot, and began to move, his head thrown back as he rode Eyck.

"Oh, Suns," Eyck whispered, licking his lips. "Schatten . . . Wex . . . *Wex*, if you don't want me to cum y-you'd better stop."

Wex didn't reply, his panting breaths and the creak of the floorboards beneath them growing louder as he picked up his pace, his hand jerking his cock quickly, flinging beads of precum into the air with the force of his movements.

"*Ohhhh.*" Eyck squeezed his eyes shut, trying to remain in control of his hands and his cock, but the latter was too far gone to pull back.

He gasped and pushed upwards as the lad came down to envelop his cock completely, and then choked out a strangled groan as Wex's sphincter clamped down hard on his dick.

Eyck opened his eyes just as the first string of cum landed on him, Wex's voiceless cry triggering his own orgasm—with a deep grunt, Eyck sent his seed into Wex as the lad continued to bounce in his lap, milking every last drop from Eyck's throbbing balls as he emptied his own onto the blacksmith's chest and belly.

Wex soon withdrew, leaving Eyck to catch his breath.

Eyck closed his eyes, relishing the warm glow that pulsed through his body. He hadn't really felt this level of pleasure, or connection, with anyone since . . . well, since Manya.

He clenched his jaw, her death like a knife in his chest for a brief moment, but he shook his head—if the priests were right and she was gazing down at him from her palace in the sky, Eyck thought she would understand. He loved her, that would never stop, and he knew she would love him to the end of time too, but she'd also want him to be happy again . . . to find love.

Eyck smiled. It might not be love *yet* with Wex, but it was close.

When Wex still hadn't cuddled up with him after a few minutes, Eyck lifted his head, remembering how the lad had reacted last time. He was dismayed to see that Wex was sitting with his arms wrapped around his knees, his eyes huge, just staring at him.

Oh no.

"Are you ok?" Eyck asked, sitting up gingerly. "Did it go . . . *wrong* again?"

"Did you enjoy it?" Wex signed slowly, his fangs pressed into his lower lip. *"Was that all right?"*

"It was more than all right, lad," he replied honestly. "It was wonderful." He frowned at Wex's expression—the boy looked terrified. "What's wrong?"

"When can we try again?" Wex signed.

"Um. Whenever you want to," Eyck replied, astonished. "Any time you like."

"I don't want to lose this. Please." Wex's gestures were rapid, and he flared his nostrils.

"Lose what? I'm not going anywhere."

"How long before we try again?"

"Wait . . . you mean . . . *now*?"

Wex nodded and signed the word *please* again.

"*Oh*. Well . . . uh . . . you're going to have to give me a few minutes."

Eyck smoothed his hair back as he looked at the mess on his furry chest, wondering what it would take to get him hard again. It seemed like it was really important to Wex, and though he couldn't begin to fathom the reason, he'd do his best.

"But, why don't you come here now and let me hold you. If you want . . . I can touch you . . ." He lifted his brows.

"Please" was all that Wex replied before curling into Eyck's embrace. He grabbed Eyck's hand and pressed it to his groin where the tip of his cock was already poking out of the furry sheath again.

"All right, lad," he whispered, pressing his lips to Wex's temple. He stroked the lad's hardening shaft and was rewarded with a shuddering sigh. "I'll take care of you, Wex. Whatever you need, just tell me."

"Yes," Wex replied. Eyes closed, he moved in time to Eyck's hand. *"Yes, thank you."*

Chapter Sixteen

I t took six days before the panic began to subside. Wex had tried to explain to Eyck what he was feeling—that every time they finished, it felt like he was falling from a high cliff and the only cure was to do it all over again.

He could see the blacksmith didn't really understand, but that didn't matter. Whenever Wex woke Eyck in the middle of the night for a frantic coupling or asked him to close the shop for a few minutes so they could run upstairs and take care of his needs, he did it without question, and always with the same words: *Whatever you need, just tell me.*

Wex buried his face in the fur between Eyck's shoulder blades, hugging him tight. It was still scary, but it no longer felt so . . . urgent. Now, after he peaked, the predominant feeling was pleasure but also of belonging. Of safety.

He was *home*. Here, in Eyck's bed—in *their* bed—he was home. His body was still learning it, but Wex knew that Eyck wasn't going to hurt him or discard him. He would be patient, and he would help Wex heal . . . because that was the kind of man he was.

Eyck let out a soft snort, then sighed. It was just past dawn, and the sun's rays were beginning to slide across the wooden floorboards.

Wex smiled and pushed his nose harder against the blacksmith's nape, then slid his hand down the coarse fur of Eyck's belly and cupped his hidden cock.

"Hm?" Eyck sounded mostly asleep.

Wex gave Eyck's cock a good squeeze, then shifted his hips up so that his erection pressed against one of Eyck's buttocks, then he prodded the base of Eyck's tail with the head of his cock.

"Uh. All right," Eyck said, his voice hoarse. He rubbed his face. "Just use more oil this time, please."

Nodding, Wex grabbed the little bottle of Sun's Flower oil and lubed his cock up well. He gently pulled Eyck's tail to the side, then pushed himself into Eyck's body.

The Levek let out a little grunt, so Wex put his arm around him again. Eyck sighed and took Wex's hand, pressing it to his chest. The blacksmith's heartbeat was strong and steady against his palm. Wex closed his eyes, his hips falling into the same rhythm.

Eyck didn't particularly enjoy being penetrated, but neither did he dislike it. It just wasn't his usual thing. Wex wasn't sure yet whether he liked one more than the other, but for the moment, nothing else mattered except this sharing of bodies.

It didn't take him long to finish, thrusting himself deeper and faster for the final strokes, then he exhaled hard, holding himself in place as he came inside Eyck. He panted, waiting for the panicky feeling to take hold, but when it did, it was just a shadow of what it had been that first day, and it was gone in an instant.

Eyck chuckled. "Are you done with me now? Can I get up? *Bloody Suns*, I need a bath. We both do."

Grinning, Wex withdrew his limp cock and climbed over Eyck to straddle him. "*Bath later*," he signed, grinding his backside on Eyck's groin.

Eyck let out a groan, rubbing his face. "I don't have it in me, lad."

But the growing hardness beneath Wex told a different story. He grabbed the oil and lifted himself up, pouring the last few drops from the bottle in his palm.

"I *just* bought that," Eyck said, his forehead wrinkled up, his expression tragic. "Mrs. Begmard is going to wonder how I've gone through two bottles of Sun's Flower oil so quickly."

"*Who cares*," Wex replied, stroking the oil over Eyck's cock. He grinned and sank down on Eyck's erection, laughing when Eyck closed his eyes and let out a deep groan of pleasure.

"Ok, I lied," Eyck said with a little growl. "I guess I *do* have it in me." He grabbed Wex by the waist and tossed him to the side, pushing his legs apart to crawl on top of him.

Wex's heart skipped a beat, and he panted quickly, fear freezing him in place as he stared up at Eyck, but then Eyck leaned forward and touched his nose to Wex's.

"This all right?" he asked softly, gently pressing the head of his cock against Wex's pucker, but not pushing further, just asking permission.

In that instant, the fear melted away.

Wex exhaled hard, putting his arms around Eyck as he nodded.

Grinning, Eyck let out another growl and slid his cock into Wex, fucking him fast and deep, more aggressive than any other time he had taken him.

Wex found himself raising his hips to meet each hard thrust with fervid enthusiasm. He closed his eyes, Eyck's pummeling cock driving him closer and closer to climax, and let out a silent moan.

Yes, it was *perfectly* all right.

"SCHATTEN!" Eyck yelled, dropping the red-hot steel on the floor.

Wex had missed with the hammer again, sending sparks flying into Eyck's fur.

"Bloody *Suns*, lad, I swear you're *trying* to burn me!"

Wex signed a small *sorry* and picked up the hot blade with the tongs. It was bent, so he sent it back into the forge, pulling down on the bellows a few times, his eyes averted. Eyck grumbled and patted at his arm where the fur still smoked, glaring at his apprentice. Wex looked so shamefaced that Eyck felt bad for shouting at him. He grinned, toying with the idea of mounting him right there on the floor to show him there was no harm done—Wex's incessant libido was definitely wearing off on him—when the bells above the door jingled.

"Pash," Eyck said, touching his temple in greeting.

"Hi, Eyck. Wex," replied the priest with a smile.

Things between them had been awkward since Wex's rape and the business about Dama Sunshine's had come out.

Eyck smiled back but it felt forced. "How're things?"

"Good. Good. Uh, I just came by to let you know, Wex, that the man that uh . . . *attacked* you will be hanged in the morning." Pash clasped his hands behind his back.

Wex stared at the priest for a long moment, then gestured.

"Just him? What about the others?" Eyck said, translating for him.

Pash looked uncomfortable, glancing at Eyck before addressing Wex again. "It's the best that could be done, considering the circumstances."

"What circumstances?"

"Wex, you have to understand . . . a *Grendall* is being hanged for what he did to you. That's unprecedented."

"I see. And if he'd been Losano? What then?"

Looking even more uneasy, Pash shrugged. "I honestly don't know, Wex. I'm sorry."

Wex clenched his jaw and stared up at the ceiling for a moment.

"The council believes that hanging the Grendall will make an example of him. I know that it doesn't feel like it's enough, but it's *something*."

Fixing him with a look of disgust, Wex shook his head, and then his expression smoothed out and he sighed, shrugging. *"No, you're right. It's not your fault. Thank you,"* he said through Eyck.

Pash's forehead crinkled, and he pressed his lips together. He nodded once. Then his eyes widened. "Oh, actually that's *not* all. The other men that were rounded up were all fined." The priest dug a pouch out of the pocket of his ivory trousers and held it out. "It's not very much, I'm afraid, but it's all yours."

Wex accepted the money pouch and opened it.

"I am going to give this to the other Duval bartender," he signed after he'd counted it.

Since Wex couldn't spell, he always referred to individuals by their breeds or their trade rather than their names. So Pash was "your priest friend," Mrs. Begmard was "the candlemaker," and Tembra the waitress was "the Ulven you cuddled." It made for some guesswork on Eyck's part, but by *"other* Duval bartender" Wex could only mean Loomis at the Giddy Dankel.

"To cover the cost of the door you broke," Wex added with a small smile. *"And the blanket that was ruined. I'll give it to the other Duval bartender at this week's end when I'm at the docks picking up the shipment of stove polish."*

Eyck nodded. "That's very good of you, lad."

"What did he say?" Pash asked.

When Eyck told him Wex's intentions, Eyck thought he could see something change in the way Pash looked at Wex. It was promising. He smiled to himself. "Want me to write an explanation for Loomis?"

Wex nodded, but Pash lifted a hand. *"I'll* write it," he said, glancing over at Eyck with a teasing smile. "The poor man won't have a Sun's chance in deciphering your scribbles."

The breathy little chuckle from Wex surprised him. Wex and Pash . . . he'd never thought they'd ever get along. Humming to himself, he pulled on the bellows again while Pash sat down at the table with a fresh leaf-quill and paper, Wex hovering over his shoulder to watch the priest jot down a brief explanation for the money in his meticulous handwriting.

Chapter Seventeen

Wex touched his temple in thanks to Ms. Tabor and left the mill with his shopping bag full of wrapped sandwiches, an onion and wheat glutty pie, a small pot of the fermented cabbage Eyck loved so much, and a fresh loaf of bread. He broke a piece off the loaf so he could snack on it as he walked to his next stop.

A woman sweeping her entranceway paused to nod a greeting at him, and he returned the nod with a smile, then waved as he passed the soapworks where the Levek brothers who owned it were outside eating lunch. They waved in return and went back to their soup and tankards of beer.

What a stark contrast to the first few times he'd run errands for the blacksmith, Wex mused. Back then, his presence was met with suspicious stares or downright malice. Once, a Losano woman had actually thrown the contents of her chamber pot in his direction, missing by only a handswidth. These days, most everyone was polite, some truly friendly.

Wex figured he was such a common sight that people had grown used to him, but working for Eyck—a respectable member of the community, as the blacksmith liked to remind everyone—certainly didn't hurt.

Working with, he reminded himself. Not *for*.

The partnership was still in word only—the papers needed to be written up and sent to the guild for approval. However, Eyck was sharing the smithy profits as if they were already legal business partners even though Wex technically hadn't even finished his apprenticeship. Wex knew it would take at least a few months for that to happen.

Then there was that . . . *other* partnership proposal. He swallowed the chunk of bread, sighed, and dug another piece out of his bag. What was he going to do with *that*? They had sex on a regular basis—what more was there? Eyck made it sound like they could live openly together, like a married couple.

He snorted and shook his head. *Romantic fool.*

Yet . . . thinking about it made him feel . . . odd.

Pushing his confusion aside as best as he could, Wex ducked into the woodshop and touched his temple in greeting as Llod rose from his workbench. The short thickset Dankel nodded at Wex, grunting as he stooped to pick up something from behind the counter. He placed a bundle of soft grey cloth on the worn wooden surface and slowly unrolled it, revealing four carved pine handles, stained a deep blue-green. Wex reached out and touched one, admiring the silky-smooth finish. They were for the metal cooking implements Ms. Tabor had commissioned. Wex was certain she would be pleased.

He dug into his pocket and handed the coins over to the woodworker who counted them with a nod. But when Llod took a step towards his workbench, Wex rapped softly on the counter to get his attention.

"Yeah?"

Wex pointed to the handles then held up two fingers. *"Need another set."*

Llod's gold eyes narrowed and let out another soft grunt. "What's that? Uh . . . another set?"

Wex nodded.

"Same again?"

This time, Wex shook his head and then mimed drawing something. Llod slid a scrap of paper towards him and handed him a wood pencil, leaning back with his arms crossed, the ever-present toothpick poking out of the side of his mouth as he waited.

Wex quickly sketched a tree then pushed the paper back to Llod. "Wall-nut?"

Nodding, Wex smiled.

"Gonna be pricey."

Wex nodded again and shrugged.

A richly dressed Samra lady had come into the shop as he and Eyck were working on Ms. Tabor's cooking implements and had all but ordered them to make a set for her too on the spot. Eyck had agreed to the commission—it was a nice change from the drudgery of making cheap soldiers' swords, after all—but told the woman she would have to wait like everyone else. That's when the woman had made all sorts of demands, like wall-nut handles and gold accents along the sides of the utensils. But, as long as she had the coin, who cared that she'd end up with a set of gaudy hard-to-clean cooking utensils? It was her prerogative.

"Colour?" Llod asked, holding up his stain chart. Wex pointed to the bright red and Llod nodded. "Right." Llod made a note in his dog-eared ledger. "Two weeks."

Wex touched his temple in thanks, then Llod surprised him.

The woodworker pointed to Wex's simple sketch. "Nice drawing, kid."

Beaming, Wex thanked him again and left. It was the most Llod had ever said to him in a single meeting. The man wasn't unfriendly . . . just taciturn.

On his way back to the smithy, Wex stopped by the shoemaker's shop so they could measure his feet for new boots. He grimaced, putting a hand over his nose as he quickly passed the big trays of resin-covered chamara drying in the sun next door. When it was fully cured, the woven seaweed made a flexible, waterproof material that was good for any number of things—footwear, belts, coats, and the aprons and felt-lined gloves that Eyck and he wore all day to work in —but *Suns* did it stink when it was fresh. He hoped his boots wouldn't smell bad for long, but even if they did, he was still excited. He'd never owned a pair of brand-new boots before.

The owner of the shop pointed Wex towards the back room where they did all the measuring, and Wex thanked him. Then, taking a deep breath to steel himself—something he immediately regretted because of the pervasive stench—he pushed past the dusty green velvet curtain and smiled wide, freezing in place when he saw who was with the shoemaker on the other side.

Schatten.

Jenshy West was a frequent customer of Eyck's, coming in at least once a week to sharpen his knives, but Wex *detested* him. The skinny little Duval chamara maker thought he was much more charming and funnier than he actually was. He drove Wex crazy with his stupid, thinly veiled comments and idiotic jokes.

"Wex! How ya been, buddy?" Jenshy said loudly, coming up to thump Wex on the back as if they hadn't just seen each other that morning.

Clenching his jaw, Wex kept his smile in place and gestured to his boots.

"Huh? What? Can't hear ya," Jenshy said, his grin lopsided as he cupped his ear.

Wex rolled his eyes and shook his head. It was the same thing every *single* time.

"Ohhhh . . . I see. *Kat's* still got your tongue, huh?"

The chamara maker's laugh was grating.

Har har har. One of these days, Wex was going to punch the braying Duval right in his stupid face.

Sighing inwardly, Wex pretended he found the inane, and frankly insulting banter amusing while his feet were measured, but it felt like an eternity before he was finally free to escape. He smiled at the stout Levek shoemaker, touching his temple in thanks to her, and left without bidding farewell to Jenshy.

As Wex turned down the next block, he shook his head, annoyed that he let Jenshy bother him so much. He wished he was more like Eyck—the big blacksmith just put up with the witless windbag and laughed in all the right spots. Eyck said Jenshy was just overcompensating because he was a very insecure fellow.

Wex frowned. Maybe Eyck didn't realize just how *much* Jenshy bothered him.

Kat's got your tongue . . . I mean what a stupid expression. What is a kat even? Kat'hoondeman and *Kat'hoondemen* were shortened to *man* and *men* accordingly, but maybe somewhere else in the kingdom they shortened it to *kat*. Or maybe that's how they shortened it in the far past. He'd ask Eyck if he knew.

Wex was supposed to stop in at Mrs. Begmard's to pick up salve and another bottle of Sun's Flower oil, but he changed his mind when he saw she was in her side garden, tending to her bees. The flying creatures just . . . unnerved him. Striped yellow and black and probably three times the size of his thumb, they buzzed menacingly and had strange unblinking eyes. Plus, Mrs. Begmard had told him they could sting if you weren't careful with them. He watched the candlemaker pull a wooden plug out of the big bee box while a number of her "pets" droned around her head, a few actually alighting on her arms and shoulders.

Ugh. Unable to watch any more, he shuddered and crossed the road to the smithy. *Eyck can go get the oil and salve himself.*

"Finally," Eyck said, when Wex walked through the door. The big blacksmith stepped up to him with a grin and looped one arm around Wex's waist to draw him close while he shut and locked the door with his free hand. Then he took Wex's shopping and deposited it gently on the floor. Nibbling at Wex's neck, Eyck pressed his groin firmly against Wex's pelvis as he wrapped his other arm around him, letting out a little growl.

Wex laughed, pushing at Eyck to free himself. *"What's gotten into you?"* he signed, stepping back out of reach.

"You kept me waiting," Eyck said, his tone playfully menacing.

"It took me longer—" Wex started signing.

He gasped when Eyck lunged at him, snatching him up into another lusty embrace. It was blatantly obvious that Eyck was hard as rock beneath the thick twill of his work pants.

Chuckling, Eyck slid a hand down the back of Wex's trousers and squeezed his backside.

Again, Wex shoved at Eyck, shaking his head. He leaned back to sign, *"Someone will see!"* and glanced pointedly over his shoulder at the curtainless windows.

Eyck took the opportunity to lean in and graze the side of his neck with his fangs again, then bit into him hard enough that Wex let out another gasp.

"I don't care. You were gone a long time, and my imagination got the better of me."

Wex closed his eyes, flaring his nostrils as Eyck's fingers circled under his tail to find his pucker, his own cock getting harder with every passing second. It snaked down the leg of his pants, and he pushed it against Eyck's straining erection.

With another deep growl, Eyck released Wex and steered him towards the table instead of the stairs.

"*What*, here?" Wex managed to sign before Eyck spun him around and forced him to bend over the table—at least to the outside observer, it might *seem* like he was forced. In reality, he was putty in Eyck's hands. A little nervous about being observed by a potential client, he swallowed and closed his eyes again, pressing his forehead to the cool wood.

Wex's pants were down around his ankles with a few rough yanks —Wex winced when the tailhole snagged some fur—and Eyck immediately mounted him, his cock evidently pre-oiled in anticipation. A harsh breath burst from Wex, and he grimaced, pushing back against the onslaught, the table's edge hard against his thighs.

Eyck grunted into his thrusts, his hands flat against Wex's back, but just when Wex thought he was about to seed him, Eyck abruptly stepped back.

"*Schatten!*"

Wex turned and saw what had interrupted Eyck—someone was approaching the door. He grabbed his pants and hauled them up, dragging Eyck up the stairs by his hand.

They collapsed on the pallet with a loud thump, both of them laughing breathlessly as the customer knocked on the door twice before giving up.

"*I thought you didn't care if anyone saw,*" Wex teased. He quickly unlaced his boots.

Eyck shrugged, grinning sheepishly, and helped Wex out of his pants.

Wex turned around and went down on his hands and knees to present, raising his tail a few times to wink his hole at Eyck.

"Oh, lad, that is just . . ." Eyck didn't bother finishing, just stuffed his cock back into Wex and resumed fucking him with the same fervour that had overcome him downstairs.

In a dozen thrusts, he let out a groan, his dick growing more slippery with every hard plunge as he drove the cum into Wex's body. Wex gasped, wrapping his hand around his own cock, getting close himself, but Eyck pulled out the instant he was done.

"Get on your back."

Wex obeyed, then hissed out a breath, arching his back, eyelids fluttering as Eyck's hot mouth enveloped his shaft. He heard a whimper—just as he was wondering who'd made it, Eyck slid two fingers into his sloppy hole, and it was over for Wex. He clutched at Eyck's thick black hair, thighs quivering and chest heaving, and filled the blacksmith's mouth with cum, his hoarse panting loud in the echoing space.

"I WANT you to promise that you'll tell me if I ever do something or make you do something you don't want to."

Wex frowned and looked over at the blacksmith. Eyck was lying on his back next to Wex, but he was staring at him with a wrinkle of worry across his brow.

"*Of course.*" Then he added a simple "*Why?*"

"Earlier, when you were pushing me away . . . you were just playing, right? I didn't really, um . . . force you into coupling with me, did I?"

Blinking at Eyck in confusion, Wex signed one-handed, "*I wanted. Why being strange?*"

Eyck let out an amused snort. "Strange?" Then his mouth twisted to the side, his forehead wrinkling up again as his green eyes went soft. "I was thinking that after everything that bastard Mangley did to you, I don't want you to ever feel like you can't say no to me."

❖

THE SILENCE STRETCHED ON, Wex's gaze locked on Eyck. Eyck worried he had overstepped by mentioning Wex's former master. Then Wex sighed and turned on his back, lifting both hands to sign upwards towards the ceiling. On his back next to Wex, Eyck had to stop him after only a few words.

"Slow down. I'm having a hard time following . . . your signs are all reversed when you do it that way. It's going to take me a bit longer to get what you're saying—you've been at this far longer than I have."

Wex nodded, and then he started over, slower this time, deftly reversing some of the gestures so they were made less ambiguous.

Watching Wex easily alter his signing language to accommodate Eyck's deficiency, it was clear as always to him that there was absolutely nothing wrong with Wex's ability to communicate his thoughts and feelings as eloquently as any speaking person . . . he just did it differently. Eyck could almost hear Wex's voice in his gestures.

"*He never touched me in that way,*" Wex signed. "*Not once. He had no interest in that. He would beat me, yes, sometimes hard enough that I was dizzy, but he never used me like that. His friends, yes, but never him.*" He paused and took a deep breath. "*The worst was Mangley's priest. I had a voice before he arrived—I remember it, even though it feels like a dream. Then he did terrible things to me . . . and my voice was gone.*"

Schatten. Eyck felt ill. *It's no wonder he's so leery of priests.*

Wex's hands had begun to tremble, so Eyck quickly took one of them between his own before Wex could continue and pressed it to his cheek. "I don't need to know what he put you through, lad. Not unless you *want* to tell me."

"*Thank you. I don't.*" Wex closed his eyes, the muscles in his jaw bulging as he clenched his teeth and shook his head. "*The past is the past.*"

"All right," Eyck said, his heart aching. "You're safe with me. Always."

Wex looked over and smiled. After a moment, the smile faded. "*There's one thing.*"

"Hm?"

"*One thing you make me do that I don't want to.*"

Eyck's breath caught in his throat. "What's that?" he said, his stomach sinking.

"I have to put up with that stupid chamara maker. I don't like it at all. I don't like him at all. I don't care if he has low self-worth, I don't want him mocking me." Wex's lips were pressed into a thin line, his brow furrowed . . .

But there was something in his eyes Eyck had seen before. A challenge.

"Oh. The man is a pompous little arse, for sure, but I had no idea he bothered you so much." Eyck remembered then that Wex *had* mentioned being irritated by Jenshy before. "I'm sorry, lad. You did say something, didn't you? I should have listened to you when you brought it up." He peered at Wex. "Though, I'm surprised you didn't bring it up again."

"I thought you'd be angry."

"Lad, why in the Three Suns would I be *angry*?"

"He's one of your best customers."

"He can go soak his tail in vinegar for all I care."

Wex breathed out a little laugh and shook his head at Eyck, his eyes fond.

"Do you want me to take care of it?"

Shaking his head, Wex signed, *"I don't need you to coddle me. I'll tell him myself."* He smiled. *"You'll just be my voice."*

"Oh boy." Eyck rubbed at the short fur on his creased forehead.

"Don't worry, blacksmith. I'll be polite."

Chuckling, Eyck nodded. Then he gave Wex a coy grin. "Since when do you worry about how I feel?"

Wex blinked twice then looked away, his expression shy. *"You know why."*

That was probably as close as Wex was going to get to expressing his feelings for him. At least for now.

"What about you?" Wex signed.

Eyck raised his brows, his heart beating faster. Was Wex looking for a declaration of some sort? Would he spook the lad by confessing his own deepening feelings? "What about me, what?" he asked a little nervously.

"Tell me about you. About your life. Your childhood. Was it happy?"

"Oh! Oh. Yeah, you could say it was happy. For the most part." Eyck was relieved but also felt a twinge of disappointment that Wex wanted to move the conversation away from their relationship.

"Do you have siblings?"

"I had a sister. Briefly. She was taken by the Five Cycle Sickness when she was barely a season old, so she didn't even have a name yet. I don't remember her at all."

The mysterious disease that swept through the kingdom at the height of summer every five, occasionally six sun-cycles killed one Kat'hoondeman in fifty. Some that fell ill survived, but with lasting reminders of the Sickness—like young Gawen and Red Falcorr's deafness—which some traditionalists regarded as worse than death. The Kat'hoondeman culture was not one that embraced any sort of impairment . . . but times were changing. The way many of the townsfolk treated Wex was evidence of that.

The Three Suns priesthood taught that the Five Cycle Sickness was the Living Suns' way of culling evil before it could take root. It was utter bullshit—if it were true, then there would be no slavery, no rape, and certainly no priest to torture Wex's voice from him. He breathed out slowly, sliding his head to the side so his temple rested against Wex.

Wex let out a little soft purr before lifting his hands to sign again. *"And what about your parents?"*

"Parent," Eyck replied. "My father left my mother when I was still a pup. He walked out one day and never returned."

"I'm sorry. That's awful."

Wex's words made Eyck's heart hurt. The lad had never even known his parents, had lived a hellish life from childhood, and yet he felt bad about Eyck's unconventional upbringing.

"Nah. According to my mother, he was a good-for-nothing. He's still knocking around somewhere, but I don't give a schatten's care in hell about him. My mother was a wonderful woman, and I'm glad she raised me to be a better man than he was."

Wex nodded. *"Was he a blacksmith like you?"*

"Silversmith. And not a very good one." Eyck chuckled then

stayed silent for a long time, just staring at the pattern of light on the ceiling. "Hey, you want to hear something funny about my childhood?"

Wex nodded again.

"When I was a pup, I was terribly shy and quiet."

At this, Wex sat up, staring down at Eyck with amusement.

"You? Quiet? Shy?" Wex gave a dry chuckle. *"I don't believe it. Not for a second."*

"Better believe it. Meek as a mouse. Actually, I have Pash to thank for changing that." Frowning, Eyck stopped, wishing he hadn't brought him up.

Wex chewed the corner of his lip as he asked, *"Will you tell me about you and the priest?"*

"Maybe another time, lad. I just want to think about what I have right now." He looked over at Wex and smiled. "With you."

"You want to mate again?"

Eyck let out a bark of laughter at the eagerness in Wex's expression.

"That's not what I meant. I mean . . . I just want to hold you and be together with you, right here in this moment. That's all that I need."

Looking a little confused and a tad disappointed that they wouldn't be spending the afternoon in bed—they'd already coupled twice that day, and Eyck needed to recover—Wex nodded and let Eyck pull him over so he lay on his stomach, half on top of Eyck, his head on Eyck's shoulder. He was heavy, but Eyck didn't care one bit.

Smiling, he held Wex and stroked the fur down his back with his free hand. Again, Wex made a quiet purring sound, his body going limp. After only a few minutes, the lad twitched and let out a sigh, obviously falling asleep.

The way Wex relaxed into his embrace made Eyck's heart ache. On the one, hand he was happy that Wex finally trusted him. On the other . . . thinking about what Wex had suffered, both physical and mental, sickened and infuriated him.

Physical and *mental.* He frowned, pondering as Wex slumbered in his embrace.

What if Wex's reading problems and lack of voice were

independent things? What if he was just terribly unlucky, and it was a coincidence that he had two hurdles to overcome when it came to communication? Maybe Wex's beatings about the head from Mangley could have caused him to have difficulties reading letters . . . But, maybe it was something else.

His wife, Manya, had told him about a small number of students she'd encountered in her many cycles of teaching who'd had a terrible time learning to spell or even properly *seeing* the letters. Could Wex have something similar? In Wex's case, he had no problem correctly forming letters and always copied them dutifully on his slate during his lessons. His problem was he couldn't seem to link the *sound* to the form.

The muteness . . . Earlier, Wex had admitted to having a voice once. Had the horrors inflicted by the priest really have taken his voice from him? Was that possible?

Someone knocked on the smithy door, paused, then knocked a second time. A few seconds passed, and whoever it was knocked again a little louder. Eyck sighed and carefully rolled the sleeping Wex off him.

"I'm coming, I'm coming," he muttered as he hastily dressed. He glanced out the window and saw that it was Pash below. Turning back to look at Wex, Eyck smiled at how peaceful the young man looked. Then he took the stairs down, his mind troubled but his heart full.

Chapter Eighteen

Refreshed from his unexpected midday nap, Wex whistled as he walked down the road to the river, the coin pouch from Pash safe in his pocket.

The sun was out, and the sky was a brilliant green, not a cloud in sight. It was warm out, but a cool breeze ruffled Wex's fur, and the scent of lavender, wild roses, and honeysuckle perfumed the air and put a smile on his face.

He was still disappointed that his abusers weren't all going to be hanged—or lose a hand at the very least—but the priest was right. It was a momentous decision, hanging the Grendall. Never in history had any member of *any* breed been hanged for violence committed against Kirmen, not even for murder. Part of him wanted to attend the hanging, but he knew it wasn't a good idea. No doubt many upper-caste Kat'hoondemen were *furious* at the verdict—he hoped that no violence would break out. Touching the coins in his pocket, he thought about sharing a drink with Loomis to celebrate . . . that is, if being back at the tavern didn't make him too uncomfortable.

Wex stopped in his tracks when he reached the wharf. Even from this distance, he recognized the last-docked ship: the *Sparkshade*. Brow furrowed, he climbed the wooden steps and walked towards the ship, wondering what it was doing there.

"Well, hello, son!" said a familiar voice. "I haven't seen you in a while!"

Wex sighed and turned to the spry old Kirmen in the ragged tunic. He gave the man a terse smile and touched his temple in greeting before setting off again.

"Wait! Wait!"

Gritting his teeth, Wex stopped.

"This one is new. Here, take some for your friends."

Wex breathed out through his nose slowly and accepted the leaflets from the old man. No matter how many times he'd tried to refuse in the past, the old man always gave him more of his cheaply printed pages. He nodded in thanks and folded the pages, stuffing them into his pocket. One of these days he should ask Eyck what the leaflets were about.

Distracted, he didn't notice Stilig until he was nearly on top of him. The lanky Grendall startled him by grasping him by the shoulders, a bright smile on his striped face.

"If it isn't my old friend, Wex!" Stilig said, squeezing Wex's shoulders. "How are ya, fella? Did you miss me?"

Wex smiled, though his stomach had gone fluttery and strange. He touched his temple.

"Wait now . . ." Stilig's eyes narrowed, and he peered up at Wex. "Hold on a sec . . . Something's different about you." He scrutinized Wex, stepping back to take him in from head to toe. "You're changed."

"*I am?*" asked Wex, looking down at himself.

"Ya look, dare I say it . . . *relaxed,*" Stilig replied, stroking his chin. "Yer puss looked like a clenched fist afore. Now yer smilin' sweet as a milk-drunk pup. What happened?"

Wex blinked a few times at the sailor, and then he shrugged, feeling awkward under Stilig's penetrating gaze.

"Oh . . . oh, wait now . . . Ah ha! I *see,*" Stilig said, his grin going coy. "You and that big blacksmith fella finally do the deed then?"

Heart pounding, Wex stared at the sailor. How did he know about Eyck?

"Well, it's a good fit on ya! Oh, you shoulda seen the way he was stammering and stuttering when I came askin' about ya, fella. And the way he was lookin' at me all jealous-like." Stilig chuckled, shaking his head.

Swallowing, Wex tried to change the subject. *"Why are you here?"*

"Are you asking me why we're back this way already?" asked the sailor, tilting his head. At Wex's nod, he said, "The *Sparkshade*'s been commandeered by the king. Bringing supplies and men to the front to fight the Oza." Stilig sighed, glancing over his shoulder at the ship. "No telling what'll happen."

Wex crossed his arms, trying to fight the jittery feeling in his belly, but the Grendall just made it worse by stepping up close again. "Shoulda stuck it in ya one last time before we left. I miss that sweet arse of yours." Stilig's eyes were wide and wistful one moment, then sly the next as his grin returned. "Unless it isn't too late . . ."

Wex shook his head, taking a hasty step back, and put his hands up. Was it guilt he was feeling? All the times he'd been mounted by Stilig were flashing in his mind's eye, and it was making him sweat.

"Woah, woah there, fella. Was simply asking," the sailor said, laughing though he was obviously disappointed. "I wish ya nothing but happiness. I swear on my tooth."

Smiling sheepishly, Wex nodded, relaxing.

"I *would* like something from you though."

"What is it?"

Stilig looked uncertain for a moment, and Wex thought he detected a little fear in the Grendall's expression. "Can ya pray for me and my brothers?" He shot another glance at the ship. "Pray we make it back safe?"

Surprised, Wex frowned. He hadn't prayed since his enslavement at Stettefyr, where he'd been forced to by that twisted fiend in priest's white, and just the thought of it made his heart pound and his mouth dry, but if it made the sailor feel better thinking that he would, what did the lie hurt? He smoothed out his brow and nodded at Stilig.

"Thanks."

Wex decided to do something he would never have done only a half-season ago. He stepped forward and embraced Stilig, hugging him tight for a moment. When he pulled away, Stilig grinned.

"Tryin' to feel me up, eh?" he asked, but there was no teasing humour in his eyes, only the wistful look from before. Then he cleared his throat and straightened his shoulders, his features sliding back into their usual sly expression. "See that Levek takes real good care of that arse." Without another word, he turned, leaving Wex feeling confused, relieved, and a little bit sad.

The drink with Loomis would wait—after he dropped off the money, he would head straight home to Eyck.

WEX FROWNED when the door wouldn't open. *Schatten.* He'd forgotten his key. Peering through the window, he saw the smithy was empty. Eyck had probably stepped out to run an errand, and with so many strange soldiers in town causing trouble, gone were the days of unlocked doors.

Wex jogged around the building to check the back door and was relieved when he found it unlocked. He paused at the forge to rake the glowing coals, and then he went to the table and sat, pulling the leaflets from his pocket to try to make sense of the writing. He could recognize some of the letters, but no matter how hard he tried to string them together, the way Eyck had shown him, no words appeared in his mind. The harder he tried, the more the letters seemed to twist together. It was so frustrating.

At the sound of a thump upstairs, Wex lifted his head and stared at the ceiling, holding his breath. There was another thump. Wex frowned. Slowly, he stepped towards the stairs. If Eyck was home, why would he lock the door? Then he froze, his gaze fixed on the stairwell. When he'd left, the priest had still been there, talking Eyck through some commission for the clergy house. Had they gone upstairs after Wex had left? But *why* would they be upstairs?

Could they be . . .

He shook his head. *No.*

It couldn't be that. He swallowed, trying to slow his speeding heart.

No.

There was no way Eyck would . . . *would* he?

But . . . Pash and Eyck *had* been lovers in the past.

Wex closed his eyes, listening hard. Was that the sound of rapid breathing, or was he imagining it? The floor above his head creaked. Did he just hear a moan, or was that the wind?

Wex balled his fists, willing himself to remain calm. He was jumping to conclusions. There was a perfectly rational explanation for why Pash and Eyck would be upstairs together. With the door locked. And Wex out of the way.

Baring his fangs, he shoved the leaflets into his pocket and took the stairs two at a time, startling the priest who was bent over the wooden chest where Wex kept his belongings.

Pash's expression went from surprise to anger almost immediately.

"I *knew* it," he said, waving the collection of leaflets Wex had stashed in the chest. "I knew you were up to something."

"What? What are you doing here? Why are you going through my stuff?" he signed rapidly.

Pash stared at him, not understanding, then lunged for him. Wex stepped back, avoiding the open hole of the stairwell, but not before Pash had snatched the crumpled papers sticking out of his pants pocket.

"Did you really think you wouldn't be found out?" Pash said, his nose wrinkled up in disgust as he looked at the creased pages. "Recruiting for the Oza right under Eyck's nose . . . I *knew* you couldn't be trusted from the second I laid eyes on you."

Wex stared at Pash, confused. *"What?"*

"Eyck brought you into his home. He trusted you. *Suns*, I think he might even be in love with you, the poor idiot. They're going to hang you for this."

"Wait, stop," Wex tried, using simplified signs and holding his hands up in a gesture of submission. *"No understand."* He pointed to his head, hoping that it would make sense to Pash. Recruiting for the Oza? What the hell was he talking about? And where was Eyck?

"Wait, stop," he gestured again. *"Where . . . blacksmith?"* Then he mimed swinging a hammer.

Pash only looked at him like he was crazy. Some people had no imagination, making them seemingly immune to gestures that should have been obvious—which was funny, considering Pash was a priest. Didn't one need a lot of imagination to believe in the hogwash they preached?

Stupid priest, what can I do to make you understand me? Wex's brain scrabbled for a solution, as Pash flipped through the leaflets, peering at the crude little drawings of Kat'hoondemen.

That's it! He could sketch out something for Pash! Wex kept some drawing charcoals in the wooden chest—all he needed was paper, and the leaflets were blank on one side.

Wex gave Pash what he hoped was a friendly smile, then reached out to take the leaflets from the priest's hand. However, Pash darted back, holding the pages aloft.

"Don't you dare," said the priest, scowling. "You can't—"

The rest of what he said was lost when he backed up further, stepping into the void of the stairwell. Wex leapt to catch his hand, but it was too late—the priest tumbled to the floor below, landing with a loud crash, the leaflets fluttering down to join him.

Oh no. No no no. Wex ran down the steps, his heart in his throat. Wasn't this the way Eyck's wife had died? Had Wex just killed his best friend the same way?

Pash lay motionless on the wooden floor, his leg twisted grotesquely beneath him.

Please be alive, please be alive, please be alive. It was like there was a wild animal inside him, clawing to get out, panic turned into a living thing.

He couldn't tell if the priest was breathing, and Wex's hands were shaking so hard he couldn't make out a heartbeat. They would hang him for certain. A Kirmen killing a Losano? And a *priest* no less?

Hang him? No, they would probably torture him to death . . . then there was the absolute certainty of Eyck's pain and fury. Pulse racing, Wex stared in horror at the puddle of blood growing under Pash's head.

There was only one thing he could do.

Wex stumbled to his feet and unlocked the door, yanking it open. There was no one on the street beyond. With a last glance at the body at the foot of the stairs, Wex began to run.

Chapter Nineteen

E yck smiled at Mrs. Begmard, handing over the silver for the Sun's Flower oil and tin of salve that Wex had forgotten to get when he went out for errands earlier.

"Are you sure you don't need anything else? I have some lovely lavender honey . . ." The stout Duval woman beamed up at Eyck.

He gave an exaggerated sigh, handing over a few coppers.

"You know I can't resist your honey, Mrs. Begmard. I daresay it's the best in the whole kingdom."

Mrs. Begmard chuckled, wrapping up Eyck's purchases in some thin brown paper. "Oh, you are sweet to say so, Mr. Stromsmith."

"Not as sweet as the honey," joked Eyck, accepting the package from her. He balanced the jug of small ale he'd picked up on top of it.

He'd left the priest to mind the shop while he stepped out to grab the ale to go with the sandwiches Wex had brought home. Hopefully, Wex would be back soon—Eyck didn't know how he felt about the lad going to the tavern by himself after what had happened.

Mrs. Begmard smiled wide, clucking her tongue at him. "Here. Take these." She picked two long yellow beeswax candles from her display case, the one Eyck had repaired so long ago, and tucked them in with Eyck's parcels. "And say hello to young Wex for me. Tell him I'll have more honeycakes day after tomorrow."

Eyck laughed. "Will do. Thank you, Mrs. Begmard. That lad is a bottomless pit." He left the shop and crossed the street, surprised to see that the smithy door hung wide-open.

"Hello?" he said.

Peering inside, he saw someone lying like a broken toy at the bottom of the steps. For a moment, it was like he had stepped into the past.

"Manya?" he choked out, feeling faint. His heart plummeted into his stomach when he saw who it was. "Oh, *Suns* . . . Pash!" He dropped to his knees next to the priest, the packages falling to the floor as he reached for his friend. *"Pash?"*

TREE BRANCHES SNAGGED Wex's fur as he crashed through Landing Woods just outside South Galetsy, running as fast as his heart and lungs would allow him.

Pash was dead. Eyck would never forgive him for that. How could he?

Wex panted, leaping over thick tree roots and dodging under vines.

Even if he could prove it was an accident, it was too late now. He shouldn't have run. That was a stupid mistake. Everyone would see his running away as proof of his guilt, so there really was nothing to do now but run and run and run until there was nothing left of him.

Wex's lungs burned, and his legs ached. He jumped over a hillock and landed badly, twisting his ankle, but that didn't slow him down. Still, he ran.

Slowly, the woods grew darker and darker until he could no longer see to avoid obstacles. He knew it was only a matter of time before he really hurt himself, but he deserved that, didn't he? However, when he soon smashed headfirst into a tree trunk, he finally decided that *maybe* stopping for the night was prudent. Tasting blood, he slumped to the leaf-strewn ground and bowed his head, pinching the bridge of his nose to staunch the flow.

Maybe after a night of sleep, I'll think more clearly. Maybe . . . maybe I should *go back. It was an accident. Just a stupid accident.*

But what about the leaflets? What did they have to do with recruiting for the Oza? And recruiting for *what*? The war? It made no sense. Why would the priest think a Kirmen would willingly work for the Oza? The Oza *ate* Kirmen, or at least that's how the rumours went.

Shivering as the cool night air dried his sweat-soaked fur, Wex began to sweep away the leaves and bark that littered the ground, digging into the humus below to create a shallow depression he could sleep in. He didn't relish the thought of sharing space with all the insects and crawling things living in the spongy ground, but it was better than freezing to death. As he worked to clear a space big enough for him to curl up on his side, his hand came into contact with an oddly smooth surface. It felt like a window. Wex frowned, wondering why there would be glass in the middle of the forest, and wearily pushed more dirt and leaves out of the way.

"Bloody *Suns*, Pash," Eyck said, his chest tight. "You scared the living daylight out of me. I thought you were dead."

Pash winced, gingerly touching the bandage on his head. "So did I."

A novice priest stopped by the bed to inspect the bark cast on Pash's leg, testing to see whether it had firmed up properly. Eyck watched quietly, feeling completely useless. At least he'd gotten the priest here in one piece, pushing him in the wheelbarrow up to the charitable house attached to the big church.

The slightly built Garza novice scribbled a note on the cast, approving it, then cast a suspicious look at Eyck before moving on to the next patient.

"I should go to the priest's dormitory," Pash said, trying to sit up. "I'm fine now, and they have need of empty beds here."

All around them lay wounded Kat'hoondeman soldiers and more lay on pallets outside in the hallway, waiting for someone to either get well or die, freeing up a bed.

"You need to stay put," Eyck said, glancing to the side. No one was watching so he pulled his chair closer and surreptitiously took Pash's hand, squeezing it. "Just for tonight. All right?"

The priest frowned but didn't try to pull away. "Ok, fine."

"Do you remember how you fell?" Eyck asked in a low voice. "Why were you upstairs to begin with?"

Closing his eyes, Pash cleared his throat. "I was . . . looking for something."

Something in Pash's tone made Eyck's hackles rise. "What?"

Pash's lips went into a tight line, and the end of his tail flicked back and forth a few times before he answered. "Something to make you send Wex packing."

Astounded, Eyck dropped Pash's hand, crossing his arms over his chest as he sat back in the chair. He shook his head. "Schatten, and here I was thinking you two were finally starting to get along. I'm an arse for believing you'd finally gotten over this *bullshit* idea that Wex can't be trusted."

"And it's *true!*" Pash said angrily.

The attending novice turned at the sound, shushing them.

Pash lowered his voice, leaning towards Eyck. "Listen to me . . . What I found was worse than I'd imagined." The priest's eyes went wide. "He is a spy for the Oza, Eyck. He's sending Kirmen over to their side to help kill our soldiers."

"*What?*" It was such a ludicrous idea Eyck couldn't hold back his bark of laughter, causing the novice priest to frown at them again. Eyck raised an apologetic hand before the man came over to kick him out. "You're crazy," he said quietly to Pash.

"I'm not," the priest said, scowling. "He's been handing out leaflets printed by Oza cultists, promising freedom and equality to any Kirmen to—*stop laughing*, you idiot."

"Wex isn't working for the Oza."

"I know what I saw. There was a whole *stack* of leaflets full of enemy propaganda sitting in his—"

"Pash . . . why in the *Living Suns* did you think you were writing that note to Loomis for Wex the other day? Just for the fun of it?"

Pash's brows met above his nose as he stared at Eyck for a few long moments.

"Wex *can't* read or write."

The priest suddenly seemed less sure of himself. "Well, maybe it's an act."

"Trust me, it's not an act. You should see how frustrated he gets— no one's that good an actor."

"But, what if the cultists just tell him what the words are?" Pash said slowly, but he no longer looked convinced. It was obvious he was grasping at straws.

Eyck put his hands on his knees, leaning forward again. "You can't be serious. Pash, he doesn't even know that there are Kirmen with the Oza. I never passed on that news."

"I don't know, Eyck. He acted suspicious when I confronted him."

"Wait, Wex was there?" Eyck asked, alarmed. "Is that why you . . . Did he . . ." He couldn't even say it—Wex had a hell of a temper but would he actually hurt the priest?

"No. Hang on . . ." Pash said, shaking his head. He grimaced, his wound obviously painful. "I locked the door so you'd have to knock to get in—you left your key on the table—that way I could run downstairs and you wouldn't know I was snooping. I forgot the back door though. Wex came in that way, and he surprised me."

"And?"

Pash sighed, shifting to get more comfortable and winced again. "I showed him the papers I found. And he started doing his . . ." He fluttered his fingers in the air. "You know I can't make heads or tails of it."

"Then what happened?" Eyck asked, his voice low and anxious.

"Then he . . . lunged at me to get the papers back, but I . . . I must have stepped the wrong way because suddenly the floor wasn't there anymore. I don't remember anything after that."

"So, it was an accident." Eyck let out a relieved sigh, rubbing the back of his neck.

Pash's lips twisted to the side, and he lifted a shoulder. "I guess. I mean, I don't think he was *trying* to hurt me. But, if he's not an Oza spy, why did he try to take the papers? Why did he run? Innocent people don't do that."

"Pash, they do when the entire world has been against them since the day they were born," Eyck said gently. "You looked as good as dead. Put yourself in his boots."

Muscles rolling in his jaw, Pash nodded. "You're right. Eyck, you're right. I . . . *Suns*, I wasn't thinking." He held out his hand, looking honestly contrite. "I'm sorry. Truly."

"I figure a broken leg and a busted head is punishment enough," Eyck said, taking Pash's hand with a sigh. He squeezed it. "I have to find Wex and make sure he knows you're all right and that it was an accident."

Pash nodded. "Go on. I'll be fine. Where do you think he could be?"

Up until Pash's confession, he'd assumed Wex was still at the tavern, or back at the smithy wondering where in the hell he was. Now he could be anywhere. "I don't even know where to begin."

"You can begin by leaving Father Tormil to sleep," said the novice appearing at Pash's bedside, a stern expression on his spotted golden face. He pointed to the door. "Out."

"Sorry," Eyck mumbled. He patted Pash's shoulder and stood, passing the scowling Garza novice with a nod of apology.

Outside, it was dark, the street torches already lit. Eyck sighed, staring up at the sky—the silver moon was only a thin crescent, marking the end of the month, and the tiny golden moon hadn't risen yet. It would be black as pitch outside of town.

Maybe Wex went back to the smithy after he calmed down a bit, he thought hopefully. *Might as well start there.*

Chapter Twenty

Dappled sunlight began playing over Wex's eyelids, and he groaned, squeezing his eyes shut harder as he hugged himself for warmth.

If he woke up all the way, that meant he'd have to face the consequences of yesterday, and he wasn't quite ready for that yet. He ground his teeth together trying to summon sleep back to him, but he was cold and uncomfortably damp from the morning dew. Also, there was some sort of insect nearby making a strange buzzing sound similar to Mrs. Begmard's bees . . . but higher pitched and rhythmic. He sighed, turning onto his back, and finally allowed his eyes to open. Scratching his cheek, he shook his head.

You shouldn't have run. It was a stupid thing to do.

Wex wondered if there were patrols out looking for him and whether they would just kill him on the spot if he tried to turn himself in.

Stupid schatten idiot.

He lay there a while longer, letting the sun dry his fur as he called himself every name he could think of. He'd almost run out of insults when a new sound abruptly interrupted the insect's buzzing.

Frowning, he sat up, looking around, startling a small group of furry brown cutzoons in the process. The little creatures scattered, growling and hissing as they went, and after a few seconds, he was surrounded only by the rustling of leaves.

Then he heard the strange sound again. He couldn't make out the words, and it was faint, but the voice was definitely female. He cocked his head, listening hard. The next time she spoke, he frowned.

That doesn't make any sense. The voice was coming from beneath him.

Wex remembered the window he'd discovered the night before and crawled over to it, sweeping aside some debris that the wind had blown onto it during the night. He'd only uncovered twenty or so handswidths of glass before succumbing to a deep, dreamless sleep, but now in the morning light, he could see this was no window. It was shiny and black, and the surface was very faintly covered in a glittering gold pattern that reminded him of the stiff bands that priests wore in their collars.

What in the Three Suns?

As he sat there staring at the strange black glass, the woman spoke again. There was no mistaking it . . . she was trapped underground.

Heart pounding, Wex sat back on his heels, wondering what he should do. What if this was some sort of . . . devilry? He rubbed his knuckles against his lips.

What would Eyck do?

That was easy—Eyck would rescue the woman.

Jaw set, Wex began excavating more of the glass. *Don't worry . . . I'll help you.*

EYCK YAWNED AGAIN, shaking his head hard to wake himself up, but it was no use. He was exhausted.

"You should get some rest," Tembra said, placing a dainty hand on his forearm as she picked up his empty dish with the other. "Your friend will turn up."

"I have to keep looking for him, Tem," Eyck replied wearily. "I have to tell him Pash is ok and everything's going to be all right and . . ." He sighed, dropping his face in his palms.

"He means a lot to you, doesn't he?" the barmaid asked quietly, stroking Eyck's shoulder.

He nodded. "He does, yeah. More'n anything, I think."

Tembra was silent for a few moments, and Eyck wondered what was going through her mind.

She squeezed his shoulder, shaking it. "Come on. I'll make you an extra-strong cup of tea, and I'll send someone to get Besdoe. He's awfully thankful for Wex teaching them some of those hand signs— I'm sure he'd be happy to help you find your missing . . . friend."

"I appreciate it, Tem." He looked up at her, smiling. "Thank you."

Her return smile was a bit forced, and the sassy wink she gave him before turning away failed to hide the subtle sadness in her eyes. Obviously, she was disappointed, but whether it was because of the way things had ended between them or because he had turned out to be "that sort" of man, he couldn't tell. Eyck chose to believe it was the former.

He sighed and sat back, rolling his shoulders to relieve the stiffness, and smiled when Tembra set a large cup of steaming tea in front of him. He thanked her for the tea and was rewarded with a gentle squeeze to his forearm. No, there was no censure there, only concern. He patted her hand before she left him, and blew on his tea, waiting for Besdoe.

THE BLACK GLASS was large enough that ten Kat'hoondeman males could lie comfortably head to toe on the long side, and seven or eight on the short. Wex had also discovered that it was made up of smaller glass panels, each about forty handswidths square. A few of them were cracked, some severely so—small golden threads twisted out from the deep, jagged cracks.

Wex felt along the edge of the black glass where it met dirt, but he was starting to lose hope. There was no way he could lift it on his own.

Also, the woman had stopped calling out.

Chewing on the inside of his cheek, Wex sat back on his heels, wondering what he should do when he spotted something glowing faintly red in the shade of a large skerl's foot fern. It looked like an ember, but he had lit no fire.

Wex crawled over to the ember-thing. It was buried under a few fingerwidths of soil. Confused, Wex reached out and carefully dug the dirt away, revealing a round red object about the size of his palm that burned bright from within. While the object certainly was perplexing, the strangest part was that there wasn't any heat, only light. Digging around the red light, Wex found it was attached to a smooth, silvery surface.

In only a few minutes, he had uncovered a very large square of the silver material. It felt like metal but not one he recognized. It was matte like cast iron, but without any texture, and it was the color of tin —bright silver with a slight bluish tinge. Shallow lines crossed over it, impossibly straight and perfect, meeting up with a large rounded rectangle. On one side of the rectangle, near the red light, a small square of black glass was embedded in the surface.

Wex's heart was beating fast, and his mouth was dry. He was frightened, certainly, but terribly curious. What was this thing, buried in the ground in the middle of the woods? How had it gotten there? Maybe it was some sort of . . . weapon. He blinked, exhaling hard. What if it was something the Oza had built?

He shook his head. No, that was impossible. The Oza were said to be primitive compared to Kat'hoondemen, and he doubted even the very best Kat'hoondeman blacksmith in the kingdom could create metal like this. This had to be something else.

He thought about the gold pattern on the black glass and the Three Suns priesthood and took a closer look at the small square in the rectangle. It had no pattern, but he could see small dots beneath the surface of the glass. Slowly, he extended a finger to touch the black square and leapt backwards, fangs bared and every hair on his body standing on end.

The small dots had burned a brilliant green at his touch before the whole rectangle had slid to the side with a quiet hiss.

❖ ❖ ❖

"He came this way," Besdoe said, kneeling on the ground, parting the high grass to show Eyck a large boot print. Besdoe's skills as a mushroom hunter were proving to be quite the boon in the search for his wayward apprentice.

Eyck nodded, and the stocky little Ulven scanned the tree line in front of them.

Besdoe pointed to a gap between the Sick-a-Mores. "And went that way."

"How can you tell?" Eyck squinted at the trees.

"There's a broken branch. Right there."

All Eyck could see were two furry brown cutzoons sitting in the crook of some heavy branches, their eyes glinting green from the shade as they warily watched the two men. One of them bared its fangs—the forest creatures were skittish but could give a nasty bite if cornered—so Eyck stepped back and gestured for Besdoe to continue leading the way.

Landing Woods was huge and densely forested—he hoped the broken branches and boot prints kept up.

Following Besdoe through the trees, Eyck tried to put his mind at ease. After all, Besdoe spent most of the dry season in Landing Woods, tracking down and collecting the little rolling puffballs that fetched such a high price at the market. He had to know the woods like the back of his hand, no?

The air smelled and tasted strange . . . stale and dusty and metallic and *other*. Wex couldn't put his finger on it. It reminded him of cellars, but not musty exactly.

He peered down into the dark tunnel, his nostrils flared and fur standing on end. The green lights twinkled in his peripheral, one of them going amber, then a pale light began to grow below, like a captured sunrise. He jerked back, alarmed.

"Please stand clear. Hatch will close in ten seconds."

Wex bared his fangs, startled. The woman's voice was now very clear and close, but he couldn't see her or smell her.

Hatch? Like the hatch on a merchant ship? Does she mean this metal doorway? He could see a ladder against one wall of the tunnel.

As a second green light went gold, Wex frowned. *Yes, she must mean the doorway is about to close. But . . . will I be able to open it again?*

He took a deep breath and, with only a second or two remaining, grabbed the top rung of the ladder and eased himself down.

"Wex!" Eyck shouted. "Wex, can you hear me? Where are you, lad?" What if Wex was hurt or trapped or unable to follow the sound of his voice? It wasn't as if he could call out to tell Eyck where he was. Nevertheless, he continued shouting until his voice began to croak and his throat burned.

When it started to get dark, they had to turn back. They had no shelter and no food with them. Staying in the woods overnight would be foolhardy.

"We'll come again tomorrow," Besdoe said gently, but it was plain from his expression that he didn't hold out much hope for finding Wex.

Disheartened, Eyck sighed and nodded. *Wex . . . where are you?*

As the Ulven led them back through the trees, Eyck did something he hadn't done since he was a small child. He began to pray.

Chapter Twenty-One

Wex timidly walked down the metal corridor towards the faint white light, his heart pounding. He was still winded from the climb down; the rungs on the ladder had been very far apart, making for a perilous descent, his struggles doubled by the nervous sweat on his palms slicking his grasp. He was amazed he'd made it down in one piece.

The hatch had shut quietly above him, sealing him into . . . *whatever* this building was, and the woman hadn't spoken again. Maybe she was at the end of the corridor? He could see some shapes beyond, but it was too dim to see what they were.

Wex stopped when he reached the threshold, peering at the blocky shapes and twinkling lights beyond. The light began to brighten, seemingly triggered by his presence, and he went slack-jawed.

It was like nothing he had ever seen. The room was large with strange metal boxes that stood at head-height to Wex, and beyond, towering above the metal boxes was a huge black square of . . . glass? He took a step forward, frowning, curiosity making him bolder.

What is this place? What is it for?

He went around one metal box only to come up against a second. Some black cords trailed from behind this one, so he stepped high to get over them, trying not to get his boots tangled.

Then Wex froze in place, his heart in his throat.

There was a leg in front of him. No, *two* legs, clad in fine silvery white cloth. They were unmistakably legs because they ended in boots that looked a little like his own . . . but three times the size. Taking a shaky breath, Wex looked up. It was a huge man, seated in a huge chair, slumped over the metal box in front of him. For a few seconds, Wex could only stare.

It had to be a Titan . . . what other creature could be so large? But the Titans had disappeared over a thousand cycles ago. What was one doing in a strange metal building buried deep in the earth?

Cocking his head, Wex listened for the sound of breathing, but there was nothing except for his own shallow breaths and the beating of his heart, loud in his ears. Slowly, he reached out to touch the Titan's leg . . . and felt nothing but bone beneath the pant leg.

Wex sagged with relief, his knees like jelly, and let his breath burst out of him in a loud sigh. This turned out to be a mistake as it sent up a choking cloud of dust which made Wex tumble backwards over the black cords to land hard on his rump, bruising his tail. Coughing, he tried waving in front of his face to clear the air but only made it worse; every surface was covered in dust.

Wex pulled the collar of his shirt over his mouth and nose and stood, moving slowly so not to disturb the dust even more. When it had settled a bit, he grabbed the edge of the Titan's metal box—a work desk, possibly—and hoisted himself up. He waited until the dust settled again and leaned forward to peer at the Titan.

It wasn't *exactly* a skeleton. A thin covering of black clung to the bones, and Wex wondered if this was what remained of its skin. If so, the Titan had been either hairless or nearly so when it had died. There was no fur on the knobby black neck, but a semicircle of brittle grey hair clung to the back of its scalp.

Strange.

The Titan was dressed in what appeared to be a shirt and pants that were sewn together seamlessly to create something similar to what newborn pups wore. On the shoulder of this bizarre outfit was the round sigil of the Three Living Suns—three golden starbursts on a field of deep blue.

Beneath it were letters, but Wex couldn't tell if they were all the same sort that Eyck had tried to teach him. He got up on one knee on the metal desk, avoiding the strange objects sticking out of it, and leaned further over the Titan. On its desiccated wrist was what looked like a priest's collar—a stiff gold filigree band with the same patterns as on the black glass he had found outside.

"Power at sixty per scent," said the woman suddenly.

Wex nearly fell off the desk in surprise. His hand landed on one of the squares, and it lit up bright red at his touch. He yanked his hand back, panting in fear, but nothing else happened. The square just stayed glowing like an ember, but it seemed innocuous enough. Wex sighed, running his dusty hands over his head, wishing he could call out to the woman.

What does she mean about scents? And sixty what per scent? He sniffed the air and frowned.

It was complete gibberish even with the woman's strange accent. She didn't sound like any Kat'hoondeman he'd ever met. Maybe she was a Titan?

Annoyed, he signed, *"Who are you?"* to the air around him. *"Where are you?"*

"That is knee-oh tear-ess-tree-all sign language, developed in 23 67 see-ee by Helen Tem-bow of the in-stee-toot for non-hue-man relations," the woman replied. "Is this correct?"

Wex had no idea what it all meant, but he understood *sign language*, so he nodded, signing *yes* at the same time.

"I am the ship's com-pew-ter," she replied.

To his amazement, the giant black square on the wall lit up and words appeared on its surface.

"I'm sorry," Wex signed. *"I can't read."*

Instantly, a pair of hands resembling his own replaced the words on the screen. The hands signed, *"I am the ship's —"* followed by a gesture he'd never seen before.

"I don't understand this." He mimicked the foreign gesture.

The hands repeated the gesture. Then the woman spoke again, but the words made little sense.

"I am an arty fish oil intelligence belonging to the inter-nash-yawn-all sigh-aunts a-cord." The disembodied hands repeated what she said, only confusing him further because half the gestures were unknown to him.

"I don't understand these words, ma'am," he signed, using politeness to mask his frustration. *"Are they Titan words?"*

"One moment. Scanning," she said. "Dee-teck-ted altered indy-gin-oos lifeform."

Wex wanted to pull out his fur. Bearing his fangs, he signed, *"Stop using words I don't understand."*

"You are primitive."

He bristled at that. *"I am* not."

"My day-da bases may have been corrupted from lengthy storage with minimal power. Your clothing is consistent with pre-in-dust-tree-all Earth."

More gibberish in both words and gestures.

"Can you please come out where I can see you? And can you stop these signs? It's not helping at all. I can hear fine, I just can't talk."

"I am here." This time, the hands on the wall didn't move.

"What does that mean? Where are you?"

"I am in the ship. I am everywhere."

A shiver of unease went through Wex. *"Where is your body? Where is this ship?"*

"I am an arty fish oil intelligence. I only exist within the ship. You are inside the ship."

"You're a spirit?" The fur on his neck rose.

"One moment." The woman seemed to ponder. "I am the voice of the ship."

"You're the voice of a haunted ship that sails underground. Great." Maybe he'd hit his head harder than he thought on his run through the woods last night. Maybe he was still lying in his little earthen hollow having the strangest dream of his life.

"Would you like to see?"

Wex could only shrug helplessly. *"Fine. Show me."*

The black wall across the room came to life.

．　．　．

Hours had passed and Wex's backside was numb, but he stayed rooted to the spot, his mind spinning like a chariot wheel.

"Do you understand?" the ship's computer asked.

"I . . . *think so.* Show me the part about the D-N-A again," he asked, forming the three letters carefully the way she'd shown him.

"Which parts?"

"All of them."

Chapter Twenty-Two

"I'm sure he's fine . . . wherever he is," Pash said, squeezing Eyck's shoulder gently. "It's not like he's a pup. He survived a hell of a lot before he met you and got through whatever happened to him in the five sun-cycles after that. He went to Hange, for Suns' sake. He can handle himself."

Eyck clenched his jaw and squeezed the bridge of his nose, closing his eyes. He was absolutely exhausted. Two days of searching Landing Woods had come to nothing.

"Maybe you're right. But maybe he's lost, wandering in the woods. *Suns*, Besdoe nearly got *us* lost, and he spends days on end there," Eyck said, shaking his head. He looked up at Pash and gave a tired, humourless chuckle. "And that's after spending nearly three hours this morning following our own schatten boot prints from yesterday."

"What did you expect? He hunts mushrooms, not people. I think those require two very different skillsets," Pash replied with a wry smile, slowly sitting down in the armchair with a wince.

He carefully lifted his leg to rest it on the padded ottoman and sat back, resting his cup of tea on his thigh above his bark cast. They were sitting in the common room of the clergy house—Pash couldn't get to the smithy with his leg the way it was, so Eyck had come to him. Despite the recent strain on their relationship, Pash remained his closest friend, and that's what he needed right now.

"*Suns*, Eyck . . . you should think about getting some sleep. You look like hell."

Eyck laughed dryly again, shaking his head. "I can't sleep knowing he's out there, on the run."

The priest stared at him in silence, his brow deeply furrowed.

"What?" Eyck asked, irritated.

"You really do care for Wex."

"Of course, I do." Eyck scratched the back of his neck.

"*Why?*"

The question took Eyck by surprise—he frowned, crossing his arms.

"I'm not judging here," Pash said with a smile. "I just . . . don't see it. You're warm, friendly, respected. Downright garrulous. Wex is, well . . . he's the opposite of all that."

"Wex is friendly."

"With you, maybe." Pash touched his neck and grimaced. "You obviously haven't been on the wrong side of his temper."

"That was different."

"Still. He's standoffish. Brooding. The fact that he can't speak makes it even more difficult to connect with him."

"He can speak just fine. Just not with his voice."

"I just don't get it, is what I'm saying, Eyck."

Eyck let out a low, frustrated growl. "I don't care if you 'get' it or not. Schatten, I didn't 'get' why you suddenly found religion, but I stuck by you, didn't I? Pash, as my friend, you're supposed to be supportive. Can you do that? *Are* you my friend?"

Pash lifted a placating hand. "Yes. Yes, of *course* I'm your friend. Don't get your fur all ruffled." He laughed quietly. "Listen . . . I screwed up and wound up getting hurt and hurting you and hurting Wex. I'm an idiot. From now on, I promise that I will trust you and trust that you know what you're doing . . . and if that means me having to trust Wex, so be it—may I fall out of the Suns' Light and my soul be remanded in Darkness if I break that trust again." He solemnly placed a hand over his heart.

Eyck laughed. "No need to get so dramatic about it, you arse."

Grinning, Pash shrugged before his expression sobered. "I mean it though. And I'll do everything in my power to help you find him. Maybe I can ask Pastor Deechuk to write to the other pastors to tell their congregants to keep an eye out."

"You think that would work?" Eyck said hopefully. "I don't want to do anything that would spook him further."

"It's worth a—"

The front door banged open, sending scattered papers somersaulting through the air.

Wex staggered into the clergy house, panting and dragging a strange shimmery white bag behind him. He scanned the room, not seeing them immediately, but when Eyck rose out of his chair, Wex rushed towards him, signing something that made little sense: *"They're not chickens."*

Eyck grabbed Wex by the shoulders, the rush of relief so great the fur along his spine rose up in an excited crest. "You worried me, lad."

Wex went stiff in Eyck's grasp, his wide-eyed gaze on Pash sitting there, alive and relatively well.

"Suns," Wex said in a raspy voice, then slowly collapsed onto the floor.

WEX DRANK down the mug of water so quickly that it seemed half of it didn't even make it into his mouth. *"More,"* he signed, holding out the mug.

"Pace yourself, lad," Eyck said, but he went to the water pail and refilled the mug anyway. "And what do you mean by 'They're not chickens'?"

"I'll explain," Wex gestured one-handed as he gulped water. He sat back, put his mug down, and stared at Pash. *"First, tell him that I'm very sorry. And that I hope he can forgive me."* He wiped water from his chin. *"And if he wishes, he can break one of my legs in return."*

Eyck burst out laughing. "That's a bit extreme."

"What did he say?" Pash asked, confused.

"Tell him."

"All right, all right. Pash . . . Wex says he's *very* sorry, hopes you'll forgive him, and gives you permission to break one of his legs so you two will be even."

Pash barked out a laugh, but quickly stopped when he saw Wex's grim look.

"I'm sorry. Wex, you're forgiven. It was an accident. No need for more limbs to be damaged. It's fine. Really."

Wex let out a breath, visibly sagging with relief, then he surprised both Eyck and Pash by sliding off the divan to kneel in front of the priest, his dark eyes wide.

"Thank you."

It wasn't the more common temple-touch of apology, but Eyck saw no translation was necessary. Pash had already leaned forward to place his hand on Wex's shoulder, instinctively understanding the gesture.

"No need. Son, I've been quick to judge, and that is a terrible, *terrible* failing on my behalf," Pash said quietly. "I hope *you* can forgive *me* . . . I'd like us to be friends, you and I. Do you think that's possible?"

Wex smiled and nodded. Then he signed something else that had Eyck chuckling again.

"What?" Pash asked, grinning.

"He says that if you need help getting around town while your leg heals, he'll pull a schatten chariot for you and only you."

Pash laughed and squeezed the Kirmen's broad shoulder—Eyck was surprised Wex didn't flinch. Maybe he was past that now. Maybe he was truly beginning to heal.

"Now . . . I need your voice," Wex signed to Eyck, getting to his feet.

"Of course. It's yours. Always," Eyck replied, frowning up at him. "Whatever you want."

"I need to tell something to all the priests . . . to everyone." Wex looked around. *"As many as you can find."*

"That's easy," Pash said when Eyck had repeated Wex's words. "Ring the church bell and all will assemble in the styrerom." He pointed to the tower door.

Wex touched his temple in thanks.

"What *I* want to know is what in *Suns* this has to do with chickens," Eyck said to Pash, shaking his head as he watched Wex go.

"Me too."

Chapter Twenty-Three

"There is a Titan in the woods," Eyck translated for the assembled crowd of priests, nuns, novices, church workers, and parishioners, blinking in surprise even as he said the words out loud.

"Oh, my goodness," said a diminutive Garza in a nurse's apron, pressing her hand to her mouth.

"Eh? What did he say?" asked an elderly Ulven with a bandage around his head.

Eyck frowned at Wex, but Wex just gestured for him to continue.

"A half-day's walk northeast through Landing Woods, there is a boat buried underground," Eyck said and stopped when Wex shook his head.

"*No. Not that word. The one that means bigger*," Wex signed.

"Bigger boat? Oh . . . you mean ship?"

Wex nodded and resumed his story.

"All right—there is a *ship* buried underground. A ship that once sailed in the sky." Eyck winced at the skeptical expression that came over everyone's faces at once. "Inside, there is a Titan, long dead."

"That's impossible," Father Sprey said, shaking his head. "Titans can't die."

"It *is* possible," Wex said through Eyck. "They were mortals. Just like us. They came from a star very far away to explore our world and study the creatures that lived here—"

"What's that Kirmen doing?" asked a young woman in the front. "Can't he talk?"

"He *is* talking," Pash cut in. "Miss, please . . . we are trying to listen. Wex, continue."

"The Titans came in three sky ships. See?" Wex pulled something out of his strange silvery bag and held it up.

The room was filled with murmurs and little exclamations of surprise. In Wex's hand was a large stiff circle of cloth with the familiar holy motif on it—the round sigil of the Three Living Suns—but beneath it was written, ISA *WATHUTI* and under that in smaller gold letters, Marc Duval.

"Duval?" Eyck repeated after reading the words out loud for the crowd.

"Yes. And read this out for everyone please," Wex said, handing him a folded sheet.

Eyck unfolded it, marvelling at how smooth and white the paper was. On it was a list of names, most of which had a prefix he'd never seen before, though it was similar to the abbreviation for *mister*.

"Dister?" he tried, glancing up at Wex for help.

Wex shook his head then made the signs for *dock* and *tear*.

"Dock-tear?"

"Like Saint Doctor?" Pash asked, pointing to the tapestry on the nearest wall where the saint could be seen with his long golden knife.

"Yes," Wex said through Eyck. "Except, doctors are not saints. They are just very skilled people who explore or create or heal . . . like our healers. Most in the sky ship were doctors. These are their names. You'll see why this is important." Eyck skimmed the list, his amazement growing. He glanced over at Wex who nodded, so he began to read the names that were written in incredibly precise black characters, skipping the prefixes: "Einar Grendhal, Hanne Ulven, Matías Lozano, Andrea Garza"—soft gasps peppered up from the crowd—"Marc Duval, Hugo . . . Le-vey-skew?" He frowned.

Wex gestured. *"It's pronounced Levek."*

"Ah! Ok." Eyck peered at the paper and resumed. "Uh, Hugo

Levesque, Ilse Dankel, Laura Kirchman, Manjit Samra, and . . ." Eyck looked again at Wex, confused. "Rajesh Oza."

The gasps had turned to exclamations as he read, but now the roar of voices was so loud, Eyck took an involuntary step back.

While some of the names were a little different—like Kirchman instead of Kirmen, and Levesque instead of Levek—it was clearly the list of castes. The fact that the Oza were included in that list . . . now *that* was interesting.

"Quiet! Quiet down. Quiet everyone," Father Alfert yelled, waving his arms in the air to no avail.

A shrill whistle split the air, and the shouting stopped. Wex took his fingers from his lips and held up a hand.

"The Titans *did* create us," Eyck translated when Wex began to sign again. "But they were only men. Only mortals like us. They just had far greater skill and knowledge than we do."

"Preposterous!" Father Sprey had his arms crossed over his chest, his light-brown eyes narrowed. "If they were mortal, how could they have the talents of gods? It's completely nonsensical."

"Now, be reasonable, Father Sprey. Tell, me . . . Do you know how to temper steel like Eyckmigh Stromsmith?" Pash asked calmly, his smile benevolent. "I certainly don't." His gaze swept the congregation. "Can everyone make glass, like Ormerod Jones? Or work chamara, like Jenshy West? How about bean pies?" He smiled at Llod, the woodworker. "Llod, can you cook like Macy Tabor?"

Llod just snorted and switched his toothpick from one side of his mouth to the other. A few people chuckled, and Eyck could hear some hushed conversations. He honestly didn't know which was more surprising—everything that Wex had said or that Pash was defending it.

"Don't be stupid. Kat'hoondemen are not bean pies," Father Sprey replied, staring at Pash like he had lost his mind.

"But we *are* like bean pies," Eyck said slowly, watching Wex's hands. "There is a recipe inside us all, and the Titans knew how to work with that. It can seem like magic. It can seem like a miracle. But it's only skill."

"Why are we letting this *greyback* talk this rubbish?" asked Father Sprey, looking around the room.

However, he had seriously misjudged the crowd—the priest's use of the slur was met with several low growls. Some in the crowd bared their fangs, and there was the distinct swish of tails flicking in displeasure.

"There's no need for that language," Father Alfert said. "Father Sprey, you're looking tired. I believe you should go lie down."

"But—"

"No, I agree," Pastor Deechuk said, stepping forward and shaking his head. "Go lie down, Gerald, before you make more of an ass of yourself."

Father Sprey glanced about as if looking for support, but when no one spoke up, he turned on his heel and left the room, his overly large ears flapping up and down from the fury in his stride.

"All right. Now . . . what were you saying, my son?" Pastor Deechuk asked, looking up at Wex.

Wex smiled in thanks, then nodded to Eyck.

Eyck cleared his throat, wishing he had a glass of water. He continued to be Wex's voice, pausing now and then when Wex corrected him or clarified a detail.

"When the Titans came from the sky, they only intended on staying here for a little while, but something bad happened. Even though our world is a lot like theirs, they discovered that tiny creatures living in the ground had stolen the essence of the coal—the *fuel*—that allows their sky ships to fly, and made it so that they couldn't leave. The Titans were stuck, but they decided to make the best of it. They planted seeds they brought from their world to make food. They had frozen baby animals of all kinds that they thawed and fertilized and made grow."

There were still skeptical expressions everywhere, but at least the crowd was quiet now. Wex's story was bizarre, yes, but why would it be more probable that three living suns were birthed from the Mother star in the night sky and created the Titans who in turn created everything else?

"But they started dying. First the big animals got sick and died, then some of the Titans became sick too."

"The Five Cycle Sickness?" asked a Losano nurse.

"Yes," Wex replied through Eyck. "The Titans tried everything they could to find a cure, but one by one they started to die. During one of the between times when the Sickness was sleeping, the Titans came up with an idea to mix creatures from their world with creatures from ours because they didn't fall sick every cycle like theirs did."

"How can someone mix creatures together? They made fish lay with bees?" someone called out.

A smattering of laughter rippled through the crowd.

"It's not so different than what Mrs. Begmard does when she mixes flowers together to create new colours," Eyck said, coming to his own conclusion.

"It's called splicing," Mrs. Begmard chimed in, smiling. "That's how I make my pink and blue rose mallows. My great grandmother taught me splicing when I was just a pup," she said proudly.

Those around her murmured and nodded.

Then a flash of understanding went off in Eyck's head, and he turned to Wex, smiling.

"Oh! The chickens! *That's* what you meant? They're not really chickens because they're a mix of Titan creatures?"

"See? You're not stupid at all," Wex signed, grinning. *"Now don't get ahead of me. Keep talking."*

Eyck apologized and continued when Wex did. "Yes, the Titans mixed creatures together to make ones that could survive on this world. Many animals were lost for good . . . but we still have them in our words. Like *bull,* in *bullshit*"—Eyck grimaced as soon as he said the words—"sorry for cursing in church. Or did you ever wonder what a *dog* is and why you should let a sleeping one lie? Or what a hog is in *hogwash*? And why a *kat* gets your tongue? The only animals that are unmixed that survived are the bees and the fish and the mice. Everything else is mixed . . . including us."

The silence was deafening.

Pastor Deechuk stroked the pale-gold fur of his cheek, obviously meditating on Wex's words.

"People have always said that I must have Titan's blood in me because I'm so big," Wex resumed through Eyck. "But we *all* do. They were dying out, one by one, so they created the Kat'hoondemen to live on as their legacy . . . as their children."

"How did you come to learn all of this?" Pastor Deechuk asked quietly.

* * *

"*THE SKY SHIP TOLD ME. She let me watch—*" Wex was faltering, trying to find suitable gestures to explain. It was frustrating. There were so many new signs that Wex wished he could use, like *scientist* or *genetics* or *technology*, but he had to make do with the signs Eyck knew.

"*She let me watch the ghost of the dead Titan, Duval, on a wall made of glass. He spoke from the past. Daily. And the black glass preserved his words. To create a history for other Titans to learn from if they came again.*"

"I see," the old pastor said. "And this ship, why do you call it *she*?"

"*It speaks in a female voice . . . she's a Titan-created intelligent mind that lives within the ship. It is she who showed me our beginnings. They made us from the tiny forest creatures, the cutzoon, who were mute and without . . . function. The Titans mixed their . . .*" He stumbled again, trying to come up with a way to describe DNA. "*Internal body recipes with the recipes inside the cutzoon, and that changed them and gave them the ability to walk on two legs and to speak and to think.*"

"Did he just say we're made from *cutzoons*?" asked a potbellied Losano of the Dankel next to him, his eyes wide.

The pastor lifted a frail-looking hand, shushing them.

"And the ghost of this dead Titan . . . he told you all this?" he asked Wex.

"*Yes, sir. He and his husband were the last Titans to survive—*"

There was a chorus of gasps, and Pastor Deechuk frowned at Eyck.

"I'm just telling you what he's saying," Eyck said, shrugging.

"It's blasphemy," said a narrow-nosed Garza in a novice's tunic. "Why are you tolerating this, Father?"

Pastor Deechuk shot him an icy glare, then nodded to Wex. "Continue."

"The Titan Duval thought he and his husband Levek survived the Sickness because there had been an illness in their . . . kingdom when they were pups. There was something in their blood that wasn't in the blood of the others, so after the other Titans died, the two of them were able to continue teaching and watching over us.

"The husband Levek died of old age, and the younger Duval lived for a long time on his own. He became very old and weak and could only watch the Kat'hoondemen from a distance using a . . ." Wex grasped for words to describe the flying drone Marc Duval had used to keep an eye on them. "A floating eye in the sky. And so we began to forget the truth about the Titans, and eventually they became strange holy creatures in the Sun Scrolls.

"The Titan Duval was one hundred and fifty-three sun-cycles when he died. He and the other Titans had taken care of us for over twenty generations.

"We do still have things the Titans gave us, like the golden collar bands, which were used for communicating with us. But, they eventually stopped working because we didn't know how to fix them, and these things just became . . . symbols."

"I see," replied the pastor. "And the ship . . . Why didn't it stop communicating like the bands?"

"It drinks the sun," Wex replied, knowing how ridiculous that sounded. "I woke it up by accident."

"I would like to see this . . . sun-drinking ship for myself," Pastor Deechuk said with a smile.

Wex couldn't tell if the old man was just humouring him.

"Did the Titans create the Oza?" called out a man from the back of the crowd. "Is that why the name is on that list?"

Wex nodded.

"Why in the Three Suns would the Titans create abominations like the Oza? What is their purpose?" asked the Garza novice, his tone cynical. A few in the crowd nodded, and the murmurs got louder.

"They are no different than we are, except in one very important way— they are born immune to the Five Cycle Sickness. The Titans Duval and Levek created a potion from their own blood and used it on mice, and it worked so well, they used it to make one last Kat'hoondeman breed—the Oza.

They were too late to protect their Titan brothers and sisters, but they found something to protect us . . . their children.

"The Oza were meant to live amongst us and mingle their bloodlines with ours so eventually no pups would get sick ever again from the Sickness."

A hush fell over the crowd as the assembled stared at him and Eyck in shock.

"That can't be true," one woman said, looking horrified. Her mate put his arm around her, comforting her.

"This is absolutely and completely ridiculous. For one, the Oza aren't even on the Caste Ladder! How do you explain *that*?" asked a sneering Samra.

Wex stared at the man for a moment, then took a breath to calm his nerves before lifting his hands again to answer him. *They are not going to like this.*

"The Titans didn't create the Caste Ladder. I don't know who did, but that happened after Duval died."

"It's in the scriptures!"

"Do you have proof of this?"

"He's out of his mind!"

"Blasphemy!"

"Someone get that dirty, lying Kirmen out of here! Lock him up!"

The crowd erupted again, but Wex couldn't help but notice it wasn't as loud as before. Several of the gathered were just quietly watching Wex with thoughtful or curious expressions.

A group of four young priests stood apart from the rest—Wex had noticed them nodding as he spoke—and now they were talking quietly amongst themselves.

However, quite a few older priests were visibly angry, as well as the mouthy Garza novice who had spoken up before—he looked mad enough to spit. It was one thing to suggest their creator gods were godlike mortals; it was quite another to attack the very foundation of Kat'hoondeman society.

One nun was quietly weeping in the corner of the room. There were quite a few dazed expressions among townsfolk. The Losano nurse was grinning from ear to ear.

"The Titans didn't create us with any specific function in mind—they

didn't do something to the Ulven to turn them into artists or to the Dankels to give them special farming abilities," Wex signed while Eyck shouted his words above the din of the crowd. *"There are ten breeds of Kat'hoondemen, but that's only because the Titans liked the way those fur patterns looked. That's it. That's all."*

Eyck actually began to laugh a little as he translated, shaking his head, and Wex grinned.

"They just thought we were pretty," Wex signed.

Eyck didn't bother relaying the last part. He just looked at Wex with amusement. "Are you *trying* to get us killed?" he asked, gesturing to the yelling crowd.

"Blasphemy!"

"Lies!"

"The Oza are not Kat'hoondemen. I *won't* believe it."

As more and more voices screamed out at Wex, he watched Pastor Deechuk. The man seemed to be having a silent argument with himself. Finally, he lifted his head, his pale-blue eyes shrewd.

"All right. We've heard enough," the old pastor said. He gestured to some robed brothers standing nearby. "Clear the room. Father Alfert, please make sure those going back to the charitable house don't rile up those convalescing. Now, you two," he said, turning to Wex and Eyck. "And you too, Father Tormil. Follow me. Harnark, assemble the neophytes . . . you know the ones I mean."

The narrow-nosed Garza frowned and opened his mouth to speak, but Pastor Deechuk just levelled a look at him. "Harnark, do as you're told, or I swear to the Three Suns that you shall remain a novice until you're as grey as I am."

Harnark clamped his mouth shut and nodded, glowering at Wex a moment before following the pastor's command.

In silence, the three of them followed Pastor Deechuk down a long corridor and through a large wooden door to his private quarters. The anteroom was lined with overflowing bookshelves on all sides, with a colourful woven carpet depicting the Passages of the Suns in warm tones, the red Mother star at its centre. Three overstuffed, comfortable-looking chairs sat in the middle of the room, but it was to a big untidy desk in the far corner they were led to.

The old pastor sat down on a creaking wooden chair, leaving Wex and Eyck standing opposite the desk. Pash sank thankfully into the single small chair at Pastor Deechuk's gesture.

Wex chewed on the inside of his cheek, wondering what the punishment would be for sharing the truth about what he'd seen—in his excitement, he hadn't thought about the repercussions.

He looked over at Eyck, his stomach twisting as he realized his reckless actions had probably condemned the blacksmith to share his fate.

But what about the priest? He glanced at Pash, wondering why he had been included. Perhaps it was because he had challenged Father Sprey? Pash was staring at the thick gold priest's ring on his finger, a frown on his bronze-furred face.

"Well, my boy, you've certainly turned our world on its head." The pastor pressed his lips together, staring up at him with narrowed eyes. He put his elbows on the desk and clasped his hands, resting his chin on top of them.

"What happens now?" asked Eyck in a quiet voice.

His tone was subdued, but his hands were clasped in front of him so tightly, Wex thought he could hear his knuckles creak from the strain. The blacksmith looked frightened. Wex clenched his jaw, the fur rising up his back, ashamed and furious with himself for putting Eyck in danger.

"I could have you all silenced," Pastor Deechuk mused. "I could say that you're suffering from delusions . . . discredit you."

"*I was only—*"

Pastor Deechuk made a harsh noise in the back of his throat, cutting off Wex's gestures even before Eyck had time to start translating.

"I could have you jailed, like a few of that lot called for," he said, gesturing to the hallway and the styrerom beyond. "I could . . . but I *won't*." The pastor let out a sigh and sat back in his chair with another loud creak.

"Father, it is with sincere gratitude that—" Pash was cut off by a stony glare from the pastor.

"Will you let me talk, for *Suns'* sake?" Pastor Deechuk waited until the three of them had nodded before resuming. "I was going to say, I won't censor you, nor clap you in irons because time and progress marches on, and we were headed in this direction anyway. Besides, I'm tired and old, and I don't give a *damn* anymore."

A gasp went up from someone, and Wex turned to find the novice Harnark staring wide-eyed at the pastor. Behind the belligerent Garza were the four young priests Wex had noticed before. Pastor Deechuk beckoned them closer.

The neophytes all smiled at Wex—by their expressions, he could tell they were burning with questions for him but were holding their tongues in the presence of the prickly old pastor.

"These young'uns have been bending my ear for months on end with their theories that the caste system was not, in fact, created by our makers, but emerged out of a power struggle that took place in the sudden *absence* of those makers. Now that you've let the proverbial *kat* out of the bag, I can attest that there are, in fact, documents and relics supporting those theories."

Wide-eyed, Wex stared at the pastor. The shocked silence was so complete it was deafening. Pastor Deechuk just looked a touch amused.

"*So, you already* knew *all the things I said earlier?*" Wex signed, appalled.

"Some. Not all. But some, yes. For instance, like you said . . . there were three ships. Not suns."

"*Do you know where the other ships are?*"

"I know where one is," Pastor Deechuk said. He tapped his foot on the tiles. "It's right beneath us in the catacombs. However, no amount of sunlight would ever get it to speak, I'm afraid. It's buried under a millionweight of stone and dirt—probably happened during the earthquake that damaged the foundation of the church when I was a pup. The sky ship is all but destroyed, but we have preserved pieces of it—silvery metal like no other . . . and black glass like you described."

Wex glared at the pastor, clenching his jaw to keep from leaping over the desk to throttle the old man.

"*Why didn't you* say *anything? Who else knows?*"

"The archbessop, me, and the other pastors. And as for why?" Pastor Deechuk gave a long sigh and scratched his chin. "The long and short of it was that I was expressly forbidden to by the archbessop. Trust me, I wanted to tell everyone the truth for many sun-cycles now, but I had to make a choice: reveal the truth and spend the rest of my life rotting in the archbessop's oubliette, or keep the church's secrets and continue supporting and nurturing the souls of my congregation. You can call me a coward, but I made my choice and stayed silent.

"But you, my boy, have no covenant with His Holy Excellency, now do you? You're free to share what you've learned."

"Fuck the archbessop." Wex glared at Eyck when he hadn't translated after a few seconds.

The big blacksmith looked miserable but repeated what Wex had said.

"And fuck you. You could have helped so many of us have better lives . . . or lives at all. Your silence kept those like me in chains."

Pastor Deechuk nodded. "I know. And for that I am ashamed and deeply sorry." He sighed again. "When I first was told of the secret documents, I didn't believe they were real. It came from a place of . . . arrogance, I suppose." He held out his arm to them. "Most just assume that I'm Losano because my fur faded to gold as the white started to take over—I don't even have spots, but no one seems to notice—and I've never corrected them . . . But, I'm not Losano. I think even those who knew me when my fur was copper-bright have forgotten that I'm Dankel, through and through. My father was a farmer, my grandfather was a farmer, my great-grandfather—" He gestured. "Well, you get it. I was the very first Dankel in South Galetsy to become a priest, and then the very first to become pastor. I thought I was special. I thought I was unique. Priests are supposed to be humble, I know, but I let pride lead me down the wrong path. I thought that if the Caste Ladder was just something someone made up, if everyone were truly equals, then how could I be special?" He chuckled and shook his head. "And *Suns* did I want to remain special. The sins of youth . . ."

"That's not an excuse," Wex signed angrily.

"I didn't say it was. Wex, I was *wrong*. The older I got, the more I realized I had made a mistake in doubting the veracity of these documents and knew it was a terrible thing that the church hid—or in some cases, destroyed—the truth of our origins . . . and I know I was complicit. There *is* no excuse. What matters to me now is what we do with what you've learned."

"What *will* we do with it?" asked Pash.

"Well, I assume this young man would like the truth shouted from every rooftop, am I correct?"

Wex nodded.

"While it sounds like a noble, wonderful idea . . . I think it would be dangerous to do so. Many will be absolutely furious with the truth that the caste system was not created by our gods . . . or that the Oza are our kin."

"That's putting it mildly, Father. You saw how they were foaming at the mouth just now, and there were only a few Samra in the crowd. Imagine telling a whole room full of schatten bluebloods that they bleed the same red as Kirmen," Eyck said.

"Exactly," replied Pastor Deechuk. "And you risk the chance of the truth being buried again. They have power and money and can sway the other breeds to their side easily—they always have. So, it needs to be done *properly*. And I have a suggestion. May I?" He folded his hands on the desktop.

All eyes were on Wex, waiting for his reply.

It felt so odd to be deferred to. It made him feel proud . . . but also sort of *itchy*. His tail-tip flicked back and forth. *"Go on."*

"With this fancy, talking sky ship, you may have just given us invaluable tools in the war with the Oza."

"But, I didn't see weapons. I don't think there are any. The Titans were peaceful."

"I didn't say weapons," replied the old pastor. "I said *tools*. Specifically, knowledge. We can share what you've learned with them as an olive branch. Maybe it will bring an end to the war, or at least make them open to peace talks. Plus, if you're right about the Oza being immune to the Sickness, perhaps it will be a boon to us all."

"You can't be serious, Father," said the Garza novice, baring his fangs. "Even if there is a single grain of truth in what the Kirmen says, which I don't believe, why in the Sun's Light would we tell the Oza?"

"Because it's the right thing to do. If they are our kin, the tenth Kat'hoondeman breed, why do we live apart? How did this happen? If we share what we have learned with them, perhaps they can shed some light on these questions—maybe they know why the schism happened."

"I've been among the Oza," Pash said. "I don't know if they can be reasoned with, or even if their culture has a way of preserving their history. They seem . . . utterly feral."

"And yet, when their leaders communicate with us, their missives aren't mad scribblings, nor do they seem at all uneducated. Right? Perhaps there's more there that we aren't seeing. The stories paint them in a dreadful light, but what if there's purpose behind it? What if these stories are meant to keep us away?"

"They started the war," Harnark pointed out.

"Only after *we* encroached on the only tiny bit of fertile land they have," said Pash, his tone pensive.

Wex thought he might be warming to the idea of approaching the Oza.

Rubbing his forehead, Pash stared off at nothing, obviously thinking. After a few moments, he spoke again. "I think information exchange would have to happen through official paths."

"Yes. Through the King's Council," said Pastor Deechuk. "That's the only way it would work. With the help of these young ones," he said, gesturing to the four priests, "I will draft up a document containing everything Wex has discovered and recommend that we approach the Oza, stressing that this could make way for peace talks. My own personal account, and my seal, will lend credibility. King Enoch has no love for priests, I know, but if the document comes from me and not the archbessop, and *against* the archbessop's wishes . . . I think he might listen to me.

"Plus, he'll have solid facts to back his own laws addressing the caste system, slavery, intermarriage, and whatever else he's got planned. People will still be furious, certainly, but having it come from the king himself should mitigate things, one would hope." The old pastor frowned up at Wex. "Well, what do you think? Is this acceptable?"

"The king is Samra. What makes you think he will welcome the truth?" Wex asked, eyes narrowed.

"I don't. But if he doesn't, I promise to you I will be one of your voices singing out the truth from the church rooftop."

Wex couldn't help but smile at the image of the old pastor perched on the church's high sloped roof. *"What about the archbessop? You aren't worried he's going to imprison you?"*

"I imagine I'll have the king's protection . . . but even if I don't, it's past time that these things come out of the shadows."

Wex nodded. *"All right. It's acceptable. But . . . when will this happen?"*

"As soon as my leg's healed," Pash said. "I will personally travel to the king's palace and deliver the letter to his hand."

Surprised, Wex turned to Pash. *"I didn't think you would agree with this. You're not angry that your religion is based on lies?"*

When Eyck translated, there was an uneasy silence as the members of the priesthood exchanged glances.

Pash took a deep breath and let it out before answering. "I wouldn't call it . . . lies, entirely. I thought Walking in the Suns' Light was the absolute truth, but now I've found out that truth was inspired by an even more . . ." Brow furrowed, Pash seemed to be searching for the right word. *"Astonishing* truth. I look forward to learning more about it. I'm not angry. I'm . . . grateful. And so, I will go to King Enoch." He smiled at Wex.

Wex smiled back. He'd expected the priest to act like Harnark was. It seemed Pash was more open-minded than he had given him credit for. Maybe he was starting to see what Eyck saw in the man.

"I'm afraid we have to act sooner than that. News will spread, and I think we need to stay ahead of it as much as possible," said the old pastor. "No . . . I think I will go myself."

"But, Father . . . you're . . .uh . . ." Harnark started.

"I'm old, yes, but not completely enfeebled. I can sit in a chariot for a day." Pastor Deechuk clapped his hands together once. "All right. The matter is settled. I will take the King's Road, and we can all pray that King Enoch is the intelligent man that I think he is," he said, picking up a quill to write himself a note on a scrap of paper while muttering what sounded like a short prayer under his breath.

Wex looked at the silvery-white bag he'd borrowed from the ship, suddenly remembering he had brought something else back with him —maybe the most important thing of all. He reached into it and handed a white card from within to Eyck. He'd had the ship—the ISA *Wathuti*—make up a stack of them, using the mineral-paper it could create at will.

"What's this?" asked the blacksmith, staring at the little drawings of hands that covered the square of paper.

Wex held up his hand and slowly made three gestures. *"W-E-X."*

For a moment, Eyck just looked confused, but then his green eyes widened. He looked down at the paper and back up at Wex. "Do that again."

Wex repeated the hand signs, waiting for Eyck to scan the card after each letter before moving on to the next.

"Holy hells! Sorry, Fathers. Wex, is this what I think it is?" Eyck's tail swished back and forth in excitement.

Grinning, Wex lifted his hand and spelled out *"I-K-E,"* and then he paused and added *"M-E."*

This time, Eyck's brow wrinkled up in confusion, and Wex repeated the letters slowly. Had he gotten it wrong? He'd practiced at least a dozen times on his way back from Landing Woods.

When Eyck shook his head, not understanding, Wex felt a crushing disappointment. Maybe he couldn't learn to spell after all, even with what the ship's computer had called a "neural loophole," using finger gestures to spell instead of written letters.

Then Eyck's face split in a huge grin, and he grabbed Wex by the shoulders to give him a few jarring shakes.

"*Suns* . . . you mean *Eyckmigh*, don't you? Oh, lad, *yes*! That's not how I spell it, but that is certainly my name. Ike Me. But . . . *how* is this possible?" Eyck searched his eyes, looking absolutely thrilled.

"The ship taught me the spelling. Sorry, I guess she got it wrong. It was difficult—there are so many sounds that go with one letter sometimes. It'll take a while to figure out, but with your help . . . I think I might be able to

spell," he said, a little embarrassed by how hard Eyck was beaming at him. *"I only know W-E-X and I-K-E M-E and D-N-A so far. It's not much."*

"I don't care. It's bloody amazing, lad," Eyck said.

Then, right there in front of the clergymen, he wrapped his arms about Wex and hugged him close, temple to temple like a mated couple.

After a few seconds, he obviously remembered where he was, because he quickly released Wex and stepped back. He scratched the back of his neck, a sheepish expression on his face, and shrugged an apology. The only member of the church not wearing a shocked or disgusted expression was Pash—he just looked a little wistful.

Anxious to shift the focus away from the scandalous show of affection, Wex dug into his bag for something else he had brought back with him. It was called a "photograph"—a picture of an event or of people frozen in time.

This one showed the Titan scientists on the day they had arrived on their planet. The ten of them wore matching silver one-piece outfits with mission patches on their shoulders and patches on their chests with their names and the name of one of the three ships they had arrived in: the ISA *Wathuti*, *Thunberg*, and *Attenborough*.

In the photograph, all of them had bright, excited smiles on their strange naked—or mostly naked—pink, tan, and brown faces. It had been taken before they had found out they were stranded, back when they were still full of hope.

Wex handed the photograph to the old pastor who gasped as he peered at it.

"My goodness," the old Dankel said. "My good Suns. These are them? The Titans?"

"Yes," Wex replied. *"The ones whose names were read out. The ones we're named after."*

Pastor Deechuk, clutched at his chest, and for a moment, Wex worried the man was going to have a heart attack.

"This is incredible. Absolutely incredible. Never did I think I would see the faces of gods. Never. Oh my Suns." The pastor shook his head, his whole face seemed lit from within with wonder.

"But, Father," Wex said. *"They weren't gods. They were mortal men."*

As Eyck translated the words, he made his voice gentle.

After a moment, Pastor Deechuk looked up from the photograph. "What is a god, my son? Isn't it a being that comes from the heavens to create new life? How, then, are these men and women not gods if that is exactly what they did?"

Wex pondered the pastor's answer and decided he didn't have a reply. He smiled politely and shrugged.

The others surrounded the desk, staring down at the Titan scientists in reverent silence.

After a few minutes, Pastor Deechuk chuckled softly to himself, then looked up at Wex again, his rheumy eyes crinkled in subtle amusement. "I have to say . . . They were very *odd*-looking creatures, weren't they?"

Wex laughed, nodding.

"Now . . . *when* can we see this sky ship of yours?" asked the pastor, folding his hands again to rest his chin upon.

"Would you take us right now?" asked one of the neophyte priests eagerly.

Now? Wex looked around, his brow furrowed.

They were all awaiting his answer with hopeful expressions, but he was tired and so schatten hungry, *and* the sun would set soon . . . not to mention how sore his feet were from walking for almost half a day. He sighed softly to himself, loath to disappoint everyone considering how all these religious men—Wex side-eyed the pugnacious Harnark—*most* of these religious men had shown themselves to have a bit of a rational side. Shoulders slumped, Wex lifted his hands to gesture his agreement, but Eyck spoke up before he had a chance.

"The lad is near-dead on his feet and sure to be starved," the blacksmith said, turning to Wex, his jade-green eyes full of warmth. "I'm sure it can wait until morning."

Weakly, Wex nodded.

Marc Duval had finished all the rations the Titans had brought with them from their world, relying entirely on his little forest garden in the last few cycles of his life. Thankfully, the ship had been able to pull water from the air outside for Wex to drink or else he might have not made it back.

"Morning's a good time for it," Pash said with a firm nod. "The symbolism is strong."

"How so?" asked Pastor Deechuk.

"It'll be the dawn of a new day," Pash said, looking over at Wex. He held his gaze with a pensive frown on his lean bronze face, still twisting his priest's ring in his fingers. "*And* the dawn of a new world."

Wex nodded, then smiled. A new world—he liked the sound of that.

EYCK WATCHED Wex sink tiredly into his usual chair at the table and cross his arms on the scarred surface so he could rest his head on them. Not sure what to do, Eyck stood there for a moment, then grabbed the basket of food from its usual place and began rummaging through it, hoping he could put together a half-decent meal for the two of them.

He felt . . . strange. It was a mix of excited and nervous, relieved and proud, all jumbled up inside him, putting a twist in his innards and making his heart beat too hard. He took a deep breath, trying to calm himself enough that his hands would stop trembling.

Earlier, he'd been so thrilled that Wex was just blurting out everything that he'd learned to the crowd, just thumbing his nose at those tiresome priests and their schatten Sun Scrolls, that he hadn't given a blasted thought towards the consequences.

But then, for one heart-stopping moment, standing in the pastor's study, he had feared he would lose Wex all over again, so soon after being reunited—and he had felt the ground open up beneath him. Eyck frowned, slicing off as many stale bits of bread as he could.

In that terrible instant, he had truly understood just how *much* Wex meant to him.

Grimacing as he searched for lettuce leaves that weren't completely wilted, he started at the touch on his shoulder. As always,

Wex moved with a silent grace that belied his size. Eyck searched Wex's expression, his chest tight with sympathy for the fatigue in the young man's eyes.

"*I'm sorry,*" Wex signed slowly, his lips pressed tight together and the lines of his face taut.

"Sorry for what?" Eyck asked, smiling. "For making me jump out of my fur?"

"*For making you afraid* earlier. *When we were with the pastor,*" Wex replied. "*I wasn't thinking ahead to what they might do to you because of me.*"

"Lad . . . the only thing I was afraid of, was losing you. I don't give a schatten's care in hell what happens to this old pelt of mine as long as you're by my side." He cupped the side of Wex's face, stroking his soft silver fur with his thumb.

Wex's eyes widened, his expression going shy, and he looked away —Eyck felt the gentle purring before he heard it. Then Wex pulled away, his brow furrowed.

"*Don't be silly, old man. I'm not going anywhere,*" Wex signed, the muscles rolling in his jaw.

His gestures were brusque from what Eyck assumed was a bout of self-consciousness and his tail-tip flicked from side to side, but his hackles hadn't raised. A moment later, all Eyck could see was teasing good humour in the lad's dark-brown eyes.

"*You haven't finished training me yet.*"

Eyck laughed and was about to tease Wex back, but a shout from outside startled them. They stood staring at the door, fists clenched and fangs bared. Wex let out a deep growl.

"What in the bloody Suns . . ." Eyck approached the door and peered through the little window in it.

He frowned and took a second look before opening the door to the two City Guardsmen outside. Heart in his throat, he wondered if the old pastor had changed his mind. He glanced over at Wex. The young man had taken a wary step back.

"Evening, Stromsmith," said the Garza on the right. "We came to keep an eye out for trouble."

"Should any come calling, that is," added the second guard, a surly looking Losano with a snaggletooth poking up over his top lip.

"Oh, thanks Suns—here I was thinking we were about to be hauled off to the stockades," Eyck replied, his shoulders sagging with relief.

"Wouldn't let that happen," the first said, rolling up his sleeve to show Eyck his arm. Eyck was confused, but then Wex clicked his tongue, getting his attention.

"He's of mixed stock. They both are," he signed, pointing to the subtle orange spots among the usual brown ones in the Garza's rich gold fur. Similarly, the other man had a very faint feathering of pale-gold along his bronze nose and up his forehead. Apparently, Wex and he were gaining supporters. *"Tell them that we appreciate their help."*

The men touched their temples and bowed their heads low when Eyck translated—he let out a hoarse chuckle, embarrassed by the fuss they were making, and cleared his throat.

"You wouldn't happen to have brought some food with you lads?" he asked.

" 'Fraid not," replied the Garza guard.

"Ah," Eyck replied, disappointed.

"But I think they might have," said the Losano, gesturing towards the street.

Brow wrinkled up, Eyck stepped out onto the porch, Wex at his side. A small group was gathering in the dusk outside the smithy, some folks he knew well, some only in passing, but they all had something in common, and it heartened him to see it—everyone wore hopeful smiles. And sure enough, a few had brought baskets and platters of food with them. News always travelled fast in South Galetsy.

He looked over at Wex. "Uh, if you're too tired . . . I can send them away . . ." But, at that moment, his stomach let out a loud, gurgling moan.

Wex grinned, poking him in the belly. *"I'm supposed to be the one who's starving. What have you been doing all day to make you so hungry, hm?"*

"Worrying, lad. Lots of worrying," Eyck replied with a crooked smile.

Wex's expression fell, and all Eyck wanted to do was pull him into his embrace . . . but that would have to wait for later.

He settled for throwing an arm around Wex's shoulders and pointing to the crowd. "Now, do we let them in? Are you really up for answering half a hundred questions?"

Wex let out a long sigh, then straightened his shoulders and nodded. *"Not really, but might as well get this over with. People need to know the truth."*

"I think you're doing a good thing, Wex," Eyck said quietly. "And, don't worry, I won't let them stay too long, just long enough for them to ask a question or two while we fill our bellies."

He winked and Wex smiled.

Lifting his head, Eyck made a sweeping gesture. "Ok, all right, then. Come on in, folks. Don't know where we're all going to bloody sit, but come on in. Everyone's welcome."

Chapter Twenty-Four

One Sun-Cycle Later

A fter dropping off the cooper's new barrel hoops, Wex decided to take a big detour around the church. Protests were still taking place in front of it almost daily, and despite the king having sent a dozen of his own men to help the City Guard keep the peace, it often turned ugly. Wex really didn't want to get caught up in the violence if he could avoid it—some blamed him for everything that had happened.

As the late pastor had predicted, the Samra had used their power and money to sway many against the new laws, focusing their ire on South Galetsy from whence they believed the "treasonous" shift in power had first emerged.

Wex could hear the yelling from two streets over as he walked. The crowd sounded bigger than normal, but he knew it was because the Samra were positively enraged by King Enoch's new wage law forcing them to pay their workers a minimum amount.

Following the abolition of slavery, hundreds of Kirmen had found themselves suddenly unhoused and starving with nowhere to turn—their freedom finally granted, but without a support system in place to ease the transition.

Lacking resources or skills to find themselves employment in the face of deep-rooted social stigma, many Kirmen had gone back to their ex-masters, earning mere coppers for their backbreaking and often demeaning labour. The king's law was meant to put a stop to that, but Wex wondered how much it would help. If *he* were king, he'd open his coffers to the ex-slaves and provide for them until they were able to take care of themselves. Smiling, he imagined himself as king but quickly sobered when he turned onto the next street and noticed yet another boarded-up home.

In addition to those protesting the ban on slavery and the end of the caste system were those who were dead set against the Oza being welcomed into the kingdom. When the provisional peace treaty with the Oza had passed, permitting restricted immigration, some folks in town had simply packed up and left, heading north to be further away from the border.

Speaking of which . . .

Whistling to himself, Wex decided to drop by Jenshy West's old chamara shop to see how the new family was settling in. He was glad the irritating little twit had shown his true colours, turning tail to run away from the "big bad Oza"—good riddance to bad rubbish.

Wex picked up the pace when he saw the Sturriges were struggling to set up a new double-wide chamara drying rack in front of their shop. They made an interesting couple—Charrie, a diminutive bright-orange Dankel and her husband Gaffroi, a broad-shouldered Duval with a curious white spot over one eye. Wex had liked them from the moment Gaffroi had clasped arms with him like an equal upon being introduced.

The Sturriges had moved into town less than a month back, seeking a home where their daughter would face less discrimination. It still amazed Wex that South Galetsy had become a sort of mecca of acceptance over the last sun-cycle—some even joked that the town should change its name to *New* South Galetsy to mark its evolution.

"*U need help?*" he finger-spelled slowly.

Before Gaffroi had even pulled out the alphabet chart from his pocket, his daughter spoke up from the stoop where she was playing with a pair of rag dolls. Kini was a pretty pup with patchwork fur in white, black, and orange and was one of the brightest of Wex's pupils.

"He's asking if you need help," she said to her father as she grinned up at Wex.

Wex touched his temple in thanks and held up the back of the drying rack while Charrie and Gaffroi set up the support posts and Kini supervised.

He'd begun teaching sign language at the school three days a week, something he'd had to force himself to do at the beginning—being around children was difficult for him because they reminded him of his own stolen childhood—but after only a few classes, he'd found himself looking forward to seeing their bright, earnest faces. They fascinated him with their eagerness, disturbed him with their dramatic emotional shifts, and confused and amused him with all their silly games.

This week's newest diversion was to take the gestures Wex had taught them to concoct all sorts of absurd insults.

"Look!" Kini said, calling him over when the last post was secured.

Wex watched her carefully sign, *"Boys smell like feet."*

He laughed, then gave her a mock scowl.

"Hey, I'm a boy too," he said, crossing his arms.

Kini put both hands over her mouth, giggling. Wex winked, then turned to the Sturriges, clasping arms with Gaffroi.

"Thanks, Wex. Say hello to Eyck and thank him again for the frame," Gaffroi said, his smile broad.

"We'll be wanting to have you two over for supper as soon as we're properly set up," Charrie added.

Wex nodded, then waved at Kini.

She grinned mischievously and quickly signed, *"Boys like mouse poop."*

Laughing, Wex shook his head. *"I should never have taught you that sign. Bye, Kini. Be good."*

"Bye, Mr. Stromsmith!"

As he walked away, he felt the strange combination of thrill and discomfort he did every time someone called him *Stromsmith*. Half of him was over the moons with bearing Eyck's name—no matter if those outside their circle thought it was simply because the blacksmith needed an heir—but the other half of him felt like he was an imposter . . . like he didn't deserve it. But thankfully, as time went on, that feeling was starting to fade.

Continuing down the steep road, he looked out over the rooftops to the glistening river beyond, searching as he always did for the *Sparkshade*. It wasn't that he *wanted* to see Stilig and his brothers again —not really anyway—he just wondered what had happened to them.

He'd broken his promise about saying a prayer for them, and even though he didn't believe in that sort of thing, he couldn't help but feel bizarre guilt over any harm that might have befallen them. With that in mind, he touched the St. Wexelmander's medallion he still wore around his neck, but instead of a prayer, he just pictured the three lanky Grendall sailors aboard their ship, their fur ruffling in the stiff breeze as they sailed off in the warm sunshine.

Wex continued downhill, turning onto Main Street, and headed for the market square. Since it was Restday, there would be a greater variety of goods for sale—he was supposed to pick up some tea, and he wanted to surprise Eyck with something fancier than the usual cheap black stuff that he drank.

As Wex was paying for the tea, a new booth at the edge of Old Road caught his attention. It was full of colourfully painted wooden carvings and signs, some of them seemingly moving of their own accord. The carvings looked interesting, but it was the Kirmen shopkeeper that made him walk over to take a closer look. She was about his age, pretty and silver-pelted, and smiled at him as he approached.

"Hello," she said, wrinkling her nose in a friendly fashion.

He nodded, then touched his temple in greeting before perusing her wares. Above her head, there were placards with flowers and leaves cunningly carved into their borders, the words still illegible to him but the letters painted with elegant swirls. On the counter in front of her and to the sides were dozens of fantastical creatures painted with bright colours and intricate designs. Planted in the dirt in front of the booth were flowers on long metal stems—the blooms spun every time a gust of wind blew through the square.

"*Clever*," he signed.

The woman surprised him by signing, "*Thank you. I made everything myself.*"

Wide-eyed, he tilted his head at her. "*You know signing language?*"

Her smile was shy when she nodded. "*I was owned by a family who had a deaf daughter. I was bought to be her companion.*"

Some of her gestures were a little different than his, but she signed with a fluidity he hadn't known since Red Falcorr.

"*I'm surprised they let her live. They were Samra?*" He liked that they were both using signs to talk—it made their conversation private in the crowded market.

She nodded. "*Yes, but they were kind. Kind to their children and kind to me.*"

Frowning, Wex stared at her, not knowing what to say.

"*Were they 'kind' when they were forced to free you?*" he asked, his gestures sharp.

The woman pressed her lips together, her brow furrowed.

"*They never should have owned me. There is a lot of wrong in what our people were permitted to do to one another, and I cannot speak to what you have gone through . . . but I did know kindness. And, no, they were not kind when they were forced to free me because they weren't forced. They had already done so when I reached maturity, of their own free will. And they paid for my woodworking apprenticeship so that I could support myself.*"

Wex flared his nostrils and tried to still his tail—he didn't like that she was making excuses for her former masters, but then again, he'd known the worst kind.

"*I'm glad you experienced kindness,*" Wex said politely, wanting to steer away from the subject. He stood there for a few seconds, wondering if he should say more or just move on. The sun was getting low—Eyck was probably wondering where he was.

"*My name is Mirem,*" she offered, spelling her name out for him. He memorized the order of the signed letters, but he would need Eyck's help sounding it out properly. Matching the right sounds to letters, even through fingerspelling, was still a daily challenge. It was all about memorization . . . repetition, repetition, repetition. It gave him a headache.

Mirem smiled shyly, her pale-brown eyes crinkling at the corners.

"Are you Wex? The one who spoke The Truth?" she asked.

Wex nodded, surprised as always when someone recognized him— but then again, was there another giant half-Kirmen out there with what the *Wathuti* called a severe case of trauma-forged selective mutism and acquired dyslexia? He figured he was probably a pretty rare creature. Sobering, he realized that maybe just the giant part was rare. He couldn't have been the only one to have suffered as he did. He flared his nostrils, taking a deep breath, and smiled faintly at Mirem.

"Would you like to accompany me to the tavern later?" Mirem asked.

Frowning, Wex wondered what prompted her to ask that, but he figured it out a second later when he realized she was looking at him the same way the silly young girls did when they came to the smithy to make doe-eyes at him, as Eyck put it, whatever that meant. He made a mental note to ask the *Wathuti* to show him a doe next time he visited the ship.

Wex didn't want to offend Mirem by just saying no, so he said, *"I'm sorry, not tonight,"* instead and hoped that was the end of it.

When she looked disappointed, Wex took a better look at her wares, feeling a little bad about turning her down. He picked a spinning pink Sun's Flower to give to Mrs. Begmard because she always had honeycakes for him. Then he spotted a heart-shaped sign with delicately carved curlicues around the edges. The sign itself was blank, and that gave him an idea.

"I'd like to purchase that," he said, pointing. *"Can you write anything on it?"*

"Of course!" She reached up and took it down from the nail. Then she bent down and retrieved a pan full of small paint pots. *"What colour would you like the words?"*

Wex chose green to go with Eyck's eyes, but when she had her paintbrush dipped, he hesitated. As she stared at him expectantly, his mind raced, trying to find the right words. Finally, he signed. *"Can you write 'Home is Never Being Apart' and underneath it, write 'E-Y-C-K and W-E-X'?"*

Mirem's eyes widened, then something in her expression softened, and she nodded.

"Of course, I can," she said quietly. "It's no problem at all." She smiled.

WEX PLANTED the spinning flower in the dirt next to Mrs. Begmard's front door, then glanced down at the gift in his hands. Mirem had wrapped the little wooden sign in delicate purple paper and had placed a silvery lace bow on it, even though he hadn't asked. It looked pretty, but would Eyck like it or would he laugh?

Wex felt embarrassed and anxious—the more he thought about it, the sillier the words painted on it seemed. *Who says something like that?* It was mushy and stupid and not like him at all.

Taking a deep breath to steady himself, he pulled open the smithy door.

Eyck was unpacking a wooden crate. "Wex! There you are, lad. Can you take this and put it on the top shelf?" He handed over a few small boxes of fittings before Wex could reply.

Wex put his gift and the tea down and organized the boxes on the top shelf, then stocked the middle shelf when Eyck gave him a few more boxes to place. When the crate was finally empty, Wex glanced at his purchases on the table and smiled nervously at Eyck.

"What's wrong?" asked Eyck, his green eyes worried.

"Well . . . I went to the market today—"

He was interrupted by the chime of the bells over the door.

Both of them turned . . . and froze.

Standing in the middle of the smithy was a tall Oza male. His fur was glossy and white as a cloud, not bone-white like the Oza were usually described, and his clothes were unusual—a slate-grey tunic that was longer in the back than the front, almost cape-like, with dark trousers underneath, and strange square-toed boots made of some sort of smooth brown material.

When the man moved, Wex saw that the tunic was split almost to the armpit and beneath he wore a brilliant red shirt. Wex also realized there was a second Oza in the shop—a little white pup peeked out from behind the man's legs, staring up at Wex with wide pale-blue eyes. When the pup moved back, darting under the drape of the man's tunic, its eyes glinted red from the shadows.

Eyck was the first to break out of his trance, stepping forward to greet the man.

"Well, hello there! Welcome. What can I do for you, sir?" he said, the usual jovial smile back on his lantern-jawed face.

Wex realized if he didn't occupy himself with something, he wouldn't be able to keep from staring, so he picked up the broom and started sweeping around the forge.

"Hello. I, ah . . . am looking for some nails. About this size," the man said, holding his fingers apart to show what he meant. His accent was pronounced but he spoke clearly, and he was easy to understand. Wex saw the pup peeking out at him again, so he leaned his broom against the forge and picked up some small copper ingots. Juggling them, he smiled when he was rewarded with a shy grin from the Oza pup.

"I think I have exactly what you're looking for," Eyck said, searching the shelf for the nails. "What are you building?"

"My home," the man replied with a reserved smile. "I thought I had bought enough nails in Olmtown, but it seems I'm a few dozen short."

Eyck found the box of nails and turned around, his brow furrowed.

"Oh! Are you the family building the homestead out by the old mill?" he asked, taking the box to the table to count out the nails. He moved the wrapped present and tea aside, glancing over at Wex curiously.

"*I'll show you after,*" Wex signed.

"Yes. I'm just putting the roof in now," the man replied.

"Well, then . . . that means we're neighbours! Welcome to South Galetsy. I'm Eyck and this is my partner, Wex."

248

Wex touched his temple in greeting. It annoyed him that *partner* was such an ambiguous word. Wex wished they could be open about their relationship, but Eyck believed that with strangers, it was always better to be on the safe side. He tried not to be so impatient—after all, in the past cycle, there had been drastic changes and there were certainly more to come—but it was hard when it meant he had to hide part of who he was.

The man nodded, visibly relaxing, and placed a hand over his heart, a gesture Wex took to be an Oza form of greeting.

"I am Alux, and this is my daughter, Niopie," he said, pulling the long drape of his tunic aside to uncover the pup hidden behind him. She wore a tunic like her father's, but hers was sky-green and covered in an interesting zigzag pattern. "*Ma puce*, say hello to Eyck and Wex."

She quickly ducked out of sight again. A moment later, her little voice emerged from her hiding spot, muffled by the cloth of the tunic. "Hello."

Wex, Eyck, and Alux chuckled, and suddenly, it didn't seem strange at all to have Oza among them.

Pleasantries aside, Alux and Eyck quickly got into an amicable discussion about how best to lay down a roof, and Wex drifted away, sweeping metal filings towards the back door, his mind on the Oza immigrant.

It had taken three attempts before King Enoch and his council were successful in presenting what was now called "The Truth" to the Oza. It was only when they realized that, not unlike their own kingdom, religious authorities held an uncomfortable amount of power over the population, complicating things for the de facto secular leadership, that any headway was made.

The solution had been to place the archbessop and members of the church in one room with the Oza cultists, and King Enoch and his council in another room with the Cobirati elders. By the end of that day, the spiritual leaders from both sides were screaming for blood while the Oza government and King's Council were finishing up the first draft of the peace treaty.

It turned out the Oza weren't the mindless, cannibalistic animals they had been made out to be—they lived in homes, had families, owned businesses, went to school, etc. There was even a large amphitheatre carved into the side of a desert mountain where Oza actors and musicians put on elaborate plays, just like they did in Tuksbury. However, the Oza population was small in comparison to their own—the land was harsh and food scarce—and the image of blood-thirsty ferals had worked well to keep them safe from attack.

That part was interesting to Wex—the fear of attack. Where had it come from? Scholars from both lands were putting their heads together to try and figure that out. One theory was that the Samra, having to come to power through some means in the Beginning Times, were worried about appearing weak compared to the Oza with their immunity to the Five Cycle Sickness. And, instead of mingling their blood with that of the Oza, the Samra had turned the other breeds against them, perhaps painting them as unnatural creatures because their pups were never targeted by the Sickness, exiling them to the desert where they remained to this day.

But there *was* no definitive answer, just theories—so much was lost to time and myth. All anyone could do was find parts of the past and piece them together like a child's puzzle and try to make a better future for everyone.

Wex crouched as he swept under the bench in the back room, lost in thought.

The first part of the peace treaty was all about the wife and daughters of the farmer who had stolen a large chunk of precious Oza farmland. It stated they were to be released at the signing of the document . . . except, the woman had actually stayed with the Oza of her own accord, having found a stoneworker among their breed who treated her far better than her drunken Dankel husband had. Thus, the "release" had been an entirely symbolic gesture, a pantomime of sorts, to satisfy the requirements of the peace treaty and put everyone's minds at ease.

The rest of the treaty laid out rules for immigration—general things like adhering to the laws of the kingdom, protecting the land, and respecting customs. Wex looked over his shoulder at the Oza man, wondering if he was finding it hard, adapting to such a different environment and culture. It was true that his own life was nothing like it had been in his youth, but that change had happened gradually. Moving from the Oza desert to South Galetsy must be a shock to the system.

Wex couldn't imagine what it must be like to live in the desert with only a tiny sliver of farmable land, being forced to rely heavily on the meat of legless, sand-burrowing creatures to stay alive. He grimaced at the thought, wondering if Alux missed the taste of flesh, then frowned when something occurred to him. He eyed the Oza's footwear, wondering whether they had been made from the skin of those creatures—perhaps he should suggest a visit to the Sturriges to pick out chamara for a new pair of shoes.

Wex opened the back door, sweeping dust, mouse droppings, and filings into the small courtyard they shared with the glassworks and weaveshop, and smiled when he heard Pash arguing with Ormerod next door.

"It has to be *thinner,*" the ex-priest said, his frustration palpable. "This won't work."

"I don't know what you want me to say," replied the glassworker. "That's as thin as I can get it."

"Did you *read* the *Wathuti*'s instructions?"

"Well . . . I . . . skimmed. Sorta."

"Shall I read them *to* you? Schatten, Orm, this is *important.*"

Chuckling, Wex leaned against the doorpost, eavesdropping on the two men as they argued. Pash always managed to make even the smallest thing sound so crucial—maybe even more so now that he wasn't a priest anymore.

The day after delivering his letters and documents to King Enoch, Pastor Deechuk had passed away peacefully in his sleep. Upon hearing the news, Pash promptly left the priesthood to form a new group along with the four young priests and the Losano nurse who had attended the momentous gathering led by Wex the previous suncycle.

The group called themselves "Researchers for the Future" and dedicated themselves to learning everything they could from the ISA *Wathuti*. Almost daily, Pash emerged from the woods, wild-eyed and bursting with new ideas.

Last week, Pash had recruited Mrs. Begmard to help splice native plants to resurrect the "coffee" plant, something the humans had been very upset about losing in the great die-out.

This week, it was Ormerod that Pash had cornered into creating glass to fix broken panes in the *Wathuti*'s solar panels—he was hoping to boost power to the ship's communications device so they could send a message to the ISA *Titan*, the mothership that still orbited around the planet, blinking red across the sky every night.

From there, if the *Titan* was still operational, a message could be sent into the great beyond, to the world where the humans lived, telling them that the Kat'hoondemen still flourished. The message would take many generations to reach that far-off planet, but perhaps one day, the humans would come back. And hopefully, the fuel-neutralizing bacteria in the soil could be dealt with before their return.

Listening to the ex-priest direct the glassmaker made Wex smile. Pash was the sort of man who needed to have a higher purpose in life, which is probably why he had thrown himself into the priesthood so eagerly—at least now, with the Researchers, his efforts benefited all Kat'hoondemen, not just the ones who liked to kneel and pray.

"Wex."

Startled, Wex turned around to find Eyck standing in the doorway, holding the still-wrapped present.

"This for me?" he asked.

Wex's embarrassment came rushing back, and he grimaced as he nodded, wishing he'd never bought the stupid thing. Eyck would think it was silly, he was sure of it.

"What's with the face?" Eyck asked, grinning. "You look like you just drank vinegar." He looked down at the gift. "Can I open it?"

"If you want," Wex replied. *"But it's dumb."*

"I'll be the judge of that," Eyck said, leading them back to the front of the shop where the light was better.

Eyck carefully peeled the paper away from the heart-shaped sign, then lifted it to the window so he could read what was written on it.

Holding his breath, Wex scrutinized Eyck's expression, looking for any sign of the disdain he was sure he would find, but then hopped a half step back as Eyck lunged at him, pulling him into a hug that squeezed the breath out of his lungs.

"I love it," Eyck said, drawing back to look at him. *"Home is never being apart . . .* did you come up with that?" He clicked his tongue, shaking his head.

Wex pulled away, his hackles raised. *"Are you making fun of me?"*

"Put the fangs away, lad." Eyck laughed. "I was only thinking that I never would have imagined in a thousand cycles that you would give me something so thoughtful . . . and sweet." He reached out to cup the back of Wex's neck, his green eyes soft with emotion.

Wex let out a low grunt, surprising himself with the noise, then shrugged.

"I thought it would look nice above the bed."

"That *is* a perfect place for it." Eyck grabbed a nail and a hammer, slipping them into his apron pocket, then headed up the stairs. One hand on the new banister, Eyck turned around to look at Wex, a slow grin creasing his cheeks.

"Well? Aren't you going to join me?"

WEX TREMBLED as Eyck scratched his claws gently along his sides, his eyes crushed closed as the blacksmith's hands neared the base of his tail, teasing him with soft strokes down his backside and back up again. Gasping, he shook his head, wishing he could force his voice to work—he was on his hands and knees on the big wooden bed Llod had built for them, unable to communicate just how much Eyck was torturing him.

"Harder," he'd say. "And stop toying with me and mount me already."

Gritting his teeth, Wex raised his tail, flicking it to the side, and squeezed his pucker, the gesture as plain as his words would have been.

"Patience," murmured Eyck as he scratched gently up along the back of Wex's thighs, continuing to torment him. "We'll get to that."

When Eyck grazed his tail, Wex's cock jerked between his legs, stiff and needy and dripping with arousal, making Eyck chuckle.

"I love it when you're like this," he said. "Your whole body is just . . . *begging* to be touched."

Panting, Wex lifted his head and looked over his shoulder. Eyck smiled, lifted a finger to his mouth to wet it, and slid it into Wex as he held his gaze. Wex gasped, and Eyck's eyes darkened at the sound, his breathing becoming audible.

Wex dropped his head between his shoulders, pushing back hard against the finger inside him, then shuddered when Eyck wrapped his other hand around the base of his tail, pulling it up so he could slip a second finger into Wex's throbbing hole.

Schatten. Wex was already getting close, but he wanted to feel Eyck's weight on top of him . . . wanted Eyck to spill his seed inside him as he climaxed. Jaw clenched, he shook his head trying to delay the inevitable.

Eyck laughed again. "What? This doesn't feel good?"

It feels too good, old man. Wex shot another desperate look over at Eyck, pleading with his eyes. *I want you.*

Eyck grinned, then tilted his head, his jade-green eyes narrowed, and slid his fingers out of Wex, leaving his hole pulsing from the sudden departure. "Should I just leave you here like this, let you cool down a bit, and start over again?"

Wex bared his fangs, his tail jerking in Eyck's hand, and he let out a low growl.

In response, Eyck threw back his head with a booming laugh.

"All right, all right." He shook his head as he reached for the bottle of Sun's Flower oil. "So schatten impatient."

Wex breathed out a harsh breath when the tip of Eyck's cock pried open his sensitive hole, the blacksmith's fingers massaging the underside of his tail as he slowly penetrated him.

It felt so good to be mounted this way, with Eyck going deeper with every thrust—Wex couldn't believe he'd once questioned the sanity of anyone who claimed to enjoy it. Purring, he moved back against Eyck, matching the blacksmith's languid pace, and heard him moan. But before he could try coaxing Eyck to go harder and faster, Eyck pulled out completely.

Wex glanced back, confused.

Eyck grinned. "Oh, don't pout, lad . . . I just wanted to do this." He got Wex to lay on his side so that they were nestled like spoons, then moved Wex's tail aside so that he could push his cock back into him. Eyck hugged Wex tight against his chest as he moved within him, fucking him slowly as he bit down on the back of Wex's neck, holding onto his scruff as he brought Wex closer and closer to the sharp edge of climax.

Panting, Wex held onto his cock, not stroking it, just willing it to behave and last a *little* longer . . . long enough that Eyck's pleasure had caught up to his own, but he didn't have long to wait. Eyck suddenly grunted, biting down harder on Wex for a second before releasing him, his thrusts quickening as his cock got slick with seed.

Wex let out a cry, finally allowing himself to peak, his hole clenching down on Eyck's slippery cock as his shaft pulsed in his grip, the cum surging out of him in thick bursts that made him pant and quiver in Eyck's arms.

With a weak gasp at the last delicious pulse of orgasm, he let himself go limp, his whole body buzzing like a flock of Mrs. Begmard's bees, and started when Eyck's hand closed over his own a moment later.

"Mmm," Eyck said, snuffling the back of his neck. "I should really go downstairs and get back to work. But I don't want to move."

"*Then don't,*" Wex replied, lifting his free hand so Eyck could see his words. "*Stay with me.*" He looked at the sign Eyck had hung above the bed and smiled. "*Home is never being apart.*"

Chuckling, Eyck snuggled closer, pressing his hips into Wex's backside so that he didn't slip out of him.

"In that case, I guess I'll stay *home*," Eyck murmured. "You're the boss. Schatten be damned, the customers . . . they can bloody wait."

"*Good,*" Wex signed. Closing his eyes, he twined his fingers with Eyck's.

Together, they were like well-tempered steel—strong yet flexible enough that when Wex's past reared its head, making him angry or scared or miserable, their bond didn't snap. There was still so much he had to learn about sharing his life with someone, but Eyck's patience with him seemed to know no bounds.

Wex knew he was a very lucky man.

Sighing happily, Wex hugged Eyck's hand to his chest, his heart warm with something he'd believed his whole life to be a myth—an emotion so far out of his experiences that he'd thought it couldn't possibly be true . . . but here it was, and it was everything the faeries' tales said it would be.

The End

Books by Bey Deckard

FOR AN UP-TO-DATE LIST OF TITLES, VISIT:

https://beydeckard.com/blog/buy-my-books/

MAX, THE SERIES

Max

Max, the Sequel

BAAL'S HEART SERIES

Caged: Love and Treachery on the High Seas

Sacrificed: Heart Beyond the Spires

Fated: Blood and Redemption

Careened: Winter Solstice in Madierus

F.I.S.T.S

Sarge

Murphy

F.I.S.T.S. Handbook For Individual Survival in Hostile Environments

THE ACTOR'S CIRCLE

The Complications of T

The Last Nights of The Frangipani Hotel

THE STONEWATCHERS

Kestrel's Talon

STANDALONE BOOKS

Better the Devil You Know

Exposed

Beauty and His Beast

The Blacksmith's Apprentice

About the Author

Artist, Writer, Dog Lover

Bey Deckard is the author of a number of novels including the *Baal's Heart books*, *Max*, *Beauty and His Beast*, and *Better the Devil You Know*.

Bey lives in Montréal, Canada where he spends most of his time writing, doing graphic work, painting portraits, speaking French, cooking tasty vegetarian eats, or watching more movies than is good for him. If you're the curious type, www.beydeckard.com is where you'll find art and free stories by Bey as well as information on his published works.

bey.deckard@gmail.com
Look for Deckard's Diablerie on Facebook

facebook.com/authorbeydeckard

twitter.com/BeyDeckard

instagram.com/beydeckard

goodreads.com/beydeckard

bookbub.com/authors/bey-deckard

pettingzoo.co/@Beybey